Cut
Both
Ways

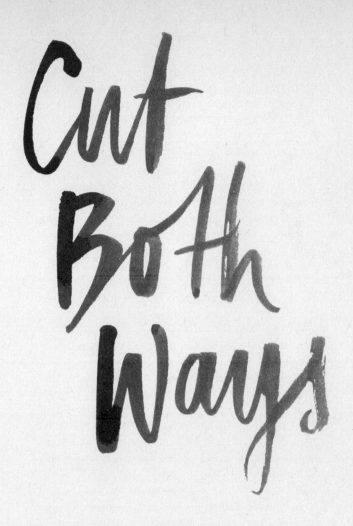

CARRIE MESROBIAN

HARPER
An Imprint of HarperCollinsPublishers

Library of Congress Cataloging-in-Publication Data
Mesrobian, Carrie.
Cut both ways / Carrie Mesrobian. — First edition.
    pages cm
Summary: "Senior Will Caynes must face unsettling feelings
for his best friend Angus after they share a drunken kiss, while
also embarking on his first real relationship with sophomore
Brandy—all as the burden of home-life troubles weigh heavily"
— Provided by publisher.
    ISBN 978-0-06-234988-0 (hardback)
    [1. Interpersonal relations—Fiction. 2. Bisexuality—Fiction.
3. Friendship—Fiction. 4. Gays—Fiction. 5. Sex—Fiction.] I.
Title.
PZ7.M5493Cu 2015   2014047809
[Fic]—dc23   CIP
                                                  AC

Typography by Ray Shappell
15 16 17 18 19   CG/RRDH   10 9 8 7 6 5 4 3 2 1

First Edition

so I wait for you like a lonely house
till you will see me again and live in me.
Till then my windows ache.
        —*Pablo Neruda, from sonnet LXV of* 100 Love Sonnets

"Home is the place where, when you have to go there,
They have to take you in."
        —*from "The Death of the Hired Man" by Robert Frost*

To Adrian

Let me paraphrase Mr. Plumbean from Daniel Pinkwater's
The Big Orange Splot:

Our house is where we long to be
and it looks like all our dreams

ONE

YOU GET USED to it, divorce. Since fourth grade, I've lived in two different houses and while that sounds kind of crazy, especially for a little kid, you get used to it. Used to your parents not being together, to scenery changing every other week. Two yards, two kitchens, two beds to jerk off in. You get used to going back and forth in the car, to traffic jams, to waiting and sitting and your dad swearing at other drivers and your mom taking work calls and pretending she wants to know how your week went. People think kids can't handle divorce, that it'll make them shatter or something, but it's not true. Just because you don't like something doesn't mean you can't get good at being used to it.

By the time I got my license, I'd worn a groove between my mom's house in Oak Prairie and my dad's house in Minneapolis, the one I'd been born in. Since I had to attend the same school in Minneapolis, while living out in the suburban asteroid belt of Oak Prairie, over the years I'd gotten to know the best routes, the quickest shortcuts, the worst times for gridlock. And I had it timed too, down to a science. The drive to where my mom lives in Oak Prairie is about a half an hour from where my dad lives in Minneapolis. Though you can do it in twenty minutes if you speed.

Lately, though, my car's kinda acting weird, so I don't speed as much. I just had a bunch of stuff fixed on it, but there's still this weird sound coming from the engine whenever I go over sixty miles an hour. Since my dad was super pissed about paying for the repairs—parts on an Audi aren't cheap, even if he got one of his mechanic friends to do the labor for less—I'd started just turning up the radio extra loud to drown out the weird sound.

"Your mother didn't *give* you this car, as far as I'm concerned," he always says. "She just transferred the debt. I didn't have a car when I was your age."

He's a pretty bitter dude, my dad. With joint custody, I have no choice but to go back and forth. Plus he barely could stand driving me to my mom's place before I got a license.

When I get to my mom's, my half sisters are playing in the sprinkler on the giant perfect lawn. All the lawns in Oak Prairie look the same. Picture, like, half a soccer field of perfect, pure green, weed-free grass. Then put one spindly, tiny tree in the corner, with the base circled with chicken fencing so the deer won't gnaw at it. Oak Prairie probably used to be some beautiful untouched forest or some bankrupt farmer's land. But try telling the deer that. They walk up to yards and chew on shrubs and eat flowers out of pots like that's natural or something. Those spindly twig-trees don't stand a chance.

Compare this to my dad's house in Minneapolis, where the lawn's torn up to mud from all the construction, but there's a huge maple tree that's over seventy years old. A big, beautiful one, with a perfect V-shaped spot in the middle where you can sit once you've climbed it. The summer of fourth grade, after the divorce, my dad and I started building a tree house in it. But our neighbors bitched that it was an "eyesore" so we had to take everything down. If you put anything heavier than a goddamn Barbie doll in the wire-surrounded twig-tree at my mom's house, it'd probably snap in half. Which might actually be kind of funny to see. But then my mom'd yell her face off at Taylor and Kinney, and Kinney would cry and Taylor would pout, which sort of cancels out the fun part.

Taylor's wearing a bikini and Kinney's wearing shorts and a T-shirt and they are chasing each other through the sprinkler. Kinney's also spraying Taylor with the hose. They have an entire backyard full of play equipment and swings and crap, but here they are, ripping it up on the front lawn, of course. They are both seven years old and not identical, in looks or behavior. Kinney's always crying about something; Taylor's always yelling at her to shut up. But they always want to be together, somehow.

Both of them rush me as I come up to the house. Kinney's holding the hose with the nozzle on it but Taylor's kinking it so she can't spray me.

"Mom's having book club!" Taylor says. "You can't go inside! The food's for the ladies only!"

"They're drinking wine!" Kinney adds. "There's three whole boxes of it!"

3

"You got new glasses," Taylor says, stopping and noticing.

"And you look like a dork!" Kinney adds.

"I like them," Taylor says, tilting her head to study me and my glasses. "They look very happy on your face."

I rush Taylor and pick her up and flip her over my shoulder and she screams, but I know she loves it. She's expecting it. Kinney sprays us and Taylor screams. I reach down, kink the hose. Kinney screams at both of us.

"Our dad's in the UK! That's England!" Taylor says, her hands on hips. "So there's no boys allowed!"

"Boys are too allowed, because I'm here," I tell her. "Deal with it."

Then my mom is on the steps, yelling. "Kinney! Taylor! What are . . . oh hi, Will," she says, seeing me. "I forgot you were coming out tonight. Turn off that hose, Kinney! Right now! Take off your shoes, Will, okay? I just mopped this floor ten times already."

I haven't been here since school let out, so I know my mom's happy I'm here. She'll just never admit it. Saying something would mean she minds that my dad's got an edge and talked me into helping him with the remodeling all summer. But she won't say she misses me, or that she's jealous. She'll just say that my half sisters miss me or that she bought me new clothes and wants me to see if they fit. I'm not even sure she misses me at all, actually. It's more like, every time I stay with her, she wins somehow. Scores a point off my dad or something.

My mom's setup for book club looks like quite a spread, even without the contributions the other women will bring. She tells

4

Kinney and Taylor to stop tracking wet all over the floor and get in the bathtub before she "loses her mind." My mom is always threatening to "lose her mind." She tells me that I can eat after the book-club ladies arrive—"there will be more than enough!" she says, several times—and that there is a babysitter coming to watch the twins.

"Can we eat with Will?" Taylor asks. I've set her down to unlace my work boots, but she's still hovering around me. Taylor likes me more than Kinney does. The feeling is mutual too, in both directions. Maybe parents have to love their kids equally, but I don't think it counts for half siblings. I mean, I don't hate Kinney or anything. But she bugs me in a way Taylor doesn't.

"No," my mom says, stabbing toothpicks into little balls of cheese. "I've already told you that. And I made your dinner and you'll eat in the TV room once Claudia gets here. But if you don't finish your bath before she gets here, then you can forget about watching movies."

"Awww . . . !" Kinney says.

"Don't!" my mom yells. "I'm serious! Don't test me!"

I don't remember my mom being such a yeller to me when I was the twins' age. She wasn't even much of a yeller to my dad. But she's jumping in the twins' shit constantly. I can kind of see the point, at least where Kinney's concerned.

"I might just stay at Angus's house," I say. "If it gets late."

"Sure, fine," my mom says. She's distracted, in a rush, clacking around the giant granite-countertop island in these sandals that don't look like they'd be loud, but they are anyway. My mom's always moving. She's skinny but she has no muscle; her arms are sticks of flab. Though she's crazy about yoga and Pilates and whatever the hell classes they do at her fitness place these days, the heaviest thing I ever see her lift is her purse and her phone. She's still a nice-looking lady, I suppose, and I look like her, but not in the same way. We both have blue eyes and the same straight, dark hair. I have glasses, though; I got my dad's astigmatism. I wonder if she notices this. If she worries I'll be like him too. When I start to think like this, I kind of hate her a little. I'm glad she's always twitching off into some new project. I don't want her to look at me and see the guy she hates so bad.

"I like your glasses," she says as she unwraps a platter of brownies. "They're very hip. Retro, even."

"Dad got them at Walmart."

She wrinkles her nose at this. She hates Walmart. Because it's where my cheapskate dad goes.

"They frame your face much nicer than those others," she says. "It was time for a change."

"Dad calls them *birth-control glasses*."

"What?" she says. I can feel her wanting to criticize my dad or maybe Walmart. Probably both.

I explain that he thinks they look like the ones they gave him when he was in Army boot camp and that they're so ugly, nobody would get near you. That he was kidding. But she just fake-laughs and starts arranging carrots around a bowl of dip.

"I suppose a little birth control at your age isn't a bad thing, right?"

"I don't think he meant—"

"Hello?" Angus's voice, coming through the screen door.

"Come in!" I yell. "It's Angus," I tell my mom. She nods, dumps some ice into a big bowl, and adds lemons.

Angus sticks his head around the corner but doesn't leave the front hall. "I'm not wearing any socks," he says. "I don't want to take off my shoes."

He smiles; I laugh at him. His mom is the same fucking way as my mom. But she's not yelling at anyone. Angus is the youngest kid in his family. His sisters are older. One's married, one's in college. After Angus goes to college, which he will, since he's smart and everything, Mr. and Mrs. Rackler get their big old giant house to themselves.

I don't want to talk about my glasses anymore so I just go to where Angus is standing on the rug in his running shoes. He's not wearing his usual bandanna over his long hair and it's going everywhere, big curly blond mess as usual, and he's wearing crappy holey jeans and a T-shirt that says MINNEAPOLIS LOCAL PIPEFITTERS 539 on it. He looks like he doesn't belong in Oak Prairie. He looks like he could wear my retro birth-control glasses and fit right in at Franklin, where I go to school in Minneapolis. Where all the hipsters go because it's an art magnet. Where there are actual kids whose parents are pipefitters. I wonder if Angus knows what a pipefitter does. I only know because of one of my dad's friends who comes over and plays poker sometimes is a pipefitter. But Angus would never wear glasses. Angus has perfect vision.

"DeKalb couldn't make it," I say, putting on my boots. They still feel a little damp with sweat.

"Bummer," Angus says. My friend DeKalb plays bass and Angus's band needs a bassist. But Angus doesn't sound that bummed. It's kind of his deal lately, to never be upset about shit. Though he definitely went through a kind of moody goth phase back in middle school. Always carrying around his journal and whatever. Angus is artistic; I think he wanted to try looking that way too. Besides his silver hoop earrings in each ear, though, now he's back to being a normal kid. If it's normal to wear blue bandannas in Oak Prairie, that is. You can't wear anything like that at Franklin or they freak out that you're wearing gang colors.

We walk down to his house, which is a block away. I've known Angus since the summer before sixth grade; he moved in during a week where I happened to be staying with my mom. I'd been bored, shooting baskets in the driveway, and Angus came up and asked if he could play. He sucked really bad, so we ended up going to the little park down the street, hanging out on the playground equipment, and then in the creek behind the little stand of woods. We didn't do anything, really, except get muddy and collect rocks and try to climb trees, but I was so happy to have him. My half sisters were still pretty little so my mom and Jay were kind of busy dealing with them every second. And Angus wasn't hard to be friends with. Though it's not like it's hard to make friends with someone when you're eleven. You just want someone to play with; it's not like I needed Angus to have the same life philosophy or anything.

Angus says he's got some weed and we might as well walk down to the playground and smoke out. I tell him that's cool; we can go back to my mom's and eat the food after all the ladies come for book club.

"They'll eat, then start guzzling the wine," I explain. "Then they'll talk about everything but the goddamn book. So we'll have tons to eat."

"Sweet," he says.

"Plus they've got a fuckton of wine we can nab," I add.

"Cool." Some guys, like DeKalb, wouldn't drink wine. Would say it sucks. DeKalb's super careful about booze, though, since his dad's a cop. So he'd front like it was too pussy to drink wine, but I'd know better.

But my mom doesn't pay attention to shit like that. She trusts me more than she should, because I've never been caught at anything. I don't love wine, but it's free. Plus no hassle in getting someone to buy for us. Easier to get weed or whatever the hell other drug if you're my age, than actual alcohol.

The park's still full of little kids so we go another block and then duck between the maintenance building and a bunch of trees, and Angus pulls out his pipe quick, because who knows when some annoying adult will come over and bust us. Oak Prairie is that kind of nosy-ass suburb, where the moms with strollers sort of act like they're the elected officials of anything taking place in the yard or street or park. Like they're the mom of everyone, no matter what age.

Angus's lighter is sparky and keeps foiling our attempts to get good hits, and we laugh a little but get the job done. Then he taps his pipe out on a tree and puts it in his pocket and we walk back to my house. The walk back—it takes much longer this time around. Weed does that—makes everything seem longer. Which can be good and bad. But this? This is good.

The whole way, we talk about stuff I can't remember the second after we talk about it. I'm starving. I'm happy. It just hits me, then, that I'm happy to be here, that I'm done working on the house for the week, and there's tons of good food in my mom's kitchen, and it's nice to be out of Minneapolis and come here. It's quiet out in Oak Prairie. Nobody on the street. Lots of stars. No trees and buildings blocking the view. Just the same house, row after row, one soccer-field lawn running into the next. I've got some change in my pockets and I'm jingling it in this rhythm, along with our footsteps. My boots, Angus's running shoes. I can keep the time, but just barely. It's a kind of enjoyable problem to deal with, flipping the quarters between my fingers and our steps and trying to keep up with what Angus is saying. He's talking about art school and music and a concert and all of these things. He does all of these things when I'm not around. He's never bored, Angus. Unlike me, he can always think up something to do.

We slip into the house. Sneaking, not just because we're high, but because we don't want to talk to anyone, even a stray tipsy book-club lady. Especially not Taylor or Kinney. Angus loads up plates for both of us while I load up a couple of my mom's fancy water Nalgene bottles with boxed wine and tuck them into the back of my shirt. Angus nods and we slip out, unnoticed, the book-club ladies talking and laughing, the cartoon noise blasting from the TV room. Successful entry and exit. We cut through yards and head to Angus's house.

"You gonna jam all by yourself?" I ask, when we get to Angus's practice space, where he keeps all his shit: drums, guitar, keyboard, amp. Angus plays a little of everything, though it's regular guitar that he's good at.

"No, let's just eat," he says. He's already shoving chips into his mouth. We sit on the old sofa he keeps out there and we eat and drink and it's just the sound of food crunching and chewing, which is kind of gross. But also, the point. The Racklers have a three-car garage, just like my mom's house, but instead of all of it being taken up with Jay's Land Rover and my mom's Mercedes wagon and their camper, the third garage is all Angus's space. All his music stuff and the old couch and a little fridge and the freedom to be as loud as he wants. Mr. Rackler insulated it acoustically and everything. It's pretty keen of his parents, I think. They go out of their way to be understanding to him.

After a while, I'm full but I keep eating, though it kills my high a little. I don't care; I still feel that shot of happiness from earlier. I don't get it that often, not constant good feelings, like normal people do. That happy feeling: it always surprises me. Makes me feel dumb, because it always comes when I'm with someone else, and I can't ever explain it. How I'm happy suddenly. Plus it's hard to hide.

"We gotta go do something," I say.

"Want to walk around a little?"

"Yeah."

I'm glad he doesn't want to drive anywhere; not just because of the gas I don't want to burn up, but because I'm a terrible driver when I'm high. I know, because I've tried, and it was fucking scary as hell. It felt like the car wouldn't move and I was afraid to step on the gas. Later, I realized I'd left the dumb-ass parking brake on the whole time. Never again.

We walk around the block. I still feel good. The moon is out now and it's finally dark. I think there might be more stars out here in Oak Prairie. Or maybe it's my improved glasses prescription. Or I don't know. Not many people have their outdoor lights on in summer, which doesn't make sense; it's not like they can't afford to, and it's not like they're not home. You can see the TV glow through the closed shades, or smell the grill from the backyards, but nothing goes on in the front. Nobody sees us stumbling and kicking rocks and laughing, lugging our Nalgenes of pink wine. Swigging from them too.

At the park, finally, there are no kids. The kids must all be in bed—their stroller moms brought the hammer down. Or they're in front of movies in the TV room, like Taylor and Kinney. Now we can own the park, the shitty fucked-up teenagers no one wants around.

Angus goes on the swings but I can't. I can't stand swings even when I'm sober. I drink more wine. Angus jumps off the swing and then goes down the slide. I stand there, watching him. He's one of those people who gets all hyper when they're high. Or maybe he's happy like I am too?

I sit on the grass, because though the gravel around the play area might keep kids from cracking open their skulls, it feels gritty and gross. Since helping with my dad's remodeling, all I think about is how to keep my hands clean. How drywall feels when you break it. How sawdust tastes. How my hands are getting worn and hard from pulling nails from buffalo board under the siding. How what I used to think counted as getting "dirty" now means nothing.

I watch Angus on the slide and the climbing-rope wall and the monkey bars, going hand over hand, his knees clenched up so he can hang properly. Angus is as tall as me, but skinnier.

"We gotta get your friend out here soon, though," he calls, going back the way he came on the monkey bars. "It's kind of getting to be an emergency."

"What? Why?"

Angus is yelling, kind of, but in a funny way, about this thing going on with his bandmates, which is crazy to me, because what they have, it's hardly a band. I mean, they never do shows. They don't have their own songs. They barely play anyone else's songs.

"Who's quitting, again?" I ask, gulping more pink wine. "The keyboards guy?"

"Andrew's not quitting. He just says he won't play if we don't let his girlfriend do bass. But she plays the violin, not the bass. They're not even the same. And you need a solid bass line, man. You can't just scramble along."

"Right. Yeah." As if I know what he means!

But what am I going to talk about instead?

Almost chopped my thumb off with the Sawzall last week?

My dad's drinking again, though just beer now?

What do you expect from your band, really, if it doesn't even have a name?

I can't be a total dickwad like that. Not to him.

"Fuck. I'm buzzed," Angus says, chucking his Nalgene toward me. It lands in the grass and then he plops down beside me.

"Yeah. Me too." I lay back on the grass, which is slightly wet, but I don't care. This summer, I've barely bothered to shower or change my clothes unless I'm leaving the house and might maybe see actual girls or whatever. Why bother getting clothes dirty for no reason, you know? Another thing Angus can't relate to; he's not a gross slob kind of guy.

I look at the stars and feel drunk. I think about people in the olden times, washing their clothes. Beating them against rocks in the river, letting them hang out from trees or laundry lines. My mom used to do that, not the river-rock beating, but the laundry-line thing, in our backyard. I'd help her pin clothes up or take them down, when I was littler. Back when I didn't care about doing chores. Now our backyard is so full of lumber and building supplies and free shit my dad got from who knows where, you couldn't even hang up anything, even if the line was still there. My dad snapped it after the divorce. We do everything at his Laundromat now.

Angus's still talking about Andrew's girlfriend. About her being an idiot. About her stupid pink hair. About what was the point, even, of dyeing her hair? This girl had been a cheerleader in junior high; who was she fooling that she was some kind of punk badass now that she was going to be a senior? Andrew swallows all this bullshit, Angus says, because she's fucking him and before that, Andrew'd been a virgin and now sex is making him stupid. Pussy stupid, Angus adds, sitting up over me and grabbing my Nalgene of wine.

I don't know Andrew or his weird girlfriend. I have no opinion about either of them.

I laugh. "Pussy stupid," I say. "There's no such thing as that."

Though I wish I could get stupid that way! From pussy! It's pretty much never going to happen. I'm seventeen and I've never even kissed a girl. I never do anything cool. I'm shit at girls. I don't have any money. I wear glasses. I'm boring. In between.

I've liked plenty of girls but they've never liked me back. It's kind of horrible.

But kind of reasonable too. Because the girls I like are always completely unaware of my liking them. I never tell anyone, not even my friends, when I like a girl. And I never talk or interact with her, either, if I like her. It's complete top-secret classified information when I like someone.

"You all right, Will?" Angus asks.

"Yeah. Drunk, though."

I link my fingers together over my head and see Angus looking down at me while slowly coiling his bandanna into the length he likes for tying it up over his forehead to get his hair out of his face. I watch one of his earrings wink from the light over the play area and then his face is one inch from my face and then Angus is kissing my mouth.

I don't do anything. For a minute, I don't move. He puts his mouth all over my mouth. My glasses are smushed between us but it's not because he's being pushy. I just feel them, suddenly, this fragile equipment, sitting there on my face. I know I should maybe move them. I can't make myself move to do that, though. The kissing keeps happening. A minute. A minute more. Then it's longer and I'm doing something back. With my own mouth. And it's a decent amount of time too, that I'm doing it back. More than a minute. A while.

I keep thinking, *I'm not gay. I'm not gay.* But I only think it. It keeps going on, the kissing. Our mouths are opening. *Angus. I'm not gay. I'm not.*

I don't know why I'm letting him do this. He lifts away from me and it's like I could stop this but I don't. I just take off my glasses and hold them in my hand. Angus kisses me again; his breath smells like pink wine and tastes salty, like potato chips. It doesn't feel bad. It feels okay. And I know he's gay: Angus. Everyone's known that, since forever. Since junior high. He'd made a big deal about it, back then, when he wore his goth costume and eyeliner and walked around acting tragic, like the poems he showed me in his journal. Angus had been the reverse of Andrew's girlfriend: weird back then, and now normal. Though still gay.

Why am I doing this? Why am I licking Angus's tongue?

Our tongues. It's very weird, that part. I want to see what that looks like, my tongue touching someone else's tongue. I wish there was some cool way I could casually open my eyes and see it. But I can't see that great without my glasses. And I don't want to look at Angus. Angus, who's been my friend since I was little. Angus, who hated T-ball with me. Angus, who ate so much candy corn one Halloween that he threw up orange bits for hours the next day. Angus, who cried when his cat died; when we buried Felix in his mom's vegetable garden, I cried too.

Plus, I don't want to move. I kind of can't really move. His hand is up in my hair, his fingers running through it. It makes my scalp shiver. My body shiver.

Then Angus puts his hand on my chest. It isn't moving around. Just rests there. And I feel trapped under it, though I'm just as big and strong as Angus, probably stronger, actually, if I think about it. Which I don't, really. Until now. Then his hand slides down my stomach, where I feel a churning of pink wine and all the goddamn food I'd slobbered down and Angus says, into my neck, "You all right? You're all right, right?"

Once he says that, I sit up. It's like something unlocks when he says that, and then I can move. Me sitting up pushes Angus out of position. His hand falls away. I wipe my glasses on the bottom of my T-shirt; they are wet from the grass. When we look at each other, he looks shocked. Like he didn't realize that I was me. Me, Will, Will Caynes; that it was me, this whole time. His friend. Who is not gay. Not gay. Clearly not.

My dick isn't even hard. I mean, not entirely. Not even half hard. About halfway to halfway hard.

You're half gay, then.

"I'm not gay, Angus."

A quarter gay.

"Okay," he says. Still looking at me all weird, his eyes bright under his bandanna.

"I'm not. I'm drunk."

"Okay," he repeats. He looks behind him, at the playground. His hands are on his knees. "Sorry. Me too. I'm drunk, I mean. I didn't . . . I wasn't thinking. I mean, I get it. I know. I know you're not."

Half hard. Half gay. Quarter gay. Can Angus tell? Does he know? Can you sense that, when you're gay? Because you have a dick too, and you know how dicks act?

Angus apologizes more. He's very slow and deliberate about it. Like he's waiting for me to tell him to stop. So I finally do.

"Angus," I say. "Stop apologizing."

"You're not mad?"

"No."

"You should hit me, Will. You can. If you want."

"Why?"

"Because. Because then you won't feel weird."

I haven't hit Angus in forever. Not since we were little kids. Hitting him now would be even weirder.

I paw my hands through the wet grass, ripping up blades of it. My T-shirt is all wet in the back and feels cold and gross. I feel gross. Spinny. High and drunk.

"I'm not hitting you, Angus. It's not a big deal."

"All right."

"I mean, don't go telling people or anything."

"Of course not," he says, sounding pissy.

"I'm just saying, you know, I don't want people to think the wrong thing. Not that it's wrong, you know? I don't care if you're gay. I don't."

"I know."

And then he stands up, like he's mad at me, and we walk back to his house, faster than we'd walked away from it, and we go back into the garage and he starts dicking around with his guitar and we act like everything's okay. And I feel okay, I guess. Not high as much, a little spinny, but still drunk. Drunk-okay, though.

It's like a thing that happened to somebody else. Like it wasn't me doing that. Like it was just Angus, not me.

Then he's nudging me, because I've fallen asleep on the sofa.

"Will," he says. "Come on."

I sit up. Look at him. My eyes water. My mouth is dry.

"I have to go home."

"You can stay here if you want. My mom won't care."

"I gotta go," I say. I stand up, make a point to appear competent. I'm very slow, but I can walk. I can. I can do this.

I walk down his driveway. I know he's behind me, watching me, but I won't turn around. I won't. For a minute, I'm kind of wobbling. I think I won't make it. I wish I was still on the garage couch. But somehow, the wide black sky above me, the stars brighter than before, I get home. My mom's house is silent. The dishwasher is humming, the light above the stove is on.

My bedroom at my mom's is across from Jay's office. There's a bathroom right there too; it's kind of my bathroom, though Jay leaves his magazines and stuff in there. I'm the only one who uses the shower. The medicine chest is full of my stuff. I turn on the light and I pee. I pee for a long time. I pee for a thousand years, swaying while I stand. Listening for signs that my mom's still awake. The sound of the television. The sound of her own toilet flushing or sink running. But nothing: just the dishwasher hum.

In my bedroom, I strip off my clothes in a damp heap. Clunk down on the bed, which has a new comforter on it. Maroon with gray trim. My mom bought it a few months ago, for no reason I could see. She just decides something needs to be replaced and does it.

I take off my glasses and set them on the dresser next to the bed. The bed is soft. The futon at my dad's is horrible. Here at my mom's, the bed's a pillowtop. Plush. Comfortable. Luxurious.

The room spins for a minute and I shut my eyes until everything's still. I think I might yack, but I breathe deep for a while and then it goes away and I feel okay.

"Okay," I say to myself. The word in the stillness hovers over my head.

Then I reach down my boxers. I'm half hard. Have I been half hard—a quarter hard?—this whole time? How long has it been hard? Since Angus kissed me? Since he woke me up?

Doesn't matter. It's all the way hard now, so I take care of it, like I normally do. The normal way, the normal things I want to think about. About girls I'd liked. Porn I'd seen. Tits in my face. Pussy. Being pussy stupid.

But I'm the one who's stupid. Stupid for doing that with

Angus. Angus and his bandanna. Angus and his mouth. His hand on my chest. All the things I don't want to think about, but am thinking about, anyway, until I come, things I'm thinking about afterward too, all through wiping myself down, because I'm not gay but what choice do I have, to spend the night of my first kiss just exactly like that.

TWO

THE NEXT MORNING, my mom is all up in my business, wanting to gab at me. My brains are sizzling inside my head, and she's asking do I want French toast. Kinney and Taylor are buzzing around the table where I'm sitting, trying to act normal even though I feel like I want to die. My mom has on the radio, some talk program. My mom always gets this way when Jay's out of town; she's saying, as Kinney and Taylor dance in and out of the room, that Jay's been gone over a week and she's going a little nuts having the girls on her own.

"Right," I say, trying to smile as she pours orange juice. She's in her yoga outfit, all purple and high-tech spandex, wearing her fitness watch, her ears plugged up with earbuds though I can't imagine she's listening to anything anymore. Not with the radio blasting like it is. My hair's dripping over the collar of my shirt like cold-water torture. I'd made myself sit through a long shower, which I only took because it was the best way to get Kinney and Taylor the hell away from me.

Kinney's listening to her iPod (of course, all seven-year-olds require their own iPods) and singing along with music no one can hear, which could have been funny because of her terrible singing, but it's so *loud*. Taylor's on her iPad, drawing things with a little stylus, asking me what she should draw next. Taylor's always asking that kind of thing: What should her video-game avatar be? What should she name her little cat guy in her comic strip? Should she draw a moon or a planet? I don't get it. If she wants to be creative so bad, why the hell does she ask someone else to tell her what to do? I can't think of anything that I could have less interest in. I can't think, period.

But I eat the French toast, slowly, so I won't upset my already burning stomach, and I nod and let my mom ask me all her questions: Do I need some new shorts? Do I have the scratch-damage plan on my new glasses? Do I have a case for the glasses? Do I want to go camping with Jay?

Answers given: No. No. Yes. Maybe. (But really? No.)

"You feeling all right?" she asks.

"Yeah, I'm just sore from the remodel stuff."

She fluffs my hair. Pushes it out of my eyes a little, which gives me a shiver. Like Angus's hand on my scalp last night. I stand up and take my plate to the sink.

"You want some Advil, maybe?" she asks.

YES, I think. Why I'd waited to take anything like that, I don't know. More proof that my brain is broken when I'm hungover. My mom's quick with the remedies, that's for sure. Whether you stain something on the floor mat of your car or have some weird allergy or need more vitamin D, she's got just the thing for you. She's kind of a whirlwind of products, my mom.

I gulp the pills with the rest of my juice as she crosses her arms over her chest and stands there, looking at me.

"Your dad doing okay?"

Fuck. Not that again.

"Yeah."

"Not drinking again? You'd tell me if he was, I know, but I can't help asking. . . ."

"No," I say. Thinking of the beers he's had every night after we finish working. Which isn't the same, isn't the thing she's talking about. Because he's handling it now. It's not like before. Plus, we talked about it and he admitted he had been out of line. He knew he was fucking up; he knew I knew too, so he fixed it.

"He's doing just fine."

She looks at me like she wants to believe me but doesn't. Like she feels sorry for me. I stare at her collarbones, the knobs under her neck sticking up through her purple yoga shirt. She wears a gold necklace with birds and gemstones on it, one for Taylor, one for Kinney. Jay gave it to her for Mother's Day. I gave her a card. Because I never have any money. It wasn't like I was going to ask her for money to buy her a Mother's Day gift.

"I gotta get going," I say. And then I duck back to my room to collect my stuff. And then I wait until they're all in the backyard, filling up the above-ground pool thing and yelling and Kinney screaming that her iPod can't get wet and I slip out the front door to my car and drive back to Minneapolis.

When I get back to my dad's, he's at home. Which is weird; lately he's always running around, tracking down something on Craigslist. A bay window, a screen door, a set of kitchen cabinets. He's always got something he's chasing after and it's never anywhere convenient. It's always off in Victoria or Elk River or halfway to Rochester. So I'm surprised to see him sitting in the kitchen, eating waffles with Roy and Garrett.

Roy's the college kid my dad hired to help with remodeling. And Garrett is one of my dad's oldest friends; they've been friends since before my parents even met. Roy's usually here at any time of day—my dad keeps strange hours and Roy can roll with that—but Garrett doesn't come around often. Garrett lives out in the middle of nowhere, between Oak Prairie and Minneapolis, on a hobby farm with his girlfriend. Plus, he runs a twenty-four-hour diner in Shoreview. He's a nice guy, and up for fun, but he's always pretty busy between the farm and the diner.

But what's weird is that Roy and Garrett are both smoking. Inside. I mean, Garrett smokes; so does Roy. That's not new. But my dad has never let anyone smoke inside before. Even after my mom left.

Except this house isn't exactly the same place anymore. It's not exactly "inside," either, with all the ripped-out insulation and removed walls and windows too.

"William," Roy says, nodding. He calls me that: William. I have no idea why. I've never corrected him.

"Hey, kid," Garrett says. Slaps me on the stomach. I clench up, not because it hurts—Garrett isn't that kind of guy—but because it reminds me of Angus.

Angus over me, Angus's hand on my stomach, Angus's hair flopping over his face.

"We working today?" I ask. I look around. There's a few rubbery-looking waffles on a plate; Garrett and my dad are drinking cups of coffee out of the coffeepot we used for camping; Roy's brought his own travel mug because he's snobby about coffee. Behind my dad, the sink's full of dishes and there's a grocery sack of recycling, mostly beer cans. The house smells strange too. Not just like smoke. Like raw wood and sour beer. Like something burned. Like someone else's house, really.

"Already finished," Garrett says. My dad smiles at him, like there's a joke I don't get.

"Finished what?"

Garrett taps his cigarette on the edge of a plate.

"Planning, mostly," my dad says. "Lots of planning. Garrett's got good ideas. This whole thing being his area of expertise." He waves his hand around at what used to be our house.

"I thought running restaurants was your thing," I say to Garrett.

Garrett shakes his head, puts out the cigarette on the plate, then stands up to open the window over the kitchen sink. I'm shy, then; can he tell I think it smells bad in here?

"I used to do carpentry and such with my old man," Garrett

says. "That was another lifetime ago. Your dad just needed someone to bounce ideas off."

"Ah, don't be all humble," my dad says to him. "You and Kristin put up that barn on your own!" My dad grabs a waffle and starts chewing, not bothering with syrup or a fork. It's kind of gross, because his mouth is open, and his fingernails are dirty, but I've had my dad's waffles. They're good, hot or cold, plain or covered in syrup and jam.

"So, are we working or what?" I mumble. I know it's the right thing to do, to be up for work, but I'm hoping I can just go back to bed, honestly.

My dad wipes his hands on his pants. "Not yet," he says. "Gotta see about some windows, then hit Harbor Freight for some supplies. Who's up for it?"

I shake my head. Garrett's looking at his phone and doesn't answer. Roy shrugs, says why not. I don't envy Roy, but maybe Roy can talk my dad down on things in a way I can't. Roy's got this long blond hair and kind of surfer-dude demeanor, but he's actually pretty no-nonsense when it comes to work. When my dad needs him, Roy's here morning till dark. Drinking his special coffee and smoking his American Spirits and sweating his balls off getting shit done. And even after all of that, some new hot girl will come pick him up in his car, which is this vintage Jeep thing that's not exactly a Jeep. I don't know what it is. But he lets all these different girls drive it while he's at work and then he hops in the car with her after a long day and then they probably go somewhere and have sex for six hours. It's kind of sickening, Roy's excellent life.

"Sure you don't want to come, Will?" my dad asks. "I'll buy you lunch."

I smile, feeling weak. "Nah," I say. "I'm not that hungry anyway. Mom made French toast."

He nods, but he looks mad about that. Like he's the only one allowed to make breakfast or something. Even though I feel shitty for turning him down, I know I've dodged a bullet. I've been on a million of these Craigslist runs with him and they always take longer than he says they will. He has to barter and haggle over the price. Or the guy selling whatever it is also has some other damn thing that he thinks my dad might want and the next thing I know, we're in someone's shitty basement looking at old cans of paint or whatever the hell. My dad goes to take a piss and Roy steps outside. The second we're alone, Garrett looks up from his phone.

"You looking for a real job, Will?"

"Sure."

"Might have something for you."

"What're the hours like?" I ask. "Because I'm helping out my dad this summer."

"I know," he says. "But I talked to your dad, and he's fine with it. Plus, we're open twenty-four-seven, so there'll be ways to work you in."

Garrett's restaurant is called Time to Eat. It's breakfast and burgers and crap. It's in what used to be an old Embers. They make way better hash browns than Embers, though.

"Hit me with your cell number," he says, getting up and handing me his phone.

28

My name's in there already, so I punch in my number. I can't believe this is that easy.

"What's the job? I've never been a waiter."

"I was thinking you'd make a good cook."

"Okay," I say. I mean, I can grill. And chop stuff. But that's about it. I kind of want to tell him this but also kind of don't.

"You'd start out in the back, learning how things on all the stations work, first. Then I'll have Carl show you the ropes." He slaps my stomach again and smiles and says he'll be in touch soon.

Cooking for Garrett? It's not completely out of range. My dad likes to cook. I mean, it's one of his things. Waffles, grilling, homemade sauce. He doesn't look like he'd be all fancy like that but he likes to eat, that's for sure. My mom never has me cook, mainly because she's always having to make two different things for Kinney and Taylor, and Jay has some weird thing about garlic and onions, so she's pretty preoccupied serving up three different dinners as it is. But my dad always has made me chop onions or wash vegetables or watch the grill when I'm at his house. I never really thought about it, I guess.

I head upstairs. My room in my dad's house used to be in the basement. A little room with a big closet and a ton of privacy. And it opened up to the back walkout, so I could sit outside on the picnic table in the backyard at night if I couldn't sleep or I was waiting for my dad to come home from somewhere. But now my dad's filled the basement with construction supplies, the flooring and the new stove and the power saw and the table saw and the mountains of ductwork and wire and Sheetrock he's accumulated for the remodel. And he had a lot of other shit in there to start with—folded-up Ping-Pong table, vats for the beer making he used to do, fuckloads of tools. Since the bedrooms on the main floor are now gone from the demo, he's been sleeping on an inflatable mattress in the living room, but I got the attic, where my mom used to have her sewing and craft room a million years ago. A room she never used, because the attic was either too cold in the winter or too hot in the summer. She always complained about this too. Which was basically their argument: she wanted more and he had enough. She wanted to expand and not just do his accounting, while he was fine with the car wash and the Laundromat. The way things were. There was a reason I was an only child, as far as I could see, because they'd been arguing about that shit since I could remember.

I guess she's still arguing about it, actually. In that same quiet way she's always been arguing about it. What she doesn't get—and what my dad has never pointed out to her, either—was that giving me Jay's old Audi was a pain in the ass. And the clothes she buys me are way too stuck-up for the school I go to. And the house she lives in? Most of my friends can't make it out to Oak Prairie, anyway. They don't drive and the bus doesn't go out there. She's still fighting with my dad, thinking she's doing shit that matters, buying me clothes at fucking Macy's when half my school gets free lunch in the cafeteria. And of course my dad won't say anything but you can tell by the way he looks at everything she sends back with me that it annoys him. That's the thing about divorce. It doesn't necessarily end after the papers are signed and the people involved move apart.

The attic's really hot now. Sticky and close. And emptied out so there's nothing of my mom in it. A bare window and a futon and a milk crate for a nightstand and a desk. A chair underneath the window that my dad found in an alley on spring-cleaning trash day. The chair is blue with little tiny pink dots on it. Dots that are flowers, if you get up close. It's supposed to make the room seem more comfortable. Make up for the fact that the pine floorboards have been stripped of the funky mildewy carpet and that the futon once belonged to Garrett's girlfriend's daughter.

There's a box fan on the floor, though, new, still in a Walmart bag. My dad promised he'd get one because it's been so hot. I set it up in the window over the chair, aim it toward the bed. Then I unlace my boots and fall onto the futon.

My headache is back. And I feel a million kinds of fucked up.

Am I so desperate that it doesn't matter who wants to get me off?

No.

I roll on my stomach. Take off my glasses. Shut my eyes.

Am I gay now? Is that what this all is?

No. Because Angus didn't get me off.

Still. I liked it. Liked him. I can't think a bad thing about it, except that I'm embarrassed. And I can't stop either thing: the liking or the being embarrassed.

But it doesn't feel like I'm gay. Because I can't see it happening with anyone else. My other friends, either. Even DeKalb, who's better looking than me. I think about it for a minute: kissing DeKalb, kissing Jack Telios.

DeKalb's a big guy. And Jack Telios, who I've been friends with since we got stuck in ninth-grade choir, is scrawny and short. Plus his skin's got this pinkish color, like he's an albino practically. But . . . nothing. Not a chance. Never ever would I want that.

I try to sleep. If I could talk to Angus about this, about what to do, about what it means, I would. But I can't.

My head hurts. The blood's thumping in my temples. I try to slow my breath, relax. My mom is always saying that, especially to Kinney when she gets all cranked up: *Relax. Slow down. Breathe.*

I slow down. My head sinks into the pillow.

It was just kissing. Just kissing. We were high and drunk.

I breathe, slow, then slower. I think about nothing but the sound going in and out of my mouth and nose. Every time I see Angus (or remember feeling him, my dick tightening underneath me) I just slow down. Breathe more. Count it out. Breathe. Breathe. Breathe. I'm like a dragon sending out fire, not breath, cooling my body off until it's just the sound of the fan and my lungs and I'm asleep.

"Hey! Brandy!"

"BRANDY!!!"

"BRANDY, COME HERE!"

"Come here right now! COME *ONNNN!* BRANDY!"

Two voices. A girl and a boy. They're hollering but not in

a *this-is-an-emergency* way. My window overlooks the back-yard, so it must be the backyard neighbors. I sit up, put on my glasses, and look out the window. There are new people there now. Before, the people owned a giant sheepdog that ripped up the lawn to bare mud, and they had a giant shed between their fence and the alley. But now the shed and the dog are gone and there's a little gate with one of those hook-and-eye latch deals. The grass is nice and green; there are pots of flowers on the deck; a garden with bamboo tripod poles that green things are climbing up in twists.

I rub my eyes. I feel a little better, though I have drool on my pillow. I get up, head to the attic bathroom to take a piss. Stare at the picture above the toilet the whole time. There's something I've always liked about this picture; it's a dog curled up and sleep-ing on a big white bed. There's something about it that makes me relaxed, makes me feel better. We've never even had a dog but it makes me want to get one.

I go downstairs, pour a huge mason jar of water and go out to the backyard. Weave through the piles of wood. There's a new jigsaw thing—at least I think it's a jigsaw?—sitting beside a stack of plastic PVC piping. I sit down on the picnic table, pushing aside the full ashtray and citronella candle.

Then I see movement in the former-sheepdog yard. Two swings heaving back and forth, two kids in them, out of sync. Yelling.

I wonder if they are saying "Andy" for a minute until I hear a loud girl's voice:

"What is going on?"

And one of the kids jumps off the swing and the other laughs and there's more yelling and I see a glimpse of the girl coming out through the sliding glass door of the deck and then I get it. It's Brandy Corvallis. She'll be a sophomore at Franklin and she was in my Studio Arts class all last year. She also lives by my dad's Laundromat and washes her family's laundry there. Which is sort of sad to me—I mean, I wash our laundry there too, sometimes— but I guess I was just surprised. Because Brandy never seemed like someone sad and poor like that. She's the kind of girl who always takes pictures for yearbook, constantly moving around the edges of basketball games or the cafeteria, taking candid shots or lining up teams or whatever. The kind of girl that's always got stuff going on like that. Busy. In Studio Arts, she was always deep into her painting or ceramic jug or whatever. Taking pictures. Folding her family's laundry while doing her algebra.

But my dad's Laundromat is where we first started talking— not in Studio Arts. Because she was good at art and I was suffering through it, mainly. But also because she was younger and while I'm desperate, I just wanted to let her do her own thing.

When Brandy started coming to the Laundromat that spring I finally said hi to her. She told me her aunt's washing machine was busted and they were saving up for a new one. She seemed a little less hassled and busy at the Laundromat, even though she was obviously doing her family's laundry. She didn't have the camera—yearbook deadlines had passed, she said—and I felt better approaching her. Because I had a reason to be at my dad's Laundromat and I could help her with stuff. Front her samples of detergent if my dad wasn't around, make sure she had her own rolling sorting cart, get her a Dr Pepper from the machine. It wasn't flirting. Just, you know. Friendly.

I'm suddenly starving. I bolt the rest of the water. A little bit of the headache comes back and I wish I had sunglasses. I never have sunglasses, though. Because I have regular glasses. And prescription sunglasses cost a lot. Plus, I think that is dorky. It's like giving up. Acknowledging that you're a full-time nerd or something. I'd rather just squint. I get up and go into the kitchen, then, because Brandy is rolling a blue circular swimming pool toward the yard, where she might see me, and I don't want to be caught staring.

At the sink, I pour another glass of water and keep staring. I'm creeping, I know. But Brandy's wearing cut-off jeans and a bikini top and it's kind of surprising, but she looks kind of good. I mean, she's a cute girl. Just younger. And I thought I'd have noticed it, her being kind of sexy. Being in one of my classes is a prime way for me to develop a huge obsession with you, actually. Nothing like sitting in class, being bored for ninety minutes and getting to stare at a girl in front of you, examine every bit of her body and face and watch her move and laugh and frown at her notebook and by the time the bell rings, you are in love with her.

Which was another reason I never talked to her in class, probably. School's bad enough as it is. No reason to add your stupid idiot boner into things.

Still, here I am, gay Will, fucked-up Will, creeping on Brandy Corvallis while she's babysitting new backyard neighbors. Her boobs are pretty nice—the bikini is green and kind of smashes them together in a way that I can't stop staring at. The window is smudged—has my dad ever cleaned the windows in this house?— but I can see Brandy helping the kids into the little pool and then grabbing a lawn chair while the boy holds the hose. Brandy sits down with her bare feet in the water and shivers and the kids laugh. Then she sits back and puts on her sunglasses.

I feel jealous of her then. How she's working but also getting to kick back like that, her feet in the pool. The kids splash around her feet and she talks to them and splashes back. I'm looking at her tits. I'm half-hard again, sad to say. Or happy to say. I feel okay, really. Though I'm hungry. Starving. I reach for the last rubbery waffle and eat it without a plate or syrup, just staring out the window.

THREE

MY DAD'S HOUSE isn't big. None of the houses next to it are, either. They're all little boxes that look like the ones you use when you play Monopoly, with matching tiny squares of lawn— so I'm shocked at all the demolition crap we fill the Dumpster with. I shouldn't be; my dad's been saying from the get-go how houses are a complex structure, not just "a wooden box that sits outside and rots."

Though once Roy whispered to me, "Actually, it is a box that sits outside and rots. It's just not a wooden one."

But the next weeks go on and on, and the shit we haul out from my dad's house? It doesn't let up. Tile and wires and duct-work and insulation and rotting Sheetrock from the main-floor bathroom and the old carpet off the attic stairs and more tile and countertops and so much shitty, abused trim. Now it's really not a house. It's just mostly enclosed space. The kitchen's a card table and a coffeepot and a whole bunch of tools. The bathroom's a toilet with half walls around it, bare studs mostly. Most of the time our breakfast is a bunch of pastries from the bakery on Johnson my dad likes.

Though I can see how much is getting done, I can also see, from the looks on people's faces (mostly Roy's), and the barer and less functional the house gets, how much it will take to build it back up, and there are less than two months of summer to do it. Minnesota's winter is too unpredictable to leave anything for fall. Roy goes back to college the last week in August. But the way the materials are piling up in the backyard—bathroom sinks and windows and cabinets and planks of new siding—you'd think my dad had all the time in the world.

One Friday, we replace two windows and start digging around the front to put in cement footings for what will be our porch. It's a long day, hot as hell. My dad has us knock off around six and so we start cleaning up the jobsite in our usual way: Roy having a smoke, my dad cracking open a beer, me cleaning my glasses for the billionth time.

The girl that comes to pick up Roy that night looks especially nice, in this short black dress, and I feel so jealous of Roy for a minute, I can barely speak. I don't know why, either. I like Roy a lot. He's always helping us and being in a good mood. We'd be fucked without him. So I don't know why I'm upset. Maybe it's just because of how easy he is with things. How he tucks his cigarettes in his shirt. Dumps his Nalgene in the neighbor's flower beds. And how, after a long day of working hard, he just gets that cute girl, that cool old Jeep-truck thing. Which is not old like my dad's truck, with its awful topper and no power steering. But old in that it's kind of vintage and cool: it's a mint green and you can take the top off if you want. It probably cost a lot but Roy acts like it's nothing. Lets any old girl drive it. Lets her roll up in it, pick him up too. Like it'd be nothing if she totaled it. I wonder if he'll fuck the black-dress girl in that car. I know I'd fuck her in that car. Or I'd want to, at least. I don't know how the version of me that could kiss a girl would ever act, but since Angus and all that, I'm kind of wishing I could find out. I don't know what I'm waiting for. Maybe Roy doesn't wait for things to happen to him?

I know Roy's parents have a lot of money—my dad mentioned this to me once—and that makes me jump from jealous to angry. I'd rather just be mad at someone than sit there feeling shitty about what I'd rather have in life. I'm supposed to be here, helping my dad, fixing this house that he's always wanted to fix, helping him get his dream and make everything the way he's always wanted, for once. My dad has been working his ass off. Finding crap from Craigslist. Coordinating schedules with his friends. Making deals on cheap materials. Even finding a kid like Roy. I shouldn't be wishing I was Roy.

But I get like this. Always wanting so much. Feeling greedy. Desperate. I hate it.

After Roy leaves, my dad and I go pick up some tacos. Though he's as sweaty and grimy as me, my dad is really happy. Smiling. Talking about what's happening tomorrow, and the week after. Saying it'll be in prime shape soon and we'll celebrate in spring, my graduation and a housewarming, all in one.

"Party like we've never had," he says. "I'm inviting the whole neighborhood, so they can't complain about the noise."

He flips on the radio, eats half a taco while he drives. Then turns in to the liquor store and lets the truck run. "Just a sec," he says, and I sit with the hot bag of tacos on my lap, the truck vibrating in idle around me.

The liquor store is next to a Walgreens, a fake nails place, and the Little Caesars where DeKalb works. I consider going to see if DeKalb's around, but I don't want to miss my dad coming back—just a sec means maybe just a six-pack?

I stare at the people going into the Walgreens. There's a lot of people. Old people. Teenagers like me. Adults alone, adults in pairs, talking, holding hands. Two little kids come out eating ice-cream treats and they're wearing swimsuits. One kid even has the floaty rings around his arms. Their dad is behind them, shoving his wallet into his back pocket and grabbing for their hands. The kids are so focused on their ice-cream treats, they aren't looking for cars in the parking lot. The one little kid yells about hand-holding and the dad yells back and then the kid's crying and dripping ice cream until they turn the corner and I can't see them anymore.

My dad comes out of the liquor store pushing a shopping cart. Fuck.

He's not looking at me. Just goes around, lifts the back hatch off the truck topper. Starts loading cases of beer and a thing of wine in a box.

I twist around and before I can say anything he says, "Got a bigger crew coming tomorrow. A couple of guys we're paying."

I nod. I hate how he's got to explain himself. Easier if he just says nothing.

All the way home, I eat tacos straight from the bag. The beer cases clunk around in the back and it annoys me. Not that he notices. He's still in an excellent mood. Someone calls his cell once we're back at the house, about something he's interested in buying and he gets even more happy. He gulps the beer he's opened, finishes his last taco, then he tells me he'll be back in twenty minutes and takes off in his truck again.

I shove all the taco garbage into the giant Rubbermaid bin that is now the trash for our kitchen. For the whole house, really. If you can call this a house.

I don't know what to do next. I'm bored. I'm feeling jittery. I fill an empty Gatorade bottle with a ton of water and hit the picnic table in the backyard. The night is lowering around the chain-link fence and I can smell grilling and burgers, and hear crickets. I think of the beer in the back of my dad's truck. He didn't even unload it. I wonder if any of it'll even make it back home. I check my almost-dead phone; it's 8:32.

"BRANDY!" Same yelling-little-kid voice.

"Yes?" Brandy, then. Part of me wants to go inside. Part of me wants to see her. Maybe even talk to her. Even though I probably reek. My shirt's still kinda damp from sweat.

"You have to say GOOD-BYE! BRANDY!" The little-kid voice again.

Then Brandy: "Good-bye, Anna. Good-bye, Rory."

"Will you come back tomorrow?"

"Tomorrow's Saturday, Rory," Brandy says. "Your parents will be home then."

I hear steps on the little cement walkway. Hear the gate unhook. I try to stay still. I don't know what to do. I feel sort of strange. Scared. But excited too.

But the gate clanks shut and then she's standing there in the alley and squinting toward me. I resist the urge to check my pits.

"Hey?" Brandy calls.

"Hey," I say back.

She walks to the chain link around our yard and I make myself move. Stand. Don't know if it's just my social idiocy or if I'm still trying to hide from her, but I have to consciously propel myself across the lawn. Making sure not to stumble over the wheelbarrow or the piles of equipment and materials covered in blue tarps in case of rain. I'm making myself go say hello to a girl at my back fence. I'm a sweaty dirty idiot. Who smells like tacos.

"Will Caynes," she says. "Thought I was seeing you all these days."

"Yeah, that's me," I say. Idiotic. "What's up? You live here now?" Though I know damn well.

"I babysit here. Rory and Anna. The Vances. I'm like their nanny. I hope there's a bus this late. They've never kept me this late."

"Oh." I should offer her a ride. Right? Or would that seem like I'm trying to get rid of her? I'm a million times sweatier all of a sudden.

We stare at each other. She nods. She smiles. I nod. I smile. This was never this hard at the Laundromat.

She's so fuckin' cute, though. She really is. Her little shirt's this white thing with little green stripes and it buttons up the front. But the front's low and the top two buttons aren't buttoned. I can't stare at it. I already stared at it. I'm looking at her face like my life depends on it.

Finally she says something. "So. This is where you live?"

"My dad lives here. I mean, I do too. But I also live out in Oak Prairie. My mom's house is out there. They're divorced."

She nods. I am studying Brandy Corvallis like there's going to be a quiz. She's kind of narrow through the shoulders, and her hair is all dark and thick and long around her shoulders. Messy but nice. Her face is splotched with sunburned skin, and her eyes have all this makeup around them, which is sort of flaking off a little. All of this makes her really cute, though.

I clear my throat and look away from her. At least with Angus, I didn't get caught looking at his boobs. Dick. Whatever. I'm trying to relax myself on the inside because just now I'm so fucking excited that she's here. But I don't want her to see it or she might get weirded out and leave.

I think for a minute. What can I tell her?

"You want something to drink?"

She looks at her watch, then looks up at me.

"Sure," she says. "Sure. Why not."

Brandy Corvallis likes white wine. I'm lucky in that, because it's an hour later and we're drinking white wine from this bottle my dad had on top of the refrigerator. It was all dusty, so I think he forgot about it. We're sitting on the picnic table and we're talking. Acting like this is normal, even though it's obviously a step beyond bullshitting in my dad's Laundromat.

And she's doing most of the talking. I'm just kind of answering. Laughing. Handing her the wine bottle. Brandy Corvallis doesn't mind that I don't have a lot to say, though I can't tell if that's because we don't know each other or if she's a little buzzed. I'm not buzzed, but I still feel all nervous and excited and I'm trying to hide it. She's asked me about all the crap in the backyard and I've tried to explain what everything is, or at least what we're doing inside. But mostly I'm just sitting here, feeling good again. Feeling that shot of happy. She smells like orange Popsicles. I wonder if she ate one or if I'm nuts. I'm smacking a mosquito on my arm when I get a text from my dad.

stopping by laundromat need anything

Brandy looks at my phone and I put it in my pocket.

I smack another mosquito. She shivers.

"Want more wine?"

"No," she says. "Who was that?"

"My dad," I say.

"Oh."

Then I kiss her. I don't plan it, either. I just do it because I can't think of anything to say. Her mouth is so soft. And I'm lucky. So lucky.

Because it's perfect, perfect timing. We're shoulder to shoulder so it's not a big move. It's just our faces close to each other and she doesn't do anything at first. Well, she kisses back. She's not just a mannequin or anything about it. Her mouth is nice, and it tastes like wine. And she isn't doing anything nuts, and so I feel normal. Good. Like it wasn't a bad idea.

I want to take my glasses off but her tongue is in my mouth. And I'm like, this is really the best thing. Her tongue in my mouth. My tongue in her mouth. Both of them together.

I put a hand on her shoulder and we get a little closer. I am still completely surging. Excited. My dick, hard. Instantly. I'm kind of impressed with myself, really. I pull back and smile. And she's looking down at her hands but she's smiling too.

"Want to come inside?" I say. I'm prepared for her to say no and then I'll just say it's to see the remodel, not anything else, in case she's worried. . . .

But she just gets up. And we go. I don't know if she likes me or there's just too many mosquitoes, but I kind of lead her through the yard and toward the side door.

I am glad the house is dark and none of the utility lights are on. And I'm glad that she doesn't stop or ask about anything. She just takes my hand and we go upstairs to my room. I'm breathing like a motherfucker and I'm trying not to, but that doesn't make it any better.

She sits down on the blue chair and sets down the little bag she's had across her body since I first saw her in the alley. I pull my keys and wallet out of my pocket and put them on my desk. I don't know what to do at all now. I feel like maybe I fucked things up.

"Will your dad get mad if I'm here?" she asks, very quiet.

This makes my dick even harder; I know she's not here just to talk or anything.

While I reach over her and flip on the fan—it's still *hot* up here—I tell her that he'll be gone for a while. I don't tell her that his code words—*need anything?*—is his way of asking me if I can be left alone so he can go get loaded. I'm guessing he's at his friend's. Or at the Laundromat. Stocking his office fridge with the beer. It doesn't matter. I've gotten that same text before, though it's been a while. Before this summer, he must have saved his benders for when I'm in Oak Prairie. But he can't avoid me now so I guess he's giving up hiding.

I go to Brandy. She stands up. We kiss in front of the fan.

Okay, Dad, I think, my hands going around her back. *Avoid me all you want, really.*

Because of the fan, her hair gets into my mouth. Her mouth too. It's kind of funny but also I feel dumb about it. I turn her and it's not a problem. And then, I pull her toward the futon. We sit down, at the same time, slowly. She takes off her flip-flops. I take off my glasses, set them on the floor with a little click. It's quiet except for the fan. I put my hand around her waist. She's wearing a belt and these shorts. They're not super-short shorts, but they are tight. I run my hand around her waist, my fingers catching along the belt. She shivers, laughs. Then we're kissing again. It's good. Every few seconds I feel something extra, something new. Happy. Then nervous. Then unsure. Then happy again.

She lies back on the futon, her hair dark against the white and blue quilt.

"Come here," she says.

Then I'm happy for real. We're making out. It goes on so long. It's all kind of the same, but all kind of not. I'm aware of everything. All of the stuff, even if it's repetitive. All of her rolling under me and me rolling under her. Every part of her I touch. How her upper arms are so soft. How her boobs feel mashed against my chest. The way she spreads her legs across my hips. We keep all our clothes on for a while and I'm okay with that too. Everything's blurry for me. I can't quite see her face, the expression. I wonder what my face looks like. I hope it's okay. Because I want to get to do this again. Because Brandy feels really good. Tastes good too.

I reach up under her T-shirt, feel her skin, the stripe of her bra across her back. Then she does the same to me, minutes later. It's like a game. Her, then me. Me, then her. Me. Her. It almost is kind of dorky, the back and forth.

"I can't believe we're doing this," she says.

"I know," I say.

"Is your dad never coming home?"

"I don't know," I say.

She sits up, then. "I have to call my aunt. I can't believe I didn't earlier."

I just lie there on the futon. I can't move. My dick is crushed under my button fly and I breathe again. I wish I wore contacts.

She stands up and starts talking. "Aunt Megan?" She goes into the hall, like she doesn't want me to hear. I can hear, though. Most of it. The tone of it sounds okay. She's making up some shit about the bus not running. Saying she's at a girlfriend's house. She'll get a ride. I wonder if she thinks I'll give her one. I look at my watch: 10:39.

Then I hear her in the room again and she's putting down her bag and she's back on the futon and I'm all over her, pulling her closer to me. I like touching her. I didn't touch Angus much. I don't know why.

Well. *Maybe* I know why.

My hands stop. The littlest bit of guilty comes into the happy. A dent in it.

"My aunt's still out in Lakeville," she says.

"Okay."

"But my nana's asleep already, so it's okay."

"All right." I know I should be asking her to fill in the blanks here, but I just flick hair off her face so I can kiss her. Smoothing out the dent.

"I live with my nana and my aunt, in case that's not obvious."

"I managed to put that together."

She laughs and the dent's gone. I don't know who I am right now, but I like him. He knows what to say. His hands don't shake. I keep kissing her.

"My nana's deaf. And super old. She just moved in with us. She was living on her own and it didn't really work."

Her hands slip up under my T-shirt. I like how her nails scrape around my skin. Not in a hurting way but good. Like I'm being clenched. Like this is all on purpose, not a mistake. And I want her so much now. I want Angus too, retroactively. I want to fuck her. I've never felt like that, even in a dream, even while jerking off. Not in this same, specific way. This tears past the happy. All the way past. It's how I know I'm an animal, all the way underneath.

Her fingers skate underneath my arms, along my collarbone. All I can think is this kind of insane I WANT TO FUCK shouting-feeling.

I realize I need to act like someone who cares about what she's saying. Respond. I clear my throat a little.

"Why's your aunt in Lakeville?"

"She's got a guy friend out there. They're canning peaches."

"What?"

She laughs. "I'm serious. Her boyfriend is kind of into that. If he's actually her boyfriend now. I'm not sure about that." Her nails slip and scratch around my collarbone. I breathe. Control myself. I'm worried she can sense it, all of my I WANT TO FUCK feelings.

"Take your shirt off," she says, her mouth at my neck. I freeze.

I do exactly what she says. She laughs.

And I think I might die of it, the happy. Her here. This bed finally feeling comfortable. Her skin touching my skin. Even the shouting feeling is okay. All of it.

At five in the morning, Brandy asks if I'll drive her home.

"My nana wakes up at, like, six a.m. every morning," she says. "It's kind of shitty."

We get our stuff back on. All business. I put my wallet in my pocket, my glasses on. She goes to the bathroom and does something in there, probably pees? All I hear is running water. I don't say anything as we go through the house. I'm hoping it looks just like a remodel. I'm hoping she won't ask any questions. I'm hoping my dick will deflate. My balls are killing me, because I've gotten hard and then soft like a hundred times, even though it was just kissing with our shirts off.

Part of me wants to tell Angus. Tell someone what happened. And part of me never wants Angus to know. Because I think of him smiling and of Brandy smiling and I don't want either of them to stop that.

The whole way to her house, I don't say much to Brandy but she doesn't say much, either. I'm totally exhausted. She's got to be too. She directs me to her house, which means we pass the Laundromat. My dad's truck's not there and I try not to think about that. She points to a house on the left, small but nice. There's a screened-in front porch and hanging baskets of flowers and stuff.

I put the car in park, shut it off. I don't want the idling engine to wake anyone up, but then I remember her nana's deaf. Oh well. Her aunt, then. If she's even around. I wonder if Brandy's used to having her aunt be gone too. Like my dad now. Like we're both these orphan children.

"Thank you for the ride," she says. All formal. Like, this is good-bye, forever. Like, she's getting on a ship to go to the New World and that's it. I can't have that. I can't; I mean, why did she stay with me all night if that's how it is?

I lean over and kiss her and she's kind of surprised and I don't care. I'm kind of surprised too. I surprise myself. I didn't know I could do this. If I'd known it would be so easy, I'd have done it long before tonight. Long before Angus did it to me.

Maybe Angus knew that? Maybe he was trying to help me.

"You want to . . . should I . . . I can call you . . . ?" she says. Looks down at her lap.

Is it terrible that it makes me smile that's she all nervous sounding? It's absolutely the best thing. But right away, I want to smooth out the dent in this too.

"Yes," I say, totally certain. She looks up at that. Smiles. I don't want her feeling bad because I don't feel bad at all. She hands me her phone and I put in my number, just like I did with Garrett.

"I'll text you after I get my nana up and stuff."

"After you get some sleep."

"Right," she says. "You get some sleep too."

"Okay."

"'Bye, Will," she says. Then she's out of the car, running up the walk and fumbling with keys. She never looks back. I drive back home just as the sun comes up.

FOUR

THE THING WITH Brandy is like I drank some potion in a comic book. And now, instead of growing or shrinking or getting radioactive superpowers, I'm this guy who does things and says things and I'm not all nervous all the time. Especially the thing with Angus.

When I go see my mom a few days later, she gives me this solution and little special chamois-cloth thing to clean my glasses and it's like everything looks a million times better. Sharper. Clearer. Even when I see Angus, everything's great. We don't talk about what happened. I don't tell him about Brandy, but we hang out in his garage and it's fun. I tell him about maybe working for Garrett. He tells me he's got an interview at a garden-center place. The happy feeling doesn't even go away. Keeps getting stronger.

Brandy and I text each other a lot and then we meet up the next time she's done babysitting. I end up walking her to the bus stop and we kiss for a minute, but nothing major, because another dude comes up to wait for the bus. Then we don't see each other for a couple weeks because the Vances take her with them on a vacation to Wisconsin Dells. I can't believe people would do that, drag a nanny on vacation, or that she'd agree, but they're paying her.

Then, at the end of July, my dad gets it up his ass to reroof the house. There was a storm back in May and hail damage, I guess. I was out at my mom's, so I missed it. But he's all busy filing an insurance claim, so work comes to a halt on the house.

I think it's a mistake, since Roy worries we're running behind schedule and it's hard enough to get used to life in the house now. It's like camping, but we're still inside. The water's cold for some weird reason, there are bugs coming in through all the open bits from the demolition, the power's iffy. There's a scorch mark on the bare plank floor near the kitchen, about six inches long. I don't know if that was the old-ass waffle iron my dad loves, or something else.

But it doesn't matter; my dad wants the new roof, because it'll be free, paid for by insurance. There's no talking to him about it, because what do I know about insurance? And Roy's hesitant, but I can tell he doesn't feel like he can tell my dad his business.

But I don't want to complain about it. Garrett calls me one Saturday while my dad's in Rochester looking at an energy-efficient furnace and I'm eating cold pizza for breakfast. He asks about the house and I tell him what's going on and then he kind of pauses.

"Hey. I know I should have called earlier, but I had a guy quit yesterday and I'm kind of shorthanded. You still interested?"

I swallow the pizza but it's not all the way chewed so it's like a lump stuck in my throat.

"Sure."

"Make sure you have ID. Social Security card, plus driver's license. Or passport, if you don't have that. I'll need two forms of ID. Wear jeans and a T-shirt—nothing fancy. Come to the front checkout and ask for me, okay?"

I say okay and hang up, guzzle a bunch of Gatorade to wash down the pizza.

I get to Time to Eat around three o'clock, which Garrett says is good because it's after the lunch rush. Garrett looks like hell. He's wearing a stained white apron over his jeans and he looks very tired. He invites me to sit at a big booth and spreads out a bunch of papers.

"Sierra, can you bring us something to drink?" he asks a passing waitress. Who is very cute. Like, hot-cute. She's got cherry-red hair and super pale skin and tattoos around her collarbones and arms and her little outfit is black and very tight. There's a clock over her left boob where *Time to Eat* is stitched in bright blue. "What do you guys want?"

"Coke's okay," I say. Because I can talk to girls now. The Brandy Magic in full effect.

"Anything for you, Mr. B?" Sierra asks. Garrett's last name is Ballantine.

"No, I'm good, thanks, Sierra," he says. "This is your new prep cook," he adds, pointing to me. "Meet Will."

"Very nice to meet you," Sierra says. She smiles and it's kind of perfect. I think about what it'd be like to kiss her.

I do the paperwork while Garrett talks about the job. When I'm done, he gives me a fresh apron and shows me around the back of the place. He shows me the time card machine, his office, where the schedule's posted, two weeks in advance. There are two cook guys leaning against the line, a blond dude who's inspecting his biceps and a redhead guy who's dumping ranch dressing into a square storage container. They nod at us. Carl's the redhead; the blond guy is something I don't catch. But I don't ask.

Then we go to the dishwasher area, which is like a tiny little room that's full of a dishwasher. The whole thing hums and smells like chemicals, and the floor is wet and then this guy comes back and he's soaking wet and his name is Everardo. Which I only remember because he hands Garrett a set of keys and hands him his apron and the name tag flops over Garrett's hand: EVERARDO. They talk a little bit, then Everardo leaves. We watch the cook guys for a minute, as they get a couple of orders in, and Garrett points to the grills, the fryers, the reach-in, the fire extinguisher, the setups. I nod, like I know what he's saying.

Then we're back at the ice machine, the walk-in cooler, the supply shelf, and the supply closet, where the mops and cleaners and piles of towels and aprons and trash bags are. Anything that's not food goes in there, he says, explaining that the blue towels should never go beyond the kitchen—only white towels in front of the house, he says.

Then it's time for keys. Keys to the Dumpster and the supply closet and the back door and the frying-grease collection bin. All of it. He says the keys rotate possession depending on who's scheduled in back. You have to pass them on to the next person listed on the schedule—that's important, because if people take them home after a shift, everyone's kind of screwed unless Garrett's around.

I nod like we've got it all figured out. Though I can just see myself taking the keys home and ruining everything. But then Garrett opens a sack of potatoes and asks me to wash them so we can start soaking them for hash; he'll put me on dish duty in a minute, but he's got to make a quick couple of calls.

Nobody really talks to me but Garrett. He keeps bringing me things to chop and wash. Ham. Onions. Green peppers. Tomatoes. Mushrooms. Even bacon. I can't use the slicer thing until I'm trained on it, so he works it and we talk about the house remodel and how it's going. I fill big plastic tubs with all these things as Garrett explains what they go into: omelets, garnishes for burgers. The prep cook stocks the coolers and reach-ins with all these ingredients, so the cooks have whatever they need ready to go.

I unpack hamburger patties and stack them in square bins. Chicken. Steak. Chicken-fried steak. Everything in boxes, stashed in the walk-in. Delivered every morning by a truck, Garrett says. We only make the hash and the fries from scratch, he says, sounding sorry. But Time to Eat has too many tables to turn over. And the hash and the fries keep people coming.

Cheese slices, unpacked and crisscrossed for easier grabbing.

Cheddar, Swiss, pepper jack. Portions of things too, for faster cooking: pulled pork, chicken breasts, sauerkraut for Reubens, bacon for club sandwiches, buffalo chicken bites, taco meat for taco salad. Everything ready for grabbing and grilling or warming or slapping together.

Because while some of it is a little detailed, most of the cooking done at Time to Eat is about slapping stuff together on a plate as fast as possible. While I'm in the dish room, loading dirty cups and plates into the washer and waiting for them to finish, I sneak glances at the cooks running the dinner-rush line. One person grills, one fries, they both meet on extras. Plates go up on the order window with the proper ticket. Everything they do moves fast and they are talking through the order window at the cute waitresses and I'm seeing where everything comes from: buns, Kaiser rolls, taco meat packets for taco salad and nachos, cheese, sliced and shredded, sides of ranch and barbecue and vinaigrette, cherry tomatoes and cucumbers for side salads, fries and chicken fingers and mozzarella sticks. The deep fryer scares me but it also smells good, and after the rush lessens and the night-shift cooks slide into place like there's nothing to it, the redhead and blond dudes clocking out like they've been waiting for this moment forever, Garrett has the new cooks make us a couple of burgers.

We eat in the break room and talk. He explains that prep cooks need to come in early, to take deliveries and start stocking. Time to Eat is open all night, but after the post-bar rush not much really goes on until about six a.m., when the daytime people come in for breakfast. So the night crew can prep too, if necessary or if things are slow.

"Anyhow, you'll see," he says. "There's always a list. One of the other cooks or managers will tell you. Or I will. I'm here most days."

I nod. I eat my burger. It's really, really good. I don't know if this is because it is good or because I'm really hungry. My dad and I have been coming to Time to Eat since I can remember, but mainly only for breakfast. My dad likes a big greasy breakfast. Still, the fries here are also good. Though I'm not sure there are fries I won't eat. I even eat the soggy baked cafeteria fries at school; DeKalb always gives me his because he thinks they're awful.

After we finish eating, Garrett has me stand behind the line to do a few orders of fries. There's a process; you don't just dump them into the grease. Plus, you have to swap the old grease out too. Which has its own process, its own list, its own place to initial things. We go back to the Dumpster area and he shows me the spot where you have to mark on another list when you dumped it. There are a lot of lists in the restaurant world, I guess. I say as much and Garrett laughs. Lights a cigarette.

"Lists and schedules," he says. "And lucky me, I get to make them." He blows out a big gray smoke cloud. It's dark now—it's after ten, according to my watch—and I feel uneven. Like I could work more or I could tip over and sleep right here in this nasty-smelling Dumpster corral.

Garrett pulls out some cash from his wallet. Gives me three twenties and I feel dumb about it but he's on to the next thing.

"Can't pay you a check until I process those forms, but I'll have it all figured out by the next time you come in."

I shove the money into my pocket. It makes a little crispy sound when I fold it down in there. I want it out of view as soon as possible. But I'm thrilled to have it.

"When do you want me to come in next?" I ask.

He scratches his head. Garrett has really big hands with lots of dark hair on the tops of them, but he doesn't have a lot of hair on his actual head. And no beard, like my dad. But I can see a little peep of chest hair coming out of the top of the T-shirt he's wearing under his Time to Eat denim shirt.

"Not tomorrow," he says. "Me and Kristin have this craft-show thing she wants to do." He thinks, smokes for a minute, like he's looking at an invisible schedule in his head. "How about Monday? That work?"

"I think so."

"I'd like if you could come in the morning, so I can show you the deliveries and such. Ask your dad if he can spare you, though."

"I think it'll be okay."

He nods. "Okay, kid. You're free to go whoop it up. It's Saturday night, after all, right?" He laughs, pats my shoulder. "Tell your dad hello, okay?"

I say okay and he opens the Dumpster corral and lets me out, like I'm a prisoner or something. A trash prisoner. A grease prisoner. For some reason, this makes me laugh. How the trash is all locked up. Because people steal the grease to use in their cars as fuel or rummage for food or whatever.

I get in my car and pull the money out of my pocket. One crisp twenty, one worn, the other in the middle. Plus a few quarters and ones in tips that Sierra slipped me after I helped her clear a few tables while Garrett was doing something else.

There's something about cash for me. I get cash from my mom a lot—to run to Walgreens for her (Taylor and Kinney are wild to go to Walgreens with me, as if it's something special, since they're in a car without their mom or dad), to pick up pizza when she's running late. I rarely get cash from my dad, though. He's just not like that. If I need shampoo or something, he'll go buy it, of course, but mainly I ask my mom for that stuff. She just kind of knows too, when I'm running out of those things. And I know she's got more money, because she makes a crapload at her job and so does Jay. My dad runs a tighter budget. He doesn't pay himself a big salary, and now he's out one income since he sold the car wash. I just don't want to bug him with what I need, really.

But this cash is mine. Because I made it. Which is, like, *No shit, Will*. But I did make it. Through all these hours and my hands smelling like chemicals and onions. Through the way my feet kind of ache from all the standing. From following Garrett around. Doing what he said. Filling up plastic tubs. Chopping things. Portions. Stacks. Racks of steaming hot clean cups. I made it. *I made it be in my pocket.*

My phone beeps and it's Angus:

whut r you doing

I'm sweating. The Audi's air-conditioning broke and my dad

60

said it was stupid to fix it. I roll down the windows and hot air from the parking lot fills the car more. It's been stupid humid lately.

I text Angus about work and then he says he's got some weed and am I staying with my mom or my dad, because his parents went out to the lake for the weekend.

Right that second, I get hard. I do. All the way. I'm sweating, sitting in a car, with a fucking boner. From a *text*.

There's a dent in the happy, then. I don't know if it's that I'm tired or if I know I'm ruining the Brandy Magic. I don't know what the fuck this is. But I don't want to think about it too much.

By the time I pull up to Angus's house, I feel like I drank a million cups of coffee, even though I don't drink coffee. Angus is standing in front of his garage when I pull up, and he tells me to park in the garage, where there's a spot because his parents' car is gone.

"You want to smoke out?" he asks.

I shrug, but it's a lie. I'm so fucking zingy. I feel like a little kid in gym class, excited to play the dog-catcher game where you chased everyone everywhere and put them in the pound, which was really just the basketball key lines on the gym floor.

"Here?"

"Come inside."

He doesn't say it sexy. Like it's supposed to mean something else. But tell that to my dick. I've got the shouting in my head again. FUCK. WANT TO. FUCK.

The Rackler house is ice cold from air-conditioning. We take off our shoes just like at my mom's house.

"Let's go on the patio."

This time he's got a joint. We step through the sliding glass door and smoke it together, standing up. Passing it back and forth. I'm aware of his spit on the paper. Maybe it's the pot, but I'm aware of how sticky my skin is. Of how it's weird to do it here; this is where the adults hang out and drink wine and beer and talk about their adult shit. Maybe that's why he wanted to do it here, instead of the garage.

The Racklers' backyard seems empty compared to my mom's backyard, where there's the above-ground pool and the play system thing, which is almost identical to the one in the park. Of course, Taylor and Kinney need their own personal one for some dumb reason. Probably it's the pot, because at the same time, the Racklers' yard seems endless. Huge. Mrs. Rackler has a garden and flower beds, and the grass goes on for what looks like a mile. The yard ends in a tall wooden fence, so you can't see the adjoining backyard. No chain link like in my dad's neighborhood. No alley.

"Look at the moon. Damn," Angus says. We stare at the moon for a minute. It's huge. Round and white. Kind of fuzzy around the edges, like it has a halo.

"Yeah," I say. Again, it's just bullshit about the moon, but all of it just makes me more excited. I wonder for a minute if I'm reading this all wrong. After all, I told him I wasn't gay. And we hung out after that and nothing happened. Maybe he's taken me at my word?

"You like the job, then?" he asks, and I say yeah. Tell him about

Garrett and the used grease and the hash and whatever. He says he likes the garden-center place okay. I think he might ask about how much I make an hour, but he doesn't and I'm glad, because that's one thing I never asked Garrett. Angus wouldn't ask that shit. He doesn't need money. He doesn't think about money like I do. I feel the money, crisp, folded in my pocket. I worry my pocket isn't deep enough. If it might fall out. I slide my hand down there. Feel for it. Still there.

I'm still hard too.

By the time we finish the joint, I'm feeling more mellow: chilling out, you could say. Maybe I'm tired. Maybe it's good weed. We go inside. Angus turns off the lights as we go. I follow him to the basement, where Angus's bedroom is, along with another TV and a Ping-Pong table and all Mr. Rackler's weights and exercise equipment. Angus asks if I want to watch a movie but I'm yawning. He tells me I can have his bed. Then I know he's not into the sex part. Then I feel even stupider for my boner. Embarrassed. Worried he can see it all over me, all these feelings. Dumb that I maybe ruined the Brandy Magic for no reason.

In his room, alone, I can smell Time to Eat all over my clothes. It's kind of awful. It's weird to think that all the food I chopped and washed and fried makes this kind of smell, especially since it goes into making things other people pay to eat. The smell doesn't belong in a bedroom. Maybe not even a restaurant. It's so bad I want to set them on fire. I strip to my boxers and set my glasses on the dresser. Then I get into Angus's bed, which is not a futon, but an actual bed. A mattress with a pillowtop and lots of pillows. Plush and soft, but it smells like a boy. Like Angus. Like his stupid body spray he insists isn't gross like Axe or Old Spice but this stuff his dad gets from Macy's or whatever. The second I lie down I can feel how exhausted I am and before I know it I'm asleep.

Later, though, I wake up, because Angus is getting in the bed. My back is to him but I feel the mattress shift and the covers flip up. Then I feel him, beside me. Feel his hand slip across my back, over my shoulder. Feel him move against me so I turn myself, eyes still closed, all the way toward him. I feel his mouth on my mouth again and it's just like the other time. Natural. Normal. But this time there is no stopping. No glasses between our faces. And I'm not just lying there. It's like I'm asleep, but I know what I'm doing. I like what I'm doing. I feel his chest and it's so smooth. I have more hair than he does. His hands are all over me too. His hair falls into my eyes. It's so relaxing, but, like with Brandy, my body's all tight too. Everywhere alive. I don't know if it's the weed or the kissing and touching.

I stop kissing for a minute. My hand's on his stomach. Angus's mouth is down around my jaw.

Angus says, "Are you okay, Will?"

And I don't say anything, but I know it's okay. I kiss him again instead of saying it and then my hand goes down lower, where we're both hard. And then it's like we just know exactly what to do. Underwear gets pushed down, sheets and covers move out of the way, and he's got my dick in his hand and I've got mine on his and it feels like being in a mirror, holding and being held and there's no wondering involved. It's automatic. Perfect. So we get to it. Get each other off.

It's not like regular jerking off. Well, it is. But it's so much better. I wonder if Brandy did this, would it feel the same? Better? Or worse? Maybe it's just because I'm surprised about how it'll go, unlike when it's my own hand and I know what'll happen next. Maybe because Angus is a guy and knows what feels good?

We're so quiet, but I don't know why. No one's here except us. But he's quiet, so I am too. Nothing but the slurpy sounds of our hands on each other's dicks. Which is gross and embarrassing but unmistakable. Maybe that's why we don't talk? Nothing but that sound, until Angus's voice catches in his throat and he comes. And then I can't help it and I come too.

A minute later, he gets one of his towels hanging off a chair and we wipe everything off. Our hands, our stomachs, everything. It kind of erases the whole thing out. Smooths it over. Makes it less gross in my mind, or something. Makes it so I'm forgiving myself.

My body feels chilled with the air-conditioning. We're still not saying anything, though I am breathing harder than a motherfucker. So's he.

And then, even though I think we shouldn't, I can tell he's going to fall asleep. I think maybe we should figure this out. Talk about what the hell this is. Because it's like I'm gay again. But I just can't find the words. So we fall asleep, my back to him, but his hands around me. When I wake up next, the sun's just coming up and when I sit up, he opens his eyes and looks at me.

It's blurry, because my glasses are on the dresser, but I kiss him on the mouth. No tongue, because I can't stay. I get dressed, put on my glasses. I don't look at him, though I know he's watching me. I leave without saying good-bye.

FIVE

ONCE THE ROOF comes off my dad's house, things change. There's insurance money and not so much with the Craigslist runs. Roy doesn't look hesitant anymore. The mismatched work crews of friends who owe my dad favors show up. There are coolers of beer and grill-outs and long days and nights. There's even an actual roofing crew with a tear-off Dumpster. My dad's laughing a lot. It goes on for a while, but I'm not around as much because of my new work schedule. I feel a little guilty about that, but it seems like my dad's got it handled.

A couple of times, Angus comes into the restaurant to say hi and I buy him a burger. Everything's cool. I don't know if it's because we're both guys that we're able to be normal about things. It's not like I have to do something drastic like buy him flowers. It's basically the same as before, except for the part underneath that only we know about.

Since it all happened when she was in Wisconsin, I tell myself that there's still Brandy Magic. No dent in it. Nothing's changed.

But when Brandy comes back, the day after the roofers finish the house, I'm nervous. I'm worried she'll know something.

We meet up in the afternoon at the Laundromat and both do our laundry. None of that is sexy, but Brandy's aunt let stuff pile up while Brandy was gone and I'm out of stuff to wear to both work and remodeling. I'm nervous, but at least we have something to do, to cover that up. Brandy kisses me and then she goes next door and gets us coffees at the coffee shop and we get all hyper on caffeine and I push her around in the rolling hampers and it's just kind of stupid but we are both laughing. Then we fold everything and put it in the backseat of my car and then she asks if I'm hungry.

"Yeah."

"Good. Let's go get dinner."

Brandy Corvallis likes veggie burgers. And french fries. And onion rings.

I have never heard of Miller Grill and would never have noticed it in a million years; it's in a strip mall next to a discount furniture store and an Indian grocery. But Brandy comes here a lot with her aunt, and her aunt spends ten bucks in the jukebox and orders a pitcher of beer and she and Brandy play cards while they eat. The waitress nods at Brandy as we seat ourselves at a little booth. The table's kind of uneven. Brandy pulls two menus from behind the ketchup and mustard in their rack and we start looking them over.

This is a date. Even though we didn't plan it. It's very clear to me, shouting over my brain: YOU ARE HAVING A DATE WITH A GIRL.

I act casual. Like it's something I've done before. In my wallet is some cash that Sierra tipped me out with. Two school buses of soccer players had showed up the day before and Garrett told me to go out and give the waitresses a hand. Move chairs around for everyone, clear tables, deliver fresh cups to the beverage station. She gave me twenty-five bucks, which made me wonder how much money she made normally.

But this is the first time I've spent any money from the summer. I have only gotten one check from Garrett, but it was pretty small and I still haven't cashed it. It's tacked up on the fridge at my mom's house.

I still have the sixty bucks Garrett paid me for my first shift too. It's in my wallet, next to Sierra's tips. Probably I should get a bank account of my own, but I keep putting it off. I like seeing the money. And I've counted it several times, a stack of slightly greasy ones, plus the twenties. Anytime I think about buying anything with it, I hesitate.

But I know I have to spend it. I can't be all weird about it in front of Brandy.

Because Brandy just orders things so easily, without doing the calculation, things that aren't even given a price on the menu. Like the extra sides: barbecue sauce with her fries and the ranch with her onion rings. And the pitcher of Dr Pepper she orders. Not diet. And not caring if there's no free refills.

But after a little nervous counting of everything, I relax. She's smiling a lot and the window we're sitting by is big and wide and it's still light out, though it's almost eight o'clock. Brandy's wearing an army-green tank top and I can see the top part of her bra, which is red. Her face is kind of sunburned from being at the water parks in Wisconsin. I get hard sneaking glances at her.

When the waitress gives us the bill, Brandy pulls out her wallet thing. Which is like a little pocketbook with a strap around her wrist. She takes out a bunch of cash and puts it on the table.

"Hey," I say. I'm horrified. She's assumed she's paying for everything. I'm still sitting on my ass. On my wallet.

"We can split it," she shrugs. "Unless you don't have cash."

"I have cash," I say.

She looks over the bill once more, like she's doing math in her head. "We always tip twenty percent here," she says. "My aunt says you have to do that, because it's out of respect for waiting tables and knowing how hard it is."

"You wait tables?"

"No, but she did," she says, adding another five to the pile, while I scramble to pull out my wallet. It's not like the bill is huge or anything, but I feel a step behind. This is the first time I've gone out to eat with a girl, but you'd think I'd be on it, working at Time to Eat.

I do the fastest math of my life, making sure the money pile is equitable, that the tip will be good for our waitress, even if she's nowhere as good as Sierra. Brandy goes to the bathroom while

I'm in the middle of this, which takes a lot of pressure off, I admit.

"Now what do you want to do?" I ask her, when she comes back from the bathroom. I hold open the door for her and we're walking out. She's chewing a toothpick and hands me one; it tastes like mint.

"I don't know," she says. "I guess it *is* Friday night. I never do anything, really. I mean, what can I do? I'm only going to be a sophomore, Will. I can't even drive. You know that, right?"

I tell her, who cares.

"School starts in a month, though," she says. "Maybe then you'll care?"

But I just go to open the car door for her and pretend she didn't say it. Because DeKalb will say something to me. Jack will tell me I'm a pedo or something. Though Jack would probably go out with a girl in junior high if he could manage even that.

We get in the car. I start it. She puts on her seat belt and opens her little thing of lip stuff and puts it all over her mouth. Then she twists toward me.

"Does that bother you? Hanging out with a sophomore?"

"Don't even talk about school right now," I say. I kiss her and get a mouth full of the lip stuff, which tastes like watermelon. We've never done anything in the backseat of the Audi yet, but just now I wish there wasn't laundry back there.

But she stops kissing, like she knows what's in my mind. I have to quick get my face to look not disappointed.

"I have to get some things from Target. Want to come with?"

* * *

White wine, Dr Pepper, veggie burgers, barbecue sauce, Target: these are all things Brandy likes. So I try to like them too, because I want the Brandy Magic back.

I don't go to Target much. One, because it's kind of the place my mom goes to get everyone stuff. And two, because my dad doesn't go anywhere except Walmart, because it's cheaper. Walmart always makes me feel like I'm one step from standing on the corner of the exit ramp and begging for change, though. It feels sad and pathetic. I don't want to be reminded of the low low prices. I don't want to see the sad fat people in their scooters or mean parents in the long checkout lines yelling at their kids. I'm not much of a shopper, and I tell Brandy this as we walk inside.

"Target just makes me feel good," she says. "Whether I buy something or not. You'll see."

I doubt this, but I get out a shopping cart and swing it toward her like I'm full of good manners. "I'll drive," I say.

She laughs. "What a dork."

"You are too," I say.

"Hang on," she says, and steps over to the snack area. She comes back a minute later with a giant cherry slushy and a box of popcorn, which she sets in the front part of the cart, where you'd put a little kid.

Then she starts walking beside me and the cart. Eating popcorn. Sipping the slushy, which makes her lips look like blood.

"The best thing is that nobody's in this Target on Friday

night. I never go in the grocery part," she adds, tugging the cart away from the produce section. We tick past the food aisles: soup, pasta, cereal.

"Eat some," she says, pushing the popcorn and slushy toward me. "I got it for us to share."

I'm not a huge fan of popcorn, but this stuff is actually kind of tasty. And I'm glad Brandy isn't all picky about sharing the same straw in the slushy. I mean, we've had our tongues in each other's mouths, so I guess what's the point of worrying about germs, anyway?

We pass the soda-and-candy aisle and I stop.

"Wait," I say, turning the cart. There's this kind of root beer that Roy always brings to our house. I wonder if Target has it. I decide that I will get it, if it's on sale. Now that I've started spending, it's like I broke the seal or something. The Savings Seal.

"What are you looking for?" Brandy asks.

"This root beer . . . ," I say. "There!" Schlager's House Brew, it's called. It's in a six-pack, bottles, and it's on sale for $5.88. I don't know if that's worth it, but I put it into the cart.

"See?" Brandy says. I shrug at her. Smile a little.

We pass through the pet aisle, the automotive aisle, the seasonal section. The outdoor/garden junk is still out, though all on sale. On the perimeter, there are stacks of Back to School supplies. Paper and notebooks and glue and pencils.

"You know, I actually like that," she says. "Getting new supplies. Plus school means Halloween's up next."

"Can't we just enjoy where we are now? How can you think of Halloween right now?"

"I love Halloween," Brandy says. "Totally love it. Even if my nana's a freak about it and doesn't like us handing out candy and stuff."

"Is she religious or something?"

"No," Brandy says, looking at a display of mud boots and gloves. "She's afraid of kids coming and stealing things. She's weird. But my aunt Megan's, like, that's ridiculous. My aunt is pretty normal like that. We just hand out candy on the screened porch. Nana's pretty deaf. She won't notice."

"When's the last time you trick-or-treated?" I ask. "Be honest."

"Seventh grade," she says.

"Huh," I say, somewhat surprised she admits that.

"How about you?" she asks.

I tell her sixth grade and she accuses me of lying, trying to one-up her, and then she sees a giant bag of Fun Dip and says, "What if we bought that? Would you help me eat it?"

"Yes," I say. She laughs, tosses the bag into the cart.

We move through toys and electronics. I don't give a shit about electronics; I think I'm the only guy alive who doesn't. But aside from my phone, I just don't need anything else. You can even get porn on your phone; I've barely opened my laptop since school let out.

We examine My Little Ponies and LEGOs and Barbies for a while, making fun of some of the Ken dolls and their plastic dickless crotches, and then she says we have to go to the magazine and book section and I didn't even know Target sold books, or magazines, except the junky celebrity ones up by the checkout lanes.

She looks through several magazines, all fashion ones with glossy covers featuring chicks in tight clothes, with their boobs or asses hanging out, their hair flying everywhere. Everyone on the cover is the exact opposite of Brandy Corvallis, but she studies each picture like it's Jesus riding a bicycle or something. I half-heartedly look through some of the men's magazines but they are all about hunting or lifting weights or sports or motorcycles. I've never really given a shit about all of that stuff. Even if it's guy stuff. I feel weird about this for a minute—realizing I have no hobbies, no interests, there aren't magazines for guys like me, at least—but then Brandy picks up a bridal magazine that's four inches thick.

"This is fifteen dollars," she says, lifting the thing up. "And it's mostly just advertisements."

"What the hell?"

"Like, people pay lots of money for these pictures," she says. "That's me someday. Not for a bunch of wedding stuff, though. I hope."

She keeps paging through the bridal magazine. I stand around like a dumbass and I ask her if she's going to buy the thing, and she's like, "Relax, already, Will. I'm never getting married. Ever."

"Oh. Okay."

I don't know what to do with this information. I'm thinking about her taking pictures. Being serious about photography. And not getting married. And Target, in general. Is it still making her feel happy? She puts the giant bridal magazine down and we move on.

We pass through the baby section, which she doesn't even acknowledge, then shoes, where she zips through the aisles touching every other shoe and making comments. ("No. No. No. Ick—that's plastic. Awful detailing.") I don't even bother to pretend to be interested in shoes. I have three pairs of shoes. Flip-flops, running shoes for gym, and work boots. And snow boots. Okay, four.

Then we're in men's clothing. "My favorite!" she says, jumping a little. I push the cart like it's my skateboard, sliding along and skidding to a stop. At first I think she'll just try on the clothes herself. But then she starts whisking out button-down shirts and jeans and stuff and holding them up to me. Like I'm her personal paper doll.

"God, no," I say to the millionth shirt she slaps against me. It's striped and has these two weird hipster pockets on the chest. "That is awful."

"I know!" she yells. "Isn't Target wonderful?"

I don't tell her I agree. But I slurp the last bit of slushy out of the cup and try not to smile.

Later, after I get a text from my dad—**need anything? going out to Garrett's**—I bring Brandy back to my house. I tell her what the "need anything?" text means and she calls her aunt and gets the okay to stay out until midnight, and I feel like spending again. Rich. Except there's nothing to buy or eat.

Like the first time, I lead Brandy into my house. The wind whips through the little flaps where we need to add trim around the new windows; she asks if it's okay to be in here and I laugh and tell her yes.

Up in my room, she slips off her flip-flops and comes straight at me. We kiss for nine million years, standing up. She takes off my T-shirt. I take off her tank top. It's so small, so thin. Such a little thing between her and the world. I take off my glasses, set them on the desk. Then I reach for the button on her shorts. I don't want to take them off, just make room for my hand. She moves my hand, though, and unbuttons them herself. She stands in front of me in her bra and panties and I wish I had my glasses on. Or that it was brighter. But it's okay, because then I kiss her. Reach around and undo her bra and then we're on the futon in a big pile. She laughs.

"I can't believe this," she says.

"What?" I ask, rearranging her so I can feel her boobs better on my chest.

"I can't believe I'm doing this with you." She's got her mouth on my chest.

"Why do you keep saying that?" I ask. I can feel the soft part under her panties. God.

She pauses, her mouth on my chest. She's kissing me there. Then lower. Her boobs up against my belly. I want to take my jeans off so bad. But I don't know if that'll freak her out. And I want her to keep being mostly naked.

"Why do you even like me, Will?" she says. But it doesn't

sound like a question. It sounds like she doesn't want an answer, good or bad. Because she's going lower and lower and now I'm on my back and she's unzipping my jeans and tugging them off me.

I almost say, "I don't know."

Instead, I say, "I just do."

She lifts her head up, from the edge of my boxers, where her mouth is just above my hard-as-hell dick. I think that I've just said the wrong answer.

But she tugs down my boxers. Says nothing.

And then? Then I can't believe my life. Because she's sucking me off. With her mouth. A girl is doing this. Really. This is happening.

I look up at the ceiling, wonder what the fuck I did to deserve this good thing. Maybe this is how you know you're in love with someone. Because they give you something that there's no way you earned.

Brandy wraps herself, her hands, her tongue, all around me. Making it all about me and no one else. Didn't earn this. No way. But I take it, anyway. Of course I take it.

SIX

YOU LEARN SO much weird shit about people when you work with them.

Like, the blond-biceps-guy cook whose name I never remember? Used to be a firefighter. He's currently getting certified to be an EMT.

And Sierra? She's really into astrology and makes people charts for money, actually. She always smells like incense and she's got all these weird tattoos that go up her legs, and her car has this bumper sticker that says I DRIVE A STICK, and it's got a broom on it. And Everardo's got three little daughters, is crazy for Mixed Martial Arts, and also makes his own barbecue sauce. And Carl, the redhead cook, barely talks if he can help it. And whenever anyone asks him what he's up to, he says, "Fucking bitches. Making money. You know."

As if that weren't ridiculous enough, Carl's shy as hell. Especially around girls. Anytime a waitress talks to him he gets all quiet and red. Plus he comes to work on a skateboard, though he's a grown-ass man. Sierra says he's got a very mixed aura. I don't know what that means, except he never says the fucking-bitches-making-money line to her or any other women at Time to Eat. Which is probably for the best. The other main thing about Carl is that he can carry three racks of clean coffee cups at a time and I can only carry one. Carl's stronger than fuck. Plus he's all about sharpening knives. It's one of these things Garrett talked about at first and said he'd show me, but things got away from him.

But Carl's on it. He catches me chopping with a knife that he says is dull and stops everything to give me a lesson in knife sharpening, even though he'd punched out already. He lays it all out on the back counter by the slicer and the Hobart mixer: the whetstones, the little bottle of oil, the special cloth to wipe everything down. By the time he finishes showing me the whole process, I'm about 99 percent sure Carl's got a samurai sword hanging up over his bed. I know he's got an army knife in his pocket; he busts that thing out all the time.

Working at Time to Eat makes me dread school. I like being at work; I like how there's always a list, always something to ask someone, always a new job to learn. Always someone's weird personality to get more details about. I even like the new people who get hired and fired; they filter through things pretty regularly and I still think about them after they're gone. Wonder about them. I have work dreams a lot too; in front of the fryer, cooking with Carl. Trying to work the cash register for Garrett, though I've never learned how. Weird stuff like that.

Though lately, I've been dreaming about Angus. Brandy too. Both of them, together, with me. All three of us.

The night before DeKalb and Angus come over to help rough in the new kitchen area, I have a dream of all three of us. I wake up sweaty and not knowing where I am. The dream was in Angus's garage, Brandy naked on the old sofa in there, Angus naked in his blue bandanna, and me, everywhere. It was so real I lie there for a while trying to make sure it didn't happen. Though it did happen. All over the sheets and my boxers. Like I'm a little kid. Jesus Christ. I get up and strip the futon sheets to wash them, because the futon only has one set.

When I get downstairs, Roy's standing there. The sheets are in a ball and I hold them in front of me.

"Hey," I say.

Roy nods. Doesn't say anything. Sips coffee from his to-go cup and looks over a note that my dad has left on the card table. He's got that uncertain look again. I see him surveying the mess of the main floor like he's calculating up the time and the value of the materials and the cost of everything, the price. He's leaving soon for school. There's no way it'll be done before then.

I know a whole bunch of shit about Roy too, though we're not formally working together. But one day, when my dad had to go to the Laundromat for something, Roy took me to get Dairy Queen and told me a bunch of stuff. He's twenty-five, for one thing, not nineteen, like I'd assumed. He's been in rehab, like, four times. For drugs. Booze, meth, coke. Snorted it, smoked it, shot it. He was in jail. Homeless. All of it. First rehab at age sixteen. And it's lucky that his parents are rich, because the cost of the last rehab was gigantic—he was there almost a full year. That was after he knocked up the girl he was with and the baby died because the girl overdosed when she was about four months pregnant or something. After that, the girl was in jail, then the psych ward, and Roy was in jail for possession and something little, like trespassing, and then he went to the year-long treatment. He only started college last year. I would never have guessed this just from Roy refusing the beer my dad always offers. I figured he preferred some specialty micro-brew, was snobby about it like he was about coffee. I would never have guessed he was any of those things. But he is. Was. Except now he attends AA or NA once a day.

I stuff the gross sheets into the canvas bag we use for the Laundromat and go back upstairs to shower. Since he told me about the rehab, Roy's uncertain look means something extra now. My dad has slipped into a pattern of cracking open the beers sometimes before the workday even ends. What Roy doesn't know, though, is how long he's gone after he's had a few. I don't know where he goes. Sometimes he says he's at Garrett's. Sometimes he says he's getting supplies or tracking down something he wants off Craigslist. Sometimes he says he's going to the Laundromat. Sometimes he doesn't say. And sometimes he doesn't come home until the next day.

When I get out of the shower, DeKalb and Angus are in the kitchen. Roy's on his phone in the driveway, smoking, but when he comes inside, I introduce everyone.

"You know where your dad's at?" Roy asks. Again, hesitant. I want to cover for my dad. Say he's at Menards or the Laundromat. But I don't know.

I offer to call him but Roy says he just did. "He didn't pick up."

"Well, should we maybe start organizing the lumber or something? What did that note say?"

Roy looks at the note on the card table.

"He's got the wood for the roughing in. But he's getting Sheetrock, the note says."

"Oh," I say.

"Problem is," Roy continues, "there's still wires to be pulled. And the furnace isn't all the way connected. Your dad needed an inspector to come sign off on that."

"Won't need the furnace for a while," I say. Since we're all pretty much sweating our balls off standing there. Angus kind of laughs. DeKalb's staring at Roy like he's an alien.

"You can't put up Sheetrock and walls until the wiring's done, though," Roy says. "Unless you want to cut into those walls after the fact. There's a kind of order involved. Do you know if your dad's got the inspector coming today or something?"

I shake my head. I have no idea what he's doing. Or not doing.

"So, what's the deal, then?" Angus asks. He and DeKalb are leaning against the new bay window that we put in. That fucker weighed a zillion pounds but it was only five hundred bucks, because we drove down to Waseca and bought it off this crazy-eyed house-flipper guy who wouldn't stop telling us about the bunker he was digging under his grandmother's root cellar for the days when the economy collapses and we all know what "real scarcity" is.

"Real scarcity," he kept saying. "It's coming." Now I can't look at that window without thinking about that guy and real scarcity.

DeKalb keeps leaning. Staring at me and Roy. Like, what the fuck already, man.

"I don't know," I tell Angus. "We're figuring it out."

It's quiet for a minute. Roy rereads the note. I pick at a little rock stuck in the bottom of my boot. DeKalb is looking at his phone. Angus sits down and puts in his earbuds.

"I don't want to tell your dad his business, William," Roy continues. "I mean, I'm a goddamn art major. Like, the cabinet-making part is the main reason I'm here."

"Cabinets?" I laugh. "Like we're even close to that part!"

Roy nods. Doesn't laugh. Just continues with his point. "But even I know that you've got to do the wires before the Sheetrock. Unless . . . does he have more people coming to work today?"

"I don't know," I say.

"You got any water?" Angus asks, his voice louder than normal.

"There's a pallet of bottled in the backyard," Roy says. Though I know Roy never drinks bottled water. Angus nods and walks out.

DeKalb puts his phone away. Crosses his arms over his chest. He's probably getting the vibe off me and Roy. I feel like a fuck-up. I'm the one who bugged Angus and DeKalb to get time off from their jobs and come help. So they could meet and whatever. And now it looks like it's all for nothing. I hate this. At Time to Eat, I never have to figure shit out. I get there, and like Garrett said, there's a list posted of opening tasks. Or Carl or someone else tells me what's been done, what's left. I don't have to think about anything. I just have to move through it. And that's how the remodel's been too. Mostly.

Roy goes out to smoke, and so me and DeKalb follow him. We all stand in the driveway, sweating. Not talking. The longer it's quiet, the more I start to get pissed at my dad. For doing this. Or not doing it. Whatever.

Roy's phone makes a little *bloopy beep* sound and he checks it, his smoke dangling from his fingertips. He reads and then shakes his head.

"Fuck it," Roy says, slipping his phone into his pocket and pulling out his keys. "He won't be back until this afternoon. You guys want to go swimming? We can go to my house."

Angus looks at me. "At your house?"

"There's a pool in the back," Roy says.

DeKalb shrugs, shakes his head like he suspected something like this. I can't figure out DeKalb's hang-up with Roy. But he just says, "I'm down for it."

"We'll come back around four, though," Roy says. "Tom said he might be back by then?" Tom is my dad. Roy looks at me, as if I should know.

Half an hour later, we pull up in Roy's Jeepster (that's the kind of car he has, and yes, it's vintage, impossible to find, and belonged to his dead uncle or something, and I only know this because Angus sits in front and asks him) to the driveway of this huge house in Arden Hills.

Angus follows Roy inside, but DeKalb kind of hangs back and waits for me. He takes off his shirt, wipes his forehead with it. DeKalb has zero chest hair. He's completely smooth. Nothing about him shirtless to notice except for some little pink scratches around his shoulders.

"Fuck, man," he says, nodding toward the giant house.

"I know." I feel a little dumb, though. Because DeKalb doesn't know what my mom's house looks like. He's only ever seen my dad's place.

And my mom's house isn't even close to being what Roy's house is. It looks like a fucking castle. And the houses next to it aren't the same beige version of it, like in Oak Prairie. There's only two other houses near Roy's house, for one thing; he lives in a little circle drive that we drove in a long twisty hill to get to, and it's surrounded by trees so you can see only parts of the other houses.

We go in through the door in the garage. No one takes their shoes off, because immediately, we're inside. We're in a giant kitchen, with marble counters and a pot rack full of copper pans and it looks like a TV show where the people are selling their house or the set of a cooking show, except it's real. Angus goes with Roy to get some shorts, because he was wearing jeans, so DeKalb and I stand there some more, looking at everything. The kitchen opens to a big giant TV room and there's a long table that looks kind of old, like it's been sitting outside in all weather, and it has benches, no chairs. There's a flat-screen TV above the fireplace, and the coffee table has stacks of magazines that look like they've never been opened.

Angus comes back with Roy, who is carrying a big pile of towels. We go down a hallway and then we're in a little screened-in porch. But it's with real furniture and everything. Then outside that there's a patio and a pool with a diving board and a whirlpool off to the side and a big silver grill built into the brick. There's also a table built into the brick and a giant awning over that and a little humming machine sliding around the bottom of the pool, probably sucking up dirt and leaves or whatever. The water is perfect, clear. DeKalb sticks his foot in the water.

"Is it warm enough?" Roy asks.

"Yeah," DeKalb says. "Hell yeah!" He takes off his shoes and jumps in.

Angus smiles and does the same.

I look at Roy. "Guess we're getting a day off?"

Roy shrugs. "No one ever swims in this pool," he says. "Might as well get some fucking use. I gotta call this girl back quick." He takes his phone and heads in. It's weird. It's like we're supposed to enjoy ourselves, but I still feel a little bit like I'm in trouble. But then I see my friends splashing each other and kicking water everywhere and I can't resist jumping in too.

I'm used to being in two places. I know how to hem around edges of a place until I get comfortable. Or at least seem that way. Obviously so does DeKalb, because he's jumped off the diving board like a hundred times and is strutting around shirtless on the patio and then pushing Roy into the water, which at first I think is aggression but then Roy's laughing and doesn't care.

Angus doesn't change how he acts at Roy's. Maybe he already did his big change, with being gay, and now he's just who he is, without worrying about it anymore?

"Your hair turns green in the chlorine, doesn't it?" Angus asks Roy, when he comes up from the surface.

"That's a white-people thing, right?" DeKalb says. "Got to be."

Roy laughs, says yes. Angus swims for his school in Oak Prairie and it turns out Roy used to swim too, so they talk about swimming and shaving their legs before races and whatever. I try to imagine Roy swimming in high school. Before rehab. Or maybe he's just saying that. I watch him dunk DeKalb then, when DeKalb's back is turned. Maybe Roy has learned to be in more than one place too.

We've been in the pool awhile when this girl shows up with food. A mess of pizza and chicken wings and a French silk pie. As she unpacks everything at the built-in brick table under the awning, like she's our mom, Roy waves at her.

"Hey," she calls to him while opening an invisible cupboard in the brick and pulling out these bright orange plates. I wonder who she is. She's wearing normal clothes, but I can see her swimsuit underneath. When Roy gets out of the pool, she hands him a towel and they talk with their heads close together. She laughs and swats at him and then Roy tells us all to come and eat.

DeKalb and me are giving each other the eye about this chick the whole time we're all eating. She gets us all Cokes from inside, except for Roy, who just drinks water. Then she takes off her stuff and goes to lie on one of the lounge chairs in her swimsuit. And she's pretty fucking hot. I try not to look, but she's kind of right in my line of sight. She's reading a book. Roy doesn't seem to even notice. He and Angus are talking about music, and I join in for a minute, just to say they all should see Angus's garage, and then DeKalb asks about the band and I tune out. Stare at the water, which is flat and blue and calm. At the match Roy leaves on his orange plate after he lights his cigarette. At the curls of hair on my arms, drying in the heat.

I'm feeling light-headed. I feel like I'm maybe coming apart. Splintering into all these versions of Will that aren't quite the right thing. Like I'm unable to be all of them. Be at all of the places. The Will who's a prep cook. The Will who can't answer for his dad. The Will who avoids his mom. The Will who takes Taylor and Kinney to Walgreens to pick up nail-polish remover and Q-tips for his mom and ends up buying his half sisters glittery jump ropes with the extra cash. The Will who kisses Angus. Touches Angus. The Will who spends money on root beer and food with Brandy. The Will who is Brandy's boyfriend.

"Help me clean this shit up, you guys," Roy says, putting out his cigarette and standing up to clear off the plates. We end up putting them in another hidden cabinet that's really a goddamn dishwasher. I look at DeKalb again, who shakes his head.

We swim some more and then it's time to head back to my house so DeKalb's dad can come collect him. The girl who fed us gets up and ties her towel around her waist and stands by Roy as we get ready to go. She looks pinkish from the sun and she's holding this book against her hip called *Ways of Seeing*. Roy asks her how it's coming along and she shrugs, "It's fine," she says. "Kind of abstract."

Roy looks bummed that she's not liking the book. As if he wrote it or something. They go back and forth about it and Angus asks what it's about.

Me and DeKalb don't say anything. Maybe it's weird that she's talking around us and none of us have asked her name. Or maybe because her boobs are unreasonable. I feel like they are everywhere. She also is kind of touchy with Roy, but he doesn't seem like he's that into her.

The whole way to my dad's, Angus is flipping through music, and he and Roy are debating that, with DeKalb popping in from the backseat to disagree or agree. I'm tired but in the best way. It's the same way after a shift of work. Just bone-ass tired. Worn. All my muscles jangly. I guess my feet don't hurt now, like they usually do after a shift at Time to Eat, but the rest of me is amped up and lazy, both at once. Maybe that's why I say, "Sure" when Angus suggests we all go out to his house and jam a little.

"Unless Tom's back," Roy says. Which is kind of buzz killing but true.

So when we pull up to my house, it's the worst-case scenario, really. Brandy, talking to my dad. Fuck.

Roy's all *who's that*, and DeKalb's like, *what the hell's the yearbook girl doing here*, and then Angus kind of raises his eyebrows at me like he knows something's up.

"Hi," Brandy says to me. "Rory threw up so Mr. Vance came home from work early."

"They pay you extra for sick duty?" My dad. Hilarious. Brandy laughs, though.

"Nothing worse than a yakking kid," DeKalb says. "My little sister's always barfing when she's nervous. You can't even predict it. Just gotta get out of the way before she blows."

Angus laughs. Roy's looking at my dad.

"So, Tom? We gonna rough in that kitchen or what? Because these guys want to go do some band-practice thing." He gestures toward DeKalb and Angus and me.

My dad scratches his beard, squints back at the house. He starts making a bunch of excuses—*getting late* and *need to do some wire work* and shit like that. Roy nods along, as if he's agreeing. But I know he's got to think my dad's full of bullshit.

Brandy, meanwhile, has her arms crossed over her chest. I catch her staring at me, looking confused, but she smiles the second she sees me.

"I should get going," she says.

"Well, but . . ."

"It's okay," she says. "We can hang out later."

"You sure?" I don't know what to say. I feel like the world's biggest asshole.

She shakes her head, smiles, and then next thing I know, my dad and Roy have moved closer to the front of the house to talk. DeKalb's texting on his phone. Angus is looking at Brandy and me in this weird way. Like he's happy for us. Or he's hiding something. I can't stand having them be right here together. Everything I'm thinking feels so close to the surface. Like it's going to pop out of my chest like an alien baby.

Brandy bites her lip and then she kind of whispers at me, as she steps backward toward the yard, "Call me later?"

I nod, trying to look as enthusiastic as you can when nodding, and she dashes back through the alley. I feel like the biggest dick alive. For spending my whole day having fun and not thinking about her. But I can't imagine telling any of them about what's going on with me, because it's too weird. Not just the Angus part; the Brandy part too. How I think of her as my girlfriend, as being her boyfriend. Like how we have dinner. Dates. Everything's different and not just because she gave me head. Though that's the part of it I can't stop thinking about.

SEVEN

"**YOU NEVER SAID** he was a fucking gay guy, man."

DeKalb, in my car later that night, as I'm driving us back to Minneapolis.

"I didn't think it mattered."

"It doesn't."

"Then why are we talking about it?"

DeKalb makes this little *pffft* noise, all pissy.

"It's kind of something you might mention. Like, you know. I'd like to know."

"I didn't tell him you were black."

He rolls his eyes at me.

"That's different," he says.

"Not really."

"I ain't gonna surprise him by suddenly turning black," he says.

I sigh, stop at a light. "What? He hit on you?"

"No."

"Then what's the deal? You guys played all fucking night. It sounded good to me."

He shrugs. He can't argue; it did sound good. Even me and my nonmusical self could tell they were "in the groove," or whatever Angus likes to call it.

"It's just a thing," he says. "You want to know that kind of thing, all right? Like, what if I'd called him a fag or something?"

"But you didn't."

"But I coulda."

"I don't think he'd care."

"What in the hell, Will?" he says. "You're outta your mind. People care about that shit."

"Obviously."

"Whatever, man," he says. "You just shoulda said."

"You don't want to be in a band with him because he's gay?"

"No," he says, looking out the window. "I didn't say that. I wasn't ever gonna say that."

He's quiet for a minute and then he brings up Brandy again. Which he did at Angus's house too. Angus didn't say anything; I just told them we hung out at the Laundromat, Brandy and me. Like it wasn't any big deal. But DeKalb kept giving me shit.

"Yeah, I like her," I say. "She's nice."

"She a baby," he says. "But you gotta start somewhere. Do what you gotta do."

I don't know what I gotta do. Or say. Because even though I was kind of distracted all night by the idea that Brandy was pissed at me blowing her off, it had been a decent time. Had been, before talking about Angus being gay. DeKalb got to smoke a little weed and play some music, and I just sat there and absorbed and sat still for a little while, which I didn't realize I needed to do. It felt good to hang out and do nothing for a change. So I'm surprised he got all hacked off that Angus is gay.

And I can't remember that ever coming up, anyway. It's like he just sensed it. Guessed it.

Which makes me nervous. Did he sense something about me and Angus? Or was it something Angus did?

When I drop him off, I'm glad his mom is the one at home and not his dad, because she's way friendlier than DeKalb's dad. Officer Ruston kind of looks at me like he thinks I'm this big fuck-up or whatever. And Mrs. Ruston doesn't kick up a fuss or come out to the car or anything like Officer Ruston does. You have to be really careful with DeKalb's dad.

It's almost midnight but I don't want to go home. The hot attic bedroom. Nobody there. Or my dad, drunk, probably.

It's automatic; I do it without even making a choice about it. Like I have no choice, I drive to Brandy's house. I haven't texted her and it's pretty late, but I just drive there anyway. Park and go knock on the door. Then, when no one answers, I text her. I know her nana's deaf, but I don't know if that's real actual deafness or old-people deafness where they just can't hear good.

The doorbell's broken. I knock a couple more times. Look at my phone.

I'm about to get all stalkery and Romeo and Juliet, toss pebbles at her window, when the door opens and it's her, Brandy. Good thing; I've never been inside Brandy's house and I have no idea what window might be her bedroom.

"Hey."

"Hey," she says back.

"What are you doing?"

"Nothing."

"You want to hang out?"

She closes the door a little, looks behind her.

"My nana's here," she says. "She's asleep. You can come in, though."

"What about your aunt?"

"She's got night shift for the next few weeks."

She opens the door and I come in and she's very quiet. The floor's got this long blue runner rug but she doesn't tell me to take off my shoes and right away I feel like I shouldn't. Even though she's barefoot herself. The house is kind of old and dark, with lots of fern-y plants and furniture that's kind of seen a lot of miles on it, but you can see little bits of Brandy here and there: a bright pink backpack, her jean jacket on a coatrack, a bowl full of colored elastic hair-tie things, a big school picture of her hanging on the wall.

She points to a staircase, and with her finger to her lips, motions for me to go up. So I do, as quiet as I can. The stairs are covered with the same blue runner rug, at least. I get to the top of the stairs and there's a bathroom and two rooms. One's really small, with a sewing machine and some dark green file cabinets in it. The other has to be her room; the door is covered in pictures and stickers, some of them so old the color's faded and you can't tell what they were originally. I open the door and go in. Her bed's half made; there are clothes on the floor, and an iPod plugged into her clock is playing something low and murmury that sounds like depression music. Everything smells like flowers, though. She's got all these lit yellow candles everywhere, on the shelf and her dresser and nightstand.

I don't want to sit on the bed, so I sit at her desk, which is mainly a place for makeup and jewelry. Little white dishes full of earrings and stuff. The wall above it has a mirror with pictures tucked into the sides and necklaces hanging off the corners. Like instead of studying your homework, you're working on yourself. I can barely look in the mirror; it seems to magnify everything, including the zits brewing on my forehead.

I take off my glasses and wipe them down on my shirt. Then look back in the mirror. Do I look gay? Once I heard a kid looking through the yearbook say that some guy had "total gayface." I always wondered what that meant; how could you see it? It had to be an expression on your face, because how you looked couldn't make you gay. How you looked at other people, maybe?

"We have to be quiet," she says. Her voice startles me, but I nod. She shuts the door. She's wearing this weird outfit. It's like, something sloppy but something girly: a dress that looks like a long sweatshirt. Like a sweatshirt that just kept on going until it was a skirt. Part of it hangs off her shoulder and there's no bra strap.

She comes over and stands in front of me. I automatically slip my hands around her hips. It feels like there's nothing under-neath the sweatshirt thing.

"You said you didn't care that I'm younger," she says. She puts her hands on my shoulders. Her face is very serious; her eyes seem very plain with no makeup on them. But she's got lip gloss on, I can tell. Her mouth's shiny and I can smell watermelon.

"I don't," I say. Though I know what's coming.

"Then how come you didn't tell your friends about me?" she asks. Her voice is very low. "I felt like such a dumbass."

"Did you want me to tell everyone? Brandy," I say. "Come on. Guys don't . . . they're not like that."

"Oh really?" she says, sounding pissed. "Is that how all those rumors get started, then? About what girls will do what, with who? Because guys aren't like *that*?"

"Okay, but *I'm* not like that," I say.

"How are they your friends, then?" she asks. "Because Shania knows everything about you. I mean, I could lie and say she doesn't, but she's my best friend. I've told her all about this." She puts her hands on my hands, which are still around her hips. I wonder if that means the sex stuff. Or just the in-general hanging-out stuff. Maybe both?

"I don't like to tell people stuff like that," I say. "I just . . . don't. It's not because I don't like you. It's not because you're younger."

"Really?"

We're looking at each other and I swear, I can't blink. My eyes are wide open, hers even wider.

"I mean, Angus doesn't even go to our school. It's not like he cares."

I don't like saying his name. Angus. Not while I'm touching her.

"And DeKalb? Well, he's kind of, I don't know." I squeeze her hips a little. "I guess I wasn't thinking about it. I'm sorry you felt dumb. I am. I just didn't think about it."

I swear, I feel her body relax toward me. I'm holding her hips in my hands and everything just feels like it tilts toward me.

"Maybe you should, though," she says. "In the future. Think about it."

"Okay."

"School starts soon," she says. "I'd rather you just tell me now than get to school and have you totally ignore me."

She's closer now. Warm against me. I'm thinking about nothing but how close I am to her panties underneath the sweatshirt thing. I'm thinking about how she's still talking like she's mad but it doesn't really sound that mad.

"I'm not going to ignore you, Brandy."

"But what if . . ."

"I'm not, okay?" I grip her a little harder. "I like you. I wasn't thinking. I shouldn't have blown you off. I'm sorry, okay? I am. I mean it. I won't ever do it again."

"Shhh!" she says. "My nana."

"Sorry," I say, lower. "I'll tell Angus. DeKalb already kinda knows."

I turn, take off my glasses, set them on her vanity-desk. I pull her closer. She sinks onto me. Onto the chair, which creaks, and she startles. But then she melts back onto me, her arms around my neck. We kiss and I feel around her waist, up her ribs. She's not wearing a bra. It's just nothing but softness. Boobs. Tits. I hate that her nana's downstairs.

"Who did you tell DeKalb I was?" she asks.

"I said you're my girlfriend," I lie, my hands underneath the little skirt thing, going all the way up, finding the edge of her panties.

"Oh," she says. I get my hand in between her legs and start rubbing. Her head kind of falls back. I can tell it's okay now, that she's forgiven me.

She stands up, takes the dress off. She's standing there in her panties, and nothing else.

I know that this is not the time. That I don't want to have sex with Brandy with her deaf grandmother sleeping one floor below us, but I know it's going to happen. It's going to. I know this. Just like I know my name. It's the reason this wasn't a choice. It's like I made this happen, just driving here. Funny how I didn't see it, but now I know. It's like I'm psychic.

I know, when I take off my shirt and my shorts, unlacing my boots and not tossing them off so they'll make a big noise, that we're going to lie on her bed. And we do, as slowly and quietly as we can. I know, when I lick her nipples, that that is a good thing to do to her. To a girl. Brandy. I know that it's going to happen and I can't think about her grandmother coming in, or the door being unlocked or anything like that, because Brandy is rubbing my dick and I'm ready. I've waited my whole life to see a girl naked, to touch a girl naked. I know nothing will get in the way of wanting that. Not a deaf grandmother. Not what I did with Angus. Nothing.

I know, when I pull her panties down, that I'm going to kiss her down there. And that she's okay with it. That it's what adults do, before sex. That when she twists around, and gets up, holding her arm over her boobs as she goes, that she's getting condoms from the nightstand drawer. The candle on the nightstand shakes and flickers when she shuts the drawer. It's a miracle she has condoms, I think. A miracle, but one that I expect. I am so lucky—I know this—as she opens the packet and hands me the little circle thing. I realize that I will need my own next time; it's like me at the restaurant, not getting out my wallet first. I unroll the condom on; it kind of feels cold. Then I get on top of her. Her knees open on either side of me.

When I'm right where I need to be, we stare at each other. I can see her up close at least, just inches from my face. We're both still, just seeing each other. Then her hand slides down to my ass and pushes and then we're having sex and I'm done thinking.

Not thinking. Just going in and out.

It feels so good that I want her to like this. I can't tell if she does. She's mysterious in a way that Angus wasn't. And I'm almost there, ready to come. I stop everything.

"Can you be on top?" I say.

She doesn't say anything; we just switch spots. It's almost like we're people in a movie theater, hedging around each other. Like we should say excuse me.

Stopping might have been to buy me time, but it doesn't work, seeing her sitting up there on me. It feels even better, her up there, even though she's not moving as much as I want her to. I can't ask her to move different though; I don't know how to explain it. And it doesn't matter, anyway. Because it's going to end, no matter what.

I wish I had more time. I wish I could be better at this. I know she will forgive me for it, though. I just know.

When I've reached the point of no return, I shut my eyes. I wish it was dark. I don't want to know what I look like. I hope she's not looking at me. Then it happens: I come and my head jerks back against the pillow and headboard, which knocks over the candle from her nightstand and there's all this fucking noise and the lamp falling to the side.

"Fuck," I say. I can hear the wax hissing on the bare floor. Brandy's still on top of me, but she's shushing me. Shushing me, reaching over to turn the candle upright. Everything fast, sure, quick. Then we're both kind of hanging our heads over the side of the bed. Looking at the puddle of yellow wax, the little black mark where the flame touched down. I think she'll be all upset. But she's not. She kisses me. She's laughing. Saying, "Oh my God, Will, I'm sorry, I didn't expect that, are you okay? Will?"

"Yeah. Sorry."

Then she's on the floor, wiping up the wax and the scorch mark. I watch her cleaning up my mess. I feel lazy. Strange. Like a king, and she's my servant. She relights the candle with matches from the nightstand drawer and then stands up and I can see her body, all of it, naked, and I like how her hips and ass are. You can't see how they are when she wears clothes, because they squash everything down. Flatten it. Make it seem less than it is, less than how it feels when I touch her. It's just a few seconds of seeing her like this, even if she hurries to get back over me, to make me stop looking. I like the idea that I get to see this and no one else gets to.

I slide down so my head's on her chest. I'm hearing her breathe. I'm feeling her fingers scraping through my hair. I'm touching her boob, watching the skin flicker and get all goose-bumpy, the nipple getting all tight. It's like I'm doing science, but blurry. My eyes are so close to her skin. You never dream you'll get that close, see that much of a person, when you like them from a distance. Getting to see it makes me feel greedy again. I never want to give it up.

So, I don't go home. It doesn't make sense—her nana could wake up any time—but I don't. But neither of us can sleep. It's like four in the morning and we're hyper. She goes downstairs and gets me a glass of water. I'm sitting in her bed naked and she's smiling like crazy and I think, *Do we do it again?* But then I don't know if she's sore or if that'd be too much and she'd be grossed out? I want to be cool about it. I don't want her to see the greedy side of me. I just smile back. We have to be so quiet.

Instead of sleeping, though, she hauls out all this yarn. Yarn, everywhere. It's hanging in one of those shoe-thingies that women put in closets; my mom has, like, seven of them. She pulls it out and dumps all this yarn on the bed.

And she sits across from me on the bed, still naked, and starts rolling hanks of yarn into balls between her fingers. I put on my glasses. Sit up myself. Grab a thing of yarn and start doing the same thing. It's hypnotic.

"Why are we doing this again?" I whisper.

"Because it's easier to work with yarn that's in balls instead of skeins," she says. As if that means one thing to me.

"It tangles less," she adds.

"What do you do with this yarn?" I ask. "Knit stuff?"

"I crochet," she says.

"What's the difference?"

"Crochet uses a hook and knitting uses needles."

"Oh."

"I like to make sweaters and stuff," she says. "But right now I'm making a blanket." She looks at me and laughs, and I look down, pull the sheet of her bed over my dick. It's kind of soft and soothing, I guess. I've never done anything with yarn. I've never had sex with a girl, either.

But now I'm doing both. Never doesn't matter. We're sitting across from each other, naked, and I am not worried. The Brandy Magic is back. I know it. Even as she's telling me about her real mom and how her dad's in prison in Stillwater and how her aunt Megan won't even visit him, not ever, because she's so pissed at him for being such a fucking loser, I still feel it. Magic. Us sitting across from each other, the bed springs squeaking as we move a little bit, stacking up the skeins of yarn. I swear, through Brandy's window, I can see the first bit of the sun nudging up the sky, making everything a light bluish-gray. The lighter it becomes, the bigger the pile of colored balls we're winding gets. I see Brandy's nipples, the same color pink as one of the things of yarn. She sees me looking and she smiles and says, I should take a picture of you.

Do it, I tell her.

And she does. She takes a picture of me with her yearbook camera. Me, under her sheet, surrounded by yarn. We laugh and I kiss her and even when she makes me go when the sun's almost up, because Megan'll be home soon, I don't care. I don't know where my dad is and I don't know if it fucking matters. I know we got away with it, and I know that's good enough.

EIGHT

ROY'S LAST DAY working on the house, my dad gets a bunch of barbecue from this place he likes in St. Paul, and we all drive to Garrett's out in Shoreview to eat it. I bring Angus with me.

Roy seems both uncomfortable and happy about the whole event. Which can also sum up his experience working with my dad in general, probably. Or maybe it's because Roy's got another girl with him. Not the girl from the day we went swimming, but another one. Equally cute too.

I like going to Garrett's house. For one thing, he has no neighbors. They literally live next to cornfields. But it's a normal house and a garage. Plus, a giant pole barn and a bunch of chicken coops. Everywhere you look, there's a tractor or a fish pond or some other weird thing. Planters made out of old tires, full of daisies. A pitchfork holding a sign that says THIS WAY TO THE BARN! Stuff like that. His girlfriend, Kristin, raises chickens and goats, and she's actually a pretty nice lady, but she's gone now, at some event with the chickens this weekend. We're out in the backyard of his house and there's a million stars out. The air smells like a farm. Like animals and manure.

The girl with Roy doesn't say anything. Just smiles and sometimes nudges him and it's so fucking weird. She doesn't seem upset or shy that everyone's talking about things that don't include her—mainly the house remodel and Time to Eat and stupid stuff Garrett and my dad used to do when they were younger. And Roy doesn't ignore her or anything. But she just kind of sits there, like an accessory. Like one of his Nalgene water bottles or something. It makes me feel sorry for her. All the girls. And bugged by Roy, for being so weird. Can't he just have a girlfriend? It feels like a question you can't ask, though.

Garrett's talking about when he was in college, some art class he took, how he couldn't keep it together for the nude life drawing class.

"It was this naked guy, right?" Garrett says. "I figured, I can handle this. I've been in locker rooms my whole life. Gang showers in the dorm, even. But this was completely different."

Roy's girl's phone goes off but she silences it and puts it in her purse. Garrett continues.

"So this kid, he's not anyone I'd ever seen before. The U's a big campus, so that's not surprising. But it was just strange, because he's wearing a blue bathrobe. Sitting on this stool. But our instructor is talking and I'm not listening. I'm just looking at the guy. But once she's done talking, the guy's completely naked.

And the whole class is completely silent and totally busy. Everyone focused on their paper, or fully focused on him, squinting at him. Like he was this puzzle you had to solve, one of those paintings that's got a sunken ship in it and you can see it if you look hard enough."

Angus laughs. I stop eating my food.

"The thing was, the kid wasn't nervous. Not at all. He's doing exactly what the instructor asks him to. Sit. Hands on his knees. His junk was . . ."

Roy's girl starts giggling. Kind of loud too.

Roy looks down. "I think I can guess where this is going," he says.

My dad leans back in his chair, downs more beer. "This ought to be good."

"Well, it wasn't ready for action, at least," Garrett continues. "I don't know why I expected it to be. It just . . . It was the saddest thing. Plus he's this really thin guy. Like a goddamn greyhound. All dick and ribs."

Roy's girl laughs again. Snorting, actually. She covers her face like she's ashamed. Roy's still looking down.

"But that's not the kicker, really," Garrett says. "It's that he's a redhead."

"Jesus," Roy says. Then he just busts out laughing with everyone else.

"Do they pay people for that?" I ask.

"Oh, of course," he says. "They get paid a lot per hour. Though they don't normally sit longer than an hour."

"Sitting like that isn't easy, either," Roy says. "They've got to remain still. That's part of the job."

"So, what happened?" Angus asks. "I mean, you couldn't handle a naked guy or he didn't like the drawing you did?"

"I couldn't do a drawing," Garrett says. "I couldn't do anything. I couldn't think of anything except how that metal stool must have felt on his ass cheeks. I swear to God! And the instructor even came over and asked me what my problem was and I could barely talk to her. She was pretty pissed off; I knew she thought I was some immature pig. But that was when I realized I couldn't do it. No way I could say I was serious about art if I couldn't look past that naked redhead guy's wang. But I couldn't. I couldn't see him like that. Like an object. A series of angles and shapes. I walked out and went straight to the registrar and dropped that class and changed my major. The next semester I dropped out and started cooking full-time at the Lamp Lighter."

After that story, everything kind of breaks up. Roy looks at his girl and says, "Shall we?" which seems pretty affected and romantic, but she just smiles. Maybe because it's the first thing he's said to her all night. She goes inside to use the bathroom and then I walk to Roy's Jeepster to say good-bye. And Roy hugs me. I don't expect him to do that, but he does. Roy's not all weird about touching. Angus isn't either.

"Listen," Roy says. "You let me know if you need anything, okay? I'm just an hour south of you."

"Okay," I say. He's so serious; I try to be serious back but I can't imagine why I'd want to bug him for anything about the house when he's busy at school.

"Don't let your dad get to you, either," he says. "This is his project. Let him own it."

"All right," I say. He nods, but I feel like I'm not getting something. He pulls out his phone and we make sure we've got each other's numbers and then Roy's girl comes back and the Serious Hug Time is over. She kind of waves at me and they get in the car and I watch the thread of dust the Jeepster kicks up the drive. Everything seems so over. Like we shouldn't even wait out the weekend. We should just give up and go back to school tomorrow. Surrender to it. Summer's over. The remodel's nowhere near done. And now Roy's gone with his girl with no name and I don't know why I feel so shitty about it.

Garrett and my dad are playing cards when I get back. There's a whiskey bottle on the table. At least we're staying over here.

It's getting dark and buggy out, so Angus and me go inside, with the plates and extra food. Garrett nods at me, like *thanks*, when we do this, and it's like we've made a deal: I clean up, you keep an eye on my dad.

"This place is fucking cool," Angus says.

I pull open the dishwasher and we start loading it.

"And Garrett's a fucking cool guy."

"Yeah," I say. "We've been coming here a long time. Since I was little."

"Roy's cool too," Angus says.

"Yeah."

I want to say, did you tell DeKalb about us? About you? But I can't. I pretend to be looking for the dishwasher soap. Once I've started the dishwasher, I look up and Angus is leaning against the counter. Staring at me.

"What?" I say.

"Nothing," he says. He looks to the side. Smiles.

I take off my glasses, wipe them on my shirt. Angus is still staring at me when I put them back on. I want to touch him. I want to. I don't know how to do it, though. The way things move with him has always been me being wasted. Things always private, in the dark. Not him standing under the kitchen light and the cuckoo clock in Garrett's kitchen.

I ask him how the band thing is going with DeKalb, if they're gonna practice or what. We walk to the back of the house, where the screen porch is. It's not far from the backyard area; we can hear Garrett and my dad talking, and there are two old sofas with a cedar chest between them like a coffee table. Angus lights the big fat candle sitting on the cedar chest and the light wobbles between us, spiking up on the ceiling of the porch. We both lie down on our sofas at the same time. Everything's kind of creepy and strange.

"DeKalb's cool," he says. "We practiced last week. I'm trying to set up a gig at this one coffee shop."

"Nice," I say.

He tells me more of it, how DeKalb's got all these old gospel spiritual songs he wants to rework, making them less folky or whatever. Lullabies and slave rebellion songs and nursery rhymes. I say, "Nice" and "Yeah" and "Cool" a bunch. I'm not being a dick. I don't know how to do this. I don't want to be the guy who just thinks about sex. But I am. I kind of hate it. And I kind of hate that there's no way for me to do this. Even if my dad and Garrett weren't here. I can't decide if it's just that I suck at this, or I don't know how to be gay. Or I don't see enough people being gay in the way I would be gay. The nonflashy gay guy. The boring-old regular gay guy. Not the one who likes theater and dresses snappy and who has a ton of girls for friends.

Maybe that doesn't exist. Maybe I'm just not gay. Maybe I'm a cheater is all. A cheater like my mom; she was with Jay before the divorce. I know this because my dad got drunk and started crying and told me all about it a couple of years ago.

Angus stops talking. Sits up.

"You don't have to be like this, Will," he says.

"What?"

"You're weird because of what we did," he says. "What we do."

I close my eyes. I wish my glasses were off.

"But you don't have to be," he says.

His voice is low. Like he knows I'm worried about Garrett and my dad hearing us. Knowing about us.

"I know you don't want to be out or anything," he says.

"What?"

"It doesn't matter," he says. "I don't, you know . . . it's not my business if you do it or not."

I'm not sure what he's saying. I mean, I could guess. I don't want to guess. I want him to stop talking.

"You can just say when you want it," he says. "It's not a big deal."

He means, I should just jump him. He means, he doesn't care what I do with him. *To* him.

Then Garrett is in the house, knocking around the kitchen.

"Guys?" he hollers.

"In here," I say.

Garrett stands in the doorway holding the half-empty whiskey bottle.

"Oh, good," he says. "There's extra blankets and pillows in that cedar chest." He points. Angus nods.

"We're hitting the sack," he says. "You guys all right?"

We tell him yes. He heads up to bed. I can hear my dad talking, low, and their footsteps. A toilet flush, the sink running. Everyone getting settled.

Angus takes the candle off the cedar chest to open it. The light on the porch gets all crazy for a minute. Then he tosses me a pillow and a blanket that smells like cedar chips. It's kind of scratchy but I don't care. I say thanks and then I unlace my boots.

I notice he takes off his shirt. I don't take off mine. We both settle into the sofas again. The candle sputters between us. I can hear, faintly, a soft thud from another part of the house.

We're quiet. It's kind of nice, though too. Would be perfect, if we hadn't had that dumb conversation. And I know it's not over, either. I can feel Angus wanting to bring it up again. I listen to the wind rustling up the cornfield and wait for it. I know he'll bring it up again.

"Is it because you're not stoned?" he finally says.

"What? No."

"I don't have any more weed," he says. "My guy's in Iowa at a family reunion."

"Oh."

"I shoulda got some from him before he left but I was working."

"It's not the weed, Angus."

"Okay."

"It's . . ." I stop. "I don't know."

"It kills me that you're like this," Angus says. "I'd rather just . . . oh, whatever. Forget it."

Forget what? I don't want to know. I want to know. I don't say anything. Angus pulls his bandanna out of his pocket, starts twisting it around. I wonder if he's going to tie it up or what.

"I wish it never happened," he says. "Now you're all uncomfortable."

"I'm not uncomfortable. I'm not."

"Whatever."

"I'm not. It's just . . ." I let out a big breath. I could be my yoga-loving mom for all the big breaths I'm holding in and letting out. I take off my glasses and set them on the cedar chest. Then I just tell him. I just have to fucking tell him. I look straight at the ceiling.

"I'm okay with it happening, Angus."

He's quiet.

"More than okay," I add.

He's still quiet.

114

"Okay?" I say.

I look over at him. He's a blur, with his hair everywhere. But he laughs. "Really? Are you *okay* with it, Will? Would *okay* be how you'd describe me?"

"Fuck you," I say. "You know what I mean."

He gets up then. Comes sits by me. Leans down and kisses me. It feels so good. And I think, *Just when I've gotten what I wanted, now I want more.*

He puts his hands on my shoulders. "You worry about a lot of shit, you know that?" He laughs. He tries to kiss me again, but I twist away from it. We can't do this here.

"I know your dad's upstairs," he says. His mouth's around my jaw. "I get it."

"You get it," I repeat.

"I'm a pretty smart guy," he says. "I have a three-point-nine GPA."

"I thought you said Oak Prairie was full of suck-up grade inflation."

"Oh, it is," he says. "But I'm still pretty smart."

"I'm not good at this," I say.

"No one's good at this."

I move over and he lies beside me and I'm so glad it's dark. My heart is beating like it might just explode and my dick's all ready for action. I want to knock it on the head, tell it, *Stop it, you're fucking embarrassing me, you don't want all that now.*

But Angus just puts his arm over my head on the pillow and I'm just next to him, I guess. He's kind of holding me, but kind of not. I like it. I like it so much I feel like I can't swallow. My throat's all tight and full of tears and I just want.

"This is all right?" he says. His mouth's near my ear.

I nod. I nod my head into his chest, so he for sure knows. Because I can't talk.

I turn away from him, but he's still there. My back against him. His arm around me. Nothing more than that. His palm presses against my stomach and I know I've left my old life. Wherever that is. My dad's house, my mom's house. If I could, I'd ask Brandy to take a picture. Take it and put it next to the one of me in her bed with the yarn. Because this is where I'm at my best. Where I'm at home. Home feels like Angus and it feels like her and I wish I could tell him that—tell both of them that.

NINE

SCHOOL STARTS AND as usual, I'm not ready for it. Like, half my crap will be at my mom's or I'll forget something at my dad's. I was spending the weekend with my mom, watching Kinney and Taylor while my mom and Jay went to a thing for Jay's work, so I was out in Oak Prairie, trying to do my laundry while making sure my half sisters didn't kill each other. My mom didn't even ask me if I needed school supplies, which was weird—shopping was usually the main thing she could check off her list of to-dos. But senior year, it's not like there's anyone checking your backpack. I brought one pen and one notebook on the first day and it didn't even matter. I just piled all the same class-policy sheets and syllabuses and whatever into in my backpack at the end of the day.

Brandy isn't in any of my classes except Photography. She isn't in the class officially—she's already taken it—but she has a study hall that hour, which she spends in the darkroom for yearbook stuff. I forgot I'd even signed up for the class. Everyone loves Photography at our school, mainly because everyone says it's an easy A. Mr. Walters just lets you go into the darkroom and play music and he doesn't care what you do the whole time, just that you hand in the projects he assigns.

But the first week, we have to learn principles of photography and take a quiz on the terms and watch slide shows of a million example photographs, and I kind of regret taking the class. Brandy is in the darkroom this whole time and it sucks that I can't even see her. Plus, I don't even like taking pictures on my fucking phone. But then to use a camera that you have to adjust a million different ways, because it's an antique or whatever? God. It kind of makes me think Brandy is magical again.

The first day is boring after Photography, until I get to Global Society. And the kid who was formerly my friend Jack Telios walks in and sits down just as the bell's ringing.

Formerly, because he's still my friend, even if he's been in Sweden all spring and summer, but he's not the same Jack. The little dickhead that everyone has called Jack-Off since middle school.

Because the Jack I remember is scrawny. He's, like, shorter than even short girls.

Or at least he was.

Now he's bigger. My height. Maybe taller. Even his face has expanded. His blond hair is even blonder. I can't figure it out. He's also wearing this white shirt, open and unbuttoned a whole bunch, and he's tan. It's like he's just walked off a safari or something.

"Greetings," Jack says. His voice is even deeper. And he doesn't have a notebook or a folder. Even a pen. Then the teacher comes in and starts telling everyone to quiet down and we can't talk anymore, because Ms. Herald is kind of a ballbuster. I had her for Communications last year and she'd mark you down if you even brought a phone to class, never mind that you didn't turn it on. It couldn't be visible, even in your back pocket.

Ms. Herald hands out syllabus sheets and goes into detail about what's expected. She also teaches AP classes and so she tends to be hard in general; that's just how she teaches. I'm taking notes, mostly because I don't want her to say anything to me—if you do what you're supposed to, you can get away with a lot more shit in school, I've learned—but Jack's sitting there, not doing anything, not even looking at the handouts, not writing. This look on his face like it's all a joke to him. I expect Ms. Herald to call him on it, but she doesn't. The class ends with us signing up for various class topic presentations and I think for a minute that Jack won't do that but he does, and ends up cornering Ms. Herald and shooting the shit with her until the bell rings.

I don't see him again until the end of the day. DeKalb's got work, so I'm sitting outside on the steps, watching the soccer players hike out to the field, and waiting for Brandy.

"Greetings, Will," Jack says again. Greetings. Who even says that? He sounds really pleased with himself.

"Hey."

Jack sprawls on the grass. I look at every changed inch of him. I can't help staring. He must know how different he looks, because he clears his throat in a formal way. Like I should buckle up before he tells me something really mind-blowing.

"School's a trip, isn't it?"

"Sure," I say. "When it's not dead boring. How was your summer?"

"My summer?" he asks, like it's no big thing. He stretches, puts his hands behind his neck. Closes his eyes against the sun. I can see he's got some muscles, though his arms are still skinny. I'm already kind of ready to strangle him. He's acting weird. Like someone's filming everything he does and says. I'm looking behind my shoulder, wondering if he's doing this to show off. Impress someone?

"Yeah, your summer," I say. "Weren't you in Sweden?"

"There. And other places," he says. "Though mostly Sweden. Airfare's a lot cheaper once you're in Europe."

"Right," I say.

"Sweden's phenomenal," he says. "Everything I expected. And a lot more. But really, the point wasn't just tourism."

"Right," I repeat. Wondering if he'd ever get to the point. Which I don't even know what that is. For him to tell me why he's so different now? I mean, what's there to say about that? He grew. His nuts finally dropped. He has neck meat around his Adam's apple. The kind of thing a mom would notice. Or a guy who was into guys would notice.

"The main thing is the people," he says. "And by people, I mean girls. Swedish girls aren't fucked up like American girls."

"What?"

"They're not all uptight about their bodies, for one thing."

"Oh."

"And they don't get all competitive," he adds. "Like, it's not a thing to share your time and yourself with someone, even if he's not the best-looking or the coolest or richest. I think a lot of that's socialism and everything. It's not socialist, per se, but Sweden's a very socially conscious society. Egalitarian. They don't have our racial problems, for instance."

"Well, everyone's white there, aren't they?"

"Not necessarily," he says. He starts talking about some tribe up in the north that is darker-skinned with "Asiatic origins," and a bunch of Asian kids walk by in their soccer cleats, and I wish he'd not talk so loud about that shit.

"So, Swedish girls are easy lays, then?" I ask.

"That's such an American way of looking at things, Will," he says. "Sex isn't a chase or a pursuit there. It's about experience. Sharing. Being human beings. Not owning each other like property. It's not a big deal like it is here. Finding meaning in life is much more important than trying to get laid."

He keeps talking like this. I don't give a shit about the meaning of life. So far, I've mostly been the kind of person who's focused on just getting through the goddamn week. Like, going to Sweden? Thinking about fucking socialism? I've got a test in bio and my mom wants me to take Kinney and Taylor to their various lessons because Jay's out of town and my dad's hiring a new guy to help him run the Laundromat and I'm out of toothpaste and

DeKalb wants to go to the movies but I don't want to spend any money. That's the speed of my life.

But then he's talking about how he did it with this girl named Tova or Tovay and how they did it out in a field or something, when her family went on a picnic and a hike and then they all went swimming, naked, and it was all very cool and she sunbathes with no top on and her little brothers were there and nobody said anything.

"Whoa," I say.

"Americans are so uptight," he shrugs. Like he's not American! I kind of want to haul off and hit him for being such a douche. But this is sort of the know-it-all way of Jack Telios. It was just easier to accept when he was a little weasel of a guy.

Thankfully, Brandy shows up. I don't know if I should be relieved or worried; Jack sits up on his elbows, still lying there in his awful safari shirt, says hello.

Brandy, to her credit, just nods at him, her eyes flicking over his body in a way that's kind of perfect, and then says she's got to go catch the bus to go to the Vances'; Mrs. Vance needs her to watch the kids tonight for a few hours.

"That reminds me; my little sisters are having a birthday party in a few weeks and my mom told me to invite you. She wants to meet you."

"Okay," she says. Then she takes my hand, really casual, and leans in and kisses me. It's weird, because my glasses are between us. Like a fence. And because Jack is fucking staring the whole time, even though it's, like, a one-second kiss with no tongue. Then she's gone and me and Jack stare at her as she goes. It's not weird; Brandy's not wearing anything that shows off her body. She doesn't walk sexy. Still, we stare and don't say anything until she's out of sight.

"Who's that?" he asks.

"Brandy Corvallis."

"Is she your *girlfriend* or something?" He says the word like I'm some kind of dumbass. Some American dumbass who owns a girl like property.

I stand up. "God, you're full of shit, Jack," I say.

He laughs at that. "I know," he says, standing up and brushing grass off his shirt. "But I want to go to film school, Will. What do you expect?"

I laugh too. Jack might be up his own ass, but at least he kind of knows it.

Later, when DeKalb's done with his band thing, Jack and him and me drive to Guitar Lab over in Uptown. DeKalb's looking for something for his bass. After dealing with the parking meter, I go in the store and see Jack and DeKalb standing together, looking at me.

"Brandy Corvallis," DeKalb says. "Can't believe you're really getting with that."

Jack spins off into the sheet music section, smirking.

"Oh fuck you," I say.

"Her little friend Shania told me all about you guys," DeKalb says. I'm standing by a giant broken accordion with a sign that says VINTAGE: $200 FIRM. Who the fuck spends that kind of money on a broken accordion?

I poke at the accordion. "What is this thing doing here? I thought this is Guitar Lab?"

"Shania say you all smacked it up a bunch of times."

"Jesus," I say. "Shania sure likes to talk."

"She's a little dim, yeah," he says. "But doesn't mean it's not information the world should know."

"We just did it once," I say, lowering my voice. "And shut up. It's not just like I'm . . . You know."

"Oh, I *know*." He laughs, walks away from me.

"She's a cool girl," I say.

"Mmm hmm."

"She is," I say.

"What the fuck do you know about that girl? Tell me one god-damn thing you know."

"Fuck you," I say.

"You can't," he says. "Nobody who dicks the shorties be doing it for love."

"She's not a fucking shorty, Jesus."

DeKalb laughs. "Name one thing."

"Okay, she's super into yarn," I say. "Like, she knits things."

"What? You making that up."

"She likes Target," I say.

"Target? Target's a fucking store. Plus Brandy's a stripper name."

"It is not."

"Is so," he says. "My dad's cousin has a daughter who's a

stripper. Or she was, until she had a baby."

"And magazines: she likes those too."

"Magazines," Jack says, from where he's flipping through stacks of 45s. "Not even a particular magazine. She just likes *all* of them. *Car and Driver, Good Housekeeping, Vogue . . .*"

DeKalb laughs so hard at this I think he's going to throw up. The manager guy at the front register looks at us weird, like he wonders if we're on drugs.

Then they both get into it:

"Brandy likes oxygen. She likes inhaling it and exhaling carbon dioxide."

"Brandy likes to buy food too. She likes grocery stores."

"Aldi," Jack says. "Rainbow. Walmart Supercenter."

"Because Brandy is one of those people who also likes eating. Food. That's the main thing she eats."

"Also, dick," DeKalb adds.

"The dick of guys named Will," Jack corrects.

Then I laugh. Because why, I don't know. I just do.

"Or just the dick of guys whose names start with *W*," DeKalb says. "Brandy real picky about dick."

And then we all lose it. "Brandy real picky about dick" is in my head like a chorus. Like a title. And because, yeah: I sound like an idiot. I like Brandy because I like her. I like getting naked with her. I like her, but I don't know her.

That weekend, Brandy and me are at my house. In the attic. My dad is somewhere in St. Paul, I don't know where. I don't care. We have sex and it's just as great as the other time, only a little longer, a little better, because I have condoms (bought myself, kept under the futon, next to my mason jar full of tips that I get sometimes for busing tables when it's busy at Time to Eat) and because we're alone and have a little more time.

We're just lying there, naked on top of the quilt, the fan blowing everywhere. Her hands are over her boobs, like she's trying to keep them quiet. It's hot as fuck. I want to take the condom off but I don't really want to do it in front of her. It's full daylight so there's nowhere to hide.

My phone beeps, so I reach over Brandy and grab my shorts. Brandy touches me as I check the phone. Her hands feel gentle, but sticky. My dad: going to Farmington to look @ jacuzzi

"Let's take a shower," I say.

"Okay," she says. Grinning. I don't expect her to be into it, but she is. I automatically think, *Things Brandy Likes: Showers. Water. Soap.*

"Go turn it on," I say. "You gotta run the water a while before the hot makes it up here."

"Okay," she says. Her hands are still on her boobs. Once she's gone, I sit up, put on my glasses, unpeel the thing. It's sticking to my ball hair in a way that's horrible, and the sound it makes when it comes off is even worse. I glance at the door. The shower is running. I wonder what it would be like to not have to use these fucking things.

"It's hot now, Will!" Brandy yells.

Taking a shower with a girl isn't as cool as you'd think. First,

I want to see everything, and wearing your glasses into the shower is not cool. Second, my shower is gross. I mean, it's small with two people in there and I don't really ever clean it and my shampoo was nearly empty and Brandy asks me if I have any conditioner and I'm like, what? Plus, after I finish washing up, we just kind of stand there getting wet and kissing, until it's clear that sex could happen again but I'm not even going to try pulling it off in here.

We get out and dry each other off. She turns to hang up the towels when we're done. I get to see her body like before and I don't want her to think I'm a creeper or anything, but it's one of my favorite parts of sex. I wish I had a picture of it, her body. I come up behind her and start touching her again, and our skin kind of squeaks against each other; my mom says that's from hard water. Of course in Oak Prairie there's a water softener. My dad thinks that shit's a waste of money.

As I'm touching her, Brandy leans back. I know she can feel my boner but she's acting all normal. She says she likes the dog picture over the toilet.

"My aunt's more into cats," she says. "But that is a pretty picture. I like the composition of it. When I have my own house, I'm getting a dog. I've always wanted a dog."

I want to tell her that my mom doesn't like pets; she doesn't like dog hair or cat boxes. That my dad never had a feeling about it, but I sensed he didn't fight her on that because of the cost. There is nothing sexy about money. Nothing. I stare at the sleeping-dog picture and wish I didn't have parents.

I turn her around and kiss her and we go back onto the futon to do it. Because that's where the condoms are. Because there was no way I'd make Brandy lie on my awful bathroom floor.

Afterward Brandy goes to get dressed, but I tell her not to. I feel super lazy. It's been a long week; I'm still working at Time to Eat, even with school, and we put up two new walls and Sheetrocked one of them too. Just me and my dad. Even though I'm back to living at my mom's and staying at my dad's every other weekend like we've always done.

"Tell me some stuff," I say.

"What?"

I put my arm around her. Her hair's still wet but I like even that. I kiss her between her tits. "I mean, what do you like?"

"You mean, like sex stuff?"

"No," I say. "Not sex. Just, I don't know. DeKalb was giving me shit."

"About me?"

"No," I say, realizing that was a mistake.

"Because I'm a sophomore?"

"No," I say. "Not that. He was asking me all this shit about you and teasing me like I don't know you."

"DeKalb is an idiot," she says. Laughs. Her hands are back on her boobs, but she curls in toward me, and her hair sprinkles water on my chest.

"Okay, so you like Target," I say. "And yarn. And Miller Grill. And taking pictures. And babysitting . . ."

"I don't like babysitting," she says. "I just do it for money."

"Okay, so you hate kids." She laughs. I smile up at the ceiling. "You live with your aunt and your nana. You do your laundry at my dad's Laundromat."

"So do you."

"Do you ever see your mom?"

She gets tense. "My mom's a loser."

I don't know what to say to that.

"You want to know good things, I will tell you good things," she says. Her hand slides around my stomach and chest, twisting around the little hairs I have there in a way that almost tickles but doesn't quite. "I like onion rings. I'm starting drivers' ed next semester. My birthday's the day after St. Patrick's Day. I think tattoos are overrated. And I don't like the color orange."

"That's good."

"I don't play any instruments, my favorite class this year is Psychology, and I have only kissed one other person besides you."

"Really? Who?" I say it without thinking that there's no way I can ever tell her about Angus.

"No," she says. "I'm not talking about that. I don't need to tell you reasons that I suck."

This makes perfect sense to me. So much sense, I feel terrible even asking her. But I repeat back in my head everything's she said: *onion rings, driver's ed, March 18, no tattoos, orange bad.*

It's a good start.

TEN

THE NEXT DAY, I go into Time to Eat to give Garrett my schedule now that I'm in school. Time to Eat's halfway between my mom's and my dad's, but with shifts starting at 4 and school letting out at 3:30, it's not like I can always get there. It's even more driving than I'm used to. Plus I need some time to get my homework done.

Carl's in the dish room, dumping soap into the silverware soak.

"What's going on, Carl?"

"Fucking bitches, making money," he says, barely looking at me.

"Right," I say.

Garrett's in his office looking at his laptop. A big sweaty Coke in a glass is sitting beside him.

"Will," he says. He's wearing a grimy apron over his Time to Eat denim shirt. I'm so glad I've never had to wear that denim shirt. I mean, on an old guy, it's fine. But in general, for me, denim shirts are absolutely terrible. "What can I do for you?"

"Got my new schedule since school started," I say, handing him the sheet of paper. "I can't work as much. Sorry."

"It's okay," he says. "Got some college guys coming back for other hours. Always juggling you all around. I've got a system."

"Cool," I say.

"Sit down," he says. "You hungry?"

I tell him no, sit in the chair by his desk.

"How's the house coming along?"

I shrug. "It's okay."

He sits back. Nods. Sips his Coke.

"Sure you don't want anything to drink? Eat?"

I shake my head.

"Your dad buy that place in St. Paul like he was talking about?"

"What?"

Garrett looks a little embarrassed. He scratches his jaw. "There's a Laundromat he had his eye on over there," he says. "By the barbecue place he likes."

"I don't know," I say. "I've never talked to him about it."

Garrett nods. "Okay. Okay." He pauses. Leans forward. "Okay, Will. Can I tell you something?"

"Yeah." But I suddenly don't want to know it.

"Here's the thing. I'm a little concerned with what's going on at your dad's place."

"All right."

"This by no means is something you need to fix or worry about," he says. "I'm just not sure he's got the whole thing under control anymore. He's running out of money. Worse yet, he's running out of time. We get an early freeze this fall and quite frankly, he's fucked."

"I know."

This is something I've been trying not to think about. And hoping nobody would notice. Or that it would change. But the truth is, nothing's really happened in the house for a while. My dad's busy like always, but I don't see much difference or progress. As uncomfortable as everything is in the house, it feels like my dad doesn't notice. He seems comfortable. At least when he's around, that is.

"The thing is, he won't stop fighting the city on that electrical and that's what'll be holding shit up. Is the furnace connected yet?"

"I think so? I don't know."

"It's not," he says. "It wasn't, last I heard, and he wouldn't pay a guy to do it. I know a good guy too, but he hasn't reached out to him yet. My guy is already booked out on other jobs, but he costs, so your dad's balking."

"Okay. So what do I do?"

"Nothing," he says. "Like I said earlier, I'm not telling you this so that you think it's your problem. It's just, I've known your dad a lot of years and I know how important redoing this house is to him. I just don't want you to think it's going to be finished faster than it is. This kind of thing always stretches out longer than anyone expects. There's been a bit of scope creep, when it comes to the original project."

"All right," I say. "I get it."

"And I know your mom might jump down his gullet about that too. I don't want to defend him—he's definitely gotten carried away with the whole thing—but I want you to understand it's also pretty common, when it comes to home remodels and construction. So you shouldn't feel caught between them, if that comes up."

"I think Roy was kind of worried about this too."

"Yeah, he said some things to me that made me wonder about it to begin with. That kid's pretty sharp, actually. Your father did good, getting him to help. I just hope he sticks with college and everything."

"Why?"

"Oh, I don't know if it's just talk, but he mentioned last night wanting to ditch out; saying he doesn't think it's real enough, real-world enough, I guess."

"Huh," I say. I don't like that idea, either. Just because it makes me think Roy's going to go back to being on drugs and homeless. College is where he needs to stay.

"Listen," Garrett says. "You ever need anything, you let me know. I know your dad pretty well and he's probably got you trained to be all self-reliant and that's great. You sure as hell need that in life. But he can be overly proud too. Pride's a big thing in this house stuff, you might have noticed. He's trying to do what Tess said he couldn't do."

"Mom told me they didn't have the money."

"Tess said she thought it was a waste of time, that you should just move to a better neighborhood entirely. But she wanted a lot of things he didn't want. So I think he's been waiting to make this move awhile now. I'm pretty sure he'd rather fall over and die than admit he's over his head."

"So, you want me to tell you how it's going? Like a spy?" I'm immediately suspicious. This is the kind of shit my mom's been doing for years. Asking about his drinking. Asking about whether he's dating anyone. Asking about why my basketball uniform wasn't clean for tournaments. Asking if he still was running the Laundro-mat, why he sold the car wash. Asking, and not just to be polite.

"No, no, no," Garrett says quickly. "I just want you to know that if you need anything and you don't feel comfortable talk-ing to your mom, my door's open. You don't have to feel weird about it, either, because I'm your boss. We've got more than that between us, okay?"

"Okay."

"I'm your boss because I've known you're a smart kid and I had a hunch you'd be a good worker. I wasn't wrong, either."

I feel embarrassed, but it's like the best thing anyone's ever said to me. I can't look at him, so I just say thanks and then tell him I've got to get home.

I'm sitting in my mom's house, watching her cook three meals at once, as usual. Chicken nuggets for Taylor and this weird cheese thing for Kinney, meatballs and spaghetti for me.

"Will, you have no hair," Taylor says to me. "Where is all your hair from before?"

"I cut it," I tell her. "It was making my neck hot." I don't tell her that Brandy cut it for me. With an electric shaver. We did it on her front porch. Her aunt Megan thought it was hilarious. After Megan left to go to take Nana to the doctor, we did it quick in Brandy's room too. Brandy couldn't stop running her hands over my stubble and that felt amazing. I'm getting hard just remembering it.

"I like the new glasses," Kinney says. "But not your hair. Sorry."

Taylor puts her hands on her hips. Taylor (and Kinney) are both kind of tiny to me. Little tiny girls with little brown haircuts going to their chins and little T-shirts that have little smart-assy sayings on them like BOW TO THE PRINCESS or HOMEWORK MAKES MY DOG SICK or whatever.

"You want mineral water or regular, Will?" my mom asks. "Or we've got milk too. And orange juice. Apple juice . . ." She's bending down, looking into the fridge. "Some cranberry, if you like that . . ."

"Water's fine," I say.

The dining-room table is huge; you could sit about fifteen people at it, but Taylor and Kinney are dicking around, spinning on the bar stools at the breakfast-counter thing, waiting for my mom to slide their individual meals on their little plates that have dancing monkeys on them. Kinney's wearing earbuds and is singing along to the music, which sounds awful, and Taylor is also singing, even though she's not wearing earbuds. I don't know if Taylor's singing along to the same song or what.

You would think my mom would be all stressed, with all the cooking and her kids singing like idiots and whatever, but she's not. She comes over to where I am and sets up two plates across from each other, pours herself a glass of red wine, lights the candles on the table. Like we're on a date, she and I. She gives me a glass of water and says we'll eat in just a minute, then she goes and gets Kinney a container of Parmesan cheese from the fridge and checks her laptop, which is sitting on the counter next to the sink, and then finally she brings over the spaghetti and meatballs and a loaf of garlic bread and some Caesar salad she made. Caesar salad for real, not from a bag; I watched her whip up the dressing for it and everything.

"There," she says, once it's all laid out. "Let's tuck in."

Tuck in: my mom always says stuff like that.

So, we serve ourselves and don't say anything, except to ask for salt and pepper, and Taylor and Kinney come over and start asking questions about the garlic bread and why it's all shiny and crunchy and my mom says, "Go finish your own dinner and let Will and me catch up."

"That doesn't make any sense," Taylor says, but she does what her mom says.

But we don't *catch up*. We just eat. My mom savors her food, closes her eyes while she chews, while she sips her wine. She gets up a bunch to clear the twins' plates and send them off into the TV room. Kinney won't go, though; after what seems like years of negotiation, she promises Mom that she won't bug us and just listen to her iPod at the breakfast nook.

"Isn't this nice?" she says. "Peaceful."

It's not totally peaceful. Kinney's still singing. My mom checks her watch, which isn't just a watch but a GPS and a fitness tracker and probably also downloads e-books and launches nuclear submarines and orders pizza.

"Jay should be home in another hour. Thank God. You'd think with the girls in school, things would be less crazy. But it's been crazier than ever."

I nod. I can hear the Disney Channel from the TV room, where Taylor is.

"And work's been crazy too."

I nod again. This, she always says. Since I can remember. She always had a normal job, even when I was younger. She steadily made more and more money, finally passing my dad and whatever he could do with his little businesses. She had just started with her current company, which was when she met Jay, and then the divorce stuff happened. Now she's been promoted a bunch, even though Jay works for the outdoors company now.

I don't like to think about her and Jay. My dad calls it cheating, but I think they were legally separated. It's not like I'm going to ask my mom when she started having sex with Jay. Obviously it's pretty gross to start up with someone before you've finalized things with your ex-husband. It's like my dad doesn't see how everything else was shitty. He just thinks, *she cheated on me*, as if that tells the whole story.

Not even Jay and her cheating really bugs me that much. This is the main problem with my mom. Though her spaghetti's good and she's made time for me and she's talking to me like I'm an adult too, and not her son, there's just not a lot I want to talk about with her. Work is probably the safest subject we've got. Even if I see it differently than she does, I get it now: how work gets crazy.

"You're still working at that restaurant?" my mom asks, sweeping up Caesar dressing with a piece of garlic bread.

"Mmm hmm," I say. My mouth's full but I can't think of anything to say otherwise.

"Do you like it?" she says. "The job, I mean? I imagine it's not an easy one."

"Yeah," I say, because for once there're no meatballs in my mouth. I wipe my mouth with the cloth napkin, which matches the cloth place mat—deep red, like the wine my mom drinks—and tell her a little about the job. About all the food people throw out. About the delivery mornings and all the stuff Garrett unloads for the week. About the waitresses who tip me out now, for busing tables when Everardo gets slammed in the dish room, Garrett giving everyone rounds of milk shakes and fries after a big rush. About Sierra who reads people's palms in the break room. About the one guy who got hired as an EMT and quit cooking, which has sent me up to the line to do more than just run the fryer.

"Wow," my mom says, folding her napkin along her place mat. "How fascinating. It's amazing they do all these other vocations at the same time."

I nod. But: *vocations*. Another word my mom would say. As if it's all so noble or exotic.

"So, how's your father doing?" she asks. And then I remember why I hate this kind of dinner with my mom. Catching up—the whole point isn't to talk to me. It's to get a read on my dad. To see if he's sucking, at both life and fatherhood. Nothing makes me want to disappear faster than this shit. But it seems like the only thing she has left, where I'm concerned; she's trying to make it up to me. She's trying to show she's not a total asshole who doesn't care, except she can't just do nice things like make me dinner and leave it at that. No, she has to act like she's all worried about my well-being and my dad's finances and how clean the goddamn house is and all that shit.

"He's fine," I say. "Doing good."

"Still running the Laundromat?"

"Yeah," I say.

"Will he buy another place, you think?"

I shrug. I have to be very careful here. Though she doesn't need a dime from my dad, she's still all over his spending habits. Still looking for places where he's being irresponsible.

"Still drinking?"

"No, he's not drinking," I say.

This is a lie, but not really. The passed-out blackout shit that was going on before isn't happening anymore. But she wouldn't see any difference. She won't believe that he could actually be a better person since she left. She'd never accept that he's happier than he's been in a long time. But I won't tell her that. I'm not on her level. She's got Jay and two new kids and money, so she thinks she won something. It's so babyish; it makes me sick.

"That you know of," she says, and then I can't hold it in.

"Mom," I say, setting down my fork. "Don't drag me into this."

"Sorry, sorry," she says, waving her hands like she can get rid of all this shit she's just asked, like she can make it go away. Erase it. "I just worry about him. Well, mostly about you."

"I'm seventeen, Mom," I say.

"I know," she says. She presses both palms down on either side of the plate, looks down at her hands. She has very nice fingernails, rounded at the edges, with a clear polish on them. "I know," she says again. "I can barely believe it. Seventeen years. It seems like you were just a little boy, just like Taylor and Kinney. Just a few minutes ago." She looks up and smiles. Kinney is now lying across both bar stools, listening to her earbuds, but she's silent. I stare at her and my mom does too, and then she laughs.

And I laugh with her but it's fake. She can't tell the difference, though. There's so much shit she doesn't know and will never know. She says she knows, but she still goes around looking at me like I'm a baby. She knows I have a girlfriend because she saw Brandy's name and number pop up on my phone. But she doesn't know that we have sex. The shit she knows barely matters.

And nobody knows about Angus but me and Angus. And I don't plan on telling them. Not just because they couldn't handle it. But because they haven't earned it. Don't deserve it.

"I just want you to know," she says. "You can always come to me. Anytime you have a problem or need anything. Okay? Need any help at all. Jay and me, we are here." She puts her palm over my hand, in a kind of ball over my knuckles. It feels weird and looks weird too. We both look at our hands together like this.

Like a huge alien hand. Knuckle tumors.

"I know," I say. Because she's told me that a million times since I was little. But the truth is that I've been an afterthought since the twins were born. I know she feels guilty about it. That's the reason for the place mats and candles and meatballs and catching up. But she doesn't get it; I've been fine without her.

And somehow, her telling me now means even less than it did before. Doesn't mean what it meant when Garrett said it.

"You know, I graduate this year," I say.

Her face perks up. "I know! We have a big party to plan! What kind of party would you like to have?"

"I don't know," I say. The idea of having a graduation thing, an open house or a party or whatever it is, sounds terrible. I mean, I want the cards with the money in them. But not the experience. And damned if I'm going to tell her about my dad's plan for my graduation.

"What does . . . does your dad want to host it? I suppose not, what with the house . . . ?"

"I'll talk to him about it," I say.

"Well, whatever you want, we can do it. We can do it here or find . . . some other place. It's up to you."

"All right." I look around my plate; there's nothing else to eat and I wish I had something to do with my hands. I take my glasses off, wipe them on the cloth napkin.

"I don't want to upset you about your father, Will," she says. She goes to touch me again but stops. Pulls her hand back. I'm sort of depressed at that, but also sort of glad. I made her see me, for once. I made that happen.

"I can't stop being concerned, when it comes to you," she continues. "Maybe you'll understand when you're older, have your own kids. There's a lot your dad doesn't understand about you, Will. About a lot of things."

I can't look at her now. I'm too pissed. There's a lot he doesn't know about me, yeah. But she's wrong. I think my dad would understand. I haven't told him about Brandy or Angus. I've never had anything like that to tell him before, but I've told him other things. The first time I drank. The time I smoked cigarettes and puked afterward. I told him and we talked and he laughed at me a little. He was cool about it. He didn't act like it was a super big deal, but he told me to be careful. To be responsible. I've never smoked cigarettes since, so it's proof that his way works. It's all in how you talk about things.

I could tell him about Brandy, for sure. About Brandy, I could see him being happy for me. And Angus, he loves Angus too. But that, I probably won't tell him. Angus is hard to explain. Even to myself. Because I'm not gay, so it doesn't really count; I'm not going to come out or anything. It's hard to describe, whether we're naked or just huddled together on the sofa on Garrett's porch, sleeping. It's good. Brandy's good too. I don't know if he'd understand them both at once, though. He'd probably see it as cheating.

I wonder what my mom would think of me and Angus naked in bed. I wonder if I went to her asking for "help" with that, what she would say.

Now Kinney is crying, though, so my mom isn't paying attention to me anymore. She's sitting on the floor, holding Kinney in a heap; Kinney fell off the bar stools somehow while she was listening to her earbuds at top volume and even above her crying, I can still hear the music through them, because they've been yanked out of her ears and are lying on the glossy hardwood floor. I stand up and clear my plate and then I pick up the earbuds and click off her iPod.

"What's going on?" Taylor is next to me, looking down at Mom and Kinney.

"Kinney wiped out, kinda," I say. We both stare at them. Kinney is sobbing now, milking it, probably. She's acting like she's dying. My mom is rubbing the back of her head, kissing her cheeks, talking softly to Kinney. Taylor seemed a little alarmed at first, but then she gets a disgusted look on her face and turns to me.

"She's such a show-off," Taylor says, spinning around in her little pink socks on the hardwood. I can practically see my reflection in this floor. "Want to watch TV with me?"

"Can't," I say. "Homework."

"Bummer for you."

Later, I'm zoning out over my homework at the dining-room table and watching my mom while she harasses Taylor and Kinney into the bathtub and pajamas. Jay is back from his trip and he's unpacking a bunch of duffel bags and sorting out his laundry in the mudroom and talking on his phone.

"That's critical," he keeps saying. "Oh, yeah. Absolutely. Critical."

I think about what Garrett said to me and for some reason, it makes me feel sick. Like, I could cry. Not about my dad and the house, though that's a little worrying. The part about how he thinks I'm smart, a good worker. For some reason, these sentences matter more to me than any other sentences I've ever heard before, from teachers, on report cards, whatever. I don't care about school shit; school shit is school shit. It's like Roy says; it's not real. Real is me filling up cambros of tomatoes, portions of guacamole and taco meat, mounds of onions and mushrooms. Real is me pushing soaked potatoes for fries until my neck aches from running the slicer. Real is me getting Carl whatever the fuck it is he needs when he hollers that he needs it and him saying, "Thanks, guy." Carl saying anything beyond "making money and fucking bitches" is the sort of thing that matters.

I know being a prep cook, or even a line cook, or even Garrett, a guy who owns a whole restaurant, isn't going to save the world, or cure hunger, or tell me the meaning of life. But I don't care about saving the world. I already know I'm not going to do that.

"No, I'm hearing you," Jay says, thumping down the lid of the washer. "Critical component of the whole project. Absolutely."

I look down at my graph paper for Advanced Math. I've erased the paper so much you can barely see the little blue boxes. Then I hear a hollering and little feet stampeding and Taylor is there, her hair all wet around her Hello Kitty pajamas. Her arms around my neck smell like raspberry soap.

"Gotta kiss you g'night, Will!" Taylor says, and plants one on both of my cheeks, as she squeezes me.

"Good night," I say. Squeezing her back. Her hair drips all over the place, reminding me of Brandy.

"Taylor! Will's doing his homework! It's time for *bed*!" my mom hollers.

"I like it better when you're here," she whispers. "Kinney can have Mom as long as I get you."

"What?"

"Don't say I told you that," she says. "Kinney's a hog of our mom. But I don't care. I'd rather have you or my dad. You're way more valuable."

"Okay," I say. I push her wet hair out of her face. "I won't tell. You need to get in bed, though, or you'll get in trouble."

She runs toward the stairs, saying over her shoulder, "I'm always in trouble, anyway!"

ELEVEN

IT'S THE LAST weekend in September and my dad and I are pulling nails out of flooring he got off a Freecycle website when I tell him I want to stay with him until he finishes the house.

I expect him to say no. I expect him to say, *I'll need to ask your mother.* I expect him to tell me the truth, then. That the house is fucked and the furnace isn't hooked up and there's no way I can stay with him. Even if it is closer to Brandy, who he now knows is my girlfriend. Even if it is closer to school and more convenient and less gas.

I expect him to say no too, because maybe he likes having his weeknights back. To drink all he wants and not feel like he's leaving me alone, like he did all summer. He'd look so guilty and embarrassed those mornings he'd show up after being gone the whole night, wearing the same clothes as the day before, red eyed and holding a box of his favorite pastries like some kind of apology to me. Like a man who beat his wife giving her flowers.

So I'm shocked when he smiles at me. Doesn't miss a beat, either.

"Of course," he says. "Of course you can. You're my son. This is your home. And you're almost eighteen. We're doing this together, you and I, Will. I'm glad you want to be a part of it."

"Okay," I say. "Cool."

He turns and grabs the magnetic sweeper, runs it over the scattered nails all over the driveway. The clatter-suck sound of it is one of my favorite things in the world. A broom that sweeps up metal is pretty much the greatest invention ever. Along with the nail gun and the thing that you bash with a hammer to staple in flooring. I am so in love with tools. I had no idea tools were so cool. Before this summer, I basically thought the world was built with a hammer and nails.

I expect him to start explaining more details about the house. About insulating the attic. About the furnace not being ready and the power being weird; we keep blowing fuses and needing a generator if we want to run the air compressor for the nail guns and stuff.

But we just keep ripping out nails. Me with a pliers, him with the claw of his hammer. The nails rain on the driveway. Every so often, we make trips to stack the flooring in piles, by length, and then one of us grabs the magnet broom to clatter-suck up the nails. When the magnet broom fills up, we dump the nails into an ice-cream bucket. Most contractors just toss nails, my dad says. But he sees no reason to waste things.

Never mind that there are tons of ice-cream buckets already full of nails, sitting in our garage. Never mind that the backyard keeps filling up with shit. Never mind that he spent two hundred bucks on a giant tent tarp to cover all the stuff from rain. It's the kind of white tent tarp that you'd use for an outdoor party and some of the neighbors asked if it was for my graduation party my dad was throwing for me, and I had to joke about it, saying, yeah, we really like to plan ahead.

But this is why I want to do something. Stay with him. Help him. Summer's long past, and it's only getting colder out. But he's still finding deals online. Free stuff. Cheap stuff. A convection oven. A bunch of loose countertops. A pedestal sink with no faucet. Half-full cans of paint. A hanging pendant light that looks like a chandelier had sex with tin cans.

And that's just the newest, latest stuff. Because instead of buying that Laundromat in St. Paul, my dad tripped upon another money-making idea. He was buying something from an unclaimed storage locker and started talking to the owner, who was selling the whole storage-unit place. So now he owns that, and all the junk that didn't get bought or claimed from some of those units, anything he thinks might be good or useful, well, it enters our garage or the big top in the backyard or the basement. I don't even go in the basement anymore.

If I don't watch it, there won't be room for me in the attic. The only reason stuff hasn't gotten dumped up there is it'd be a pain in the ass to haul it up the stairs. I've got to try to work with him. Steer this the right way.

That night, when I don't come home for dinner, my mom calls. "What's going on?"

"I'm just gonna stay at Dad's the rest of this week, Mom."

"Okay. What . . ." She stops. "Is there a reason for that?"

"I just . . . we're working on something and I've got homework and I don't want to drive all that way."

She's quiet. "All right. You'll be here on Saturday, though? It's the girls' birthday."

"For sure," I say.

Later, I'm showering upstairs, and the water's barely warm. The hot-water heater isn't working right; my dad replaced the old one with a tankless thing, which is supposed to be energy efficient, but either he didn't install it right or it's a lemon, because half the time it doesn't work.

I get out of the shower and it's freezing. The burst of hot weather is over now. I've pretty much stopped with summer clothes. We've had the windows closed for a while, but it doesn't help; there are too many gaps in the walls and siding now. The wind just sings through the cracks. Looking at the dog asleep on the bed in the picture above the toilet, I dry off as fast as I can and run to my room to get clothes back on. I don't have much here; I need to remember to dig out my warm clothes when I go back for Kinney and Taylor's birthday, because most of what I keep at my dad's is summer shit and stuff for construction.

My dad's downstairs, heating up canned soup on the hot plate for us. He's got a TV rigged up on a sawhorse table, but there's nothing but network for channels. He's watching some news show, the kind where they talk about kidnapped kids or people getting cancer from living on a toxic-waste dump without realizing it. Serious people in business suits interviewing all these poor bastards.

I call Brandy but she doesn't pick up.

So I text her, tell her I'm going to bed soon. We usually text each other in bed until about eleven. But I'm way too fucking beat tonight and could probably fall asleep in my bowl of soup. I don't want her to think I blew her off. Since that one day this summer, I try to always do what I say I'm going to do.

My dad changes the channel to football. I finish my text, just as he's saying to the television, "There we go." The Vikings have gotten a first down. He opens another beer and gets out silver mixing bowls, dumps soup in one, then hands me a sleeve of saltine crackers.

"Nothing fancy tonight, sorry," he says.

"I don't mind," I say. "Steak and potato is my favorite."

We eat the soup, sitting on stools, holding mixing bowls, watching football. I've never liked football enough to want to play it, but I've always watched it with my dad. He'd fill a dish full of peanut M&M's and make chili or stew and corn bread and we'd just sit on our asses and watch it and eat and it wasn't anything big, but it was fun. Usually Garrett or some of his other friends would stop by. They would all eat and holler at the TV and talk shit and laugh. He didn't do this every Sunday, but nearly. It was the main way he relaxed. The most he ever talked was in those situations. When I was younger, I could ask a million football questions and all these guys would answer them. It was funny and noisy and everyone would want to explain things to me.

Now, I want to ask him a million questions again. But not about football.

More like: *Is the furnace hooked up?*

And, why don't you tell me anything?

And, are you actually happy or just when you're drunk?

Are you an alcoholic? Or something else? Something worse? Is there some reason you can't stand life the way it is? And is it some reason I can do anything about? Garrett said there was nothing I could do, but I don't think that's completely right. I think I can do things. I know how to work; I know how to do what I'm told. I know how to fold myself up into anything. I'm like the batter that Carl mixes up in the morning in the Hobart. It could be anything, depending on what you fold into it: pancakes, berry crisp, lemon cake, devil's food. It all starts out with this one box of powdery flour and you follow the lists taped up on the wall, depending on what you want. That's me. You can fold anything into me and it'll blend. I can write research papers and do group projects, not that I like either of them, but I can fucking do them, without complaining. I can go watch Angus's band play; I can play pickup ball with DeKalb. I can go to Target on a Friday night with Brandy. I can live in Oak Prairie; I can live in the city. I can live here with you, Dad, in this wreck of a house, and I can live with Mom in her mansion that feels like a hotel. I can be your only son and I can be a big brother. I can be with Angus; I can be with Brandy.

But I don't say any of that. I ask him why the fuck Joe Buck still has a job announcing football when the whole world knows he's a giant ass. My dad laughs, lifts his mixing bowl to drink the last bits. Then he opens a beer.

"You want a beer, Will?"

I don't respond.

"I know that you've drank beer before," he says, cracking open the fridge. Which is full of nothing but beer, really. Well, beer and ketchup.

I still don't say anything.

"And you've got nowhere to be, either, right?"

I shrug. He takes that for yes and hands me one of his beers. It's a Grain Belt Nordeast in a tall can. I open it and he seems happy. Smacks me on the back. I drink the beer, we watch the game. Then, during a commercial, he says, "Help me with this mattress, will you?"

Every morning the blow-up mattress he sleeps on deflates a little, and then he pushes all the air out and rolls it up into a loose heap, sticks it in the corner. He used to just use a sheet, but now he's like me in the attic, and has a sleeping bag with a bunch of other quilts that I've never seen before. They've probably been abandoned at the Laundromat. He's been bringing home that kind of crap for years now. My mom would go crazy, when I was littler. They'd have the same fight, over and over.

"Tom, what the hell is this?"

"What do mean, what is it? It's a kind of tablecloth thing."

"Where'd you get it?"

"The Laundromat."

"We don't even have a table that size, though," she would say. "And gross—it's someone else's tablecloth!"

"It was in the damn washer and dryer, Tess!" he'd yell back, leaving me unsure which of them to side with, since they both had decent points.

He attaches the little pump to the mattress and then I help him spread it out over the floor. He doesn't seem to mind that there's sawdust and crap all over the place. It seems impolite, somehow, to point this out.

He flips on the pump and the whole house feels like it's shaking to death from the noise. My dad doesn't seem to notice, though. Just tips back his beer and guzzles like it's a contest. Once the bed's inflated, he puts down his beer and says, "All right, then."

And he sits down and the game's back on, and so he lies there, drinking on the mattress while I sit on the stool, and we watch the Vikings get killed by New England, while Joe Buck talks in his Supreme Douche of the Universe voice and I have more questions I won't ask.

Do you hate this or is it okay with you?

Do you think I'm a baby for thinking living like this is shitty?

Do you actually like this beer or do you just buy it because it's on sale?

Why the hell was Mom the one who bitched about child support, not you? Why did you let her roll over you, and make me go back and forth, week after week? When she had the good job, anyway? Everyone says you're the cheap one, but people don't get rich by spending money, either; is that why she wouldn't pay it? Because she couldn't stand to give you a cent? Even if it was for her only son? Or was that a bad investment too? The better investments being Kinney and Taylor, who come from a better father. Someone who looks good in a suit and doesn't drink whatever's on sale. The biggest quantity for the least amount.

The sound of this in my head is too much. I can hear it over fucking Joe Buck, even. My dad seems like he's made of liquid, lying on the jiggly mattress, sipping his beer, watching the TV and his phone in equal measure. He's got his eye on every little ping from Craigslist and Freecycle and who knows what else. The latest thing is this giant draftsman's desk he got from some dude online. It's in the backyard, this blinding white thing, all aerodynamic and fancy, next to the piles of wood and scrap and stacks of cabinets he wants to reuse. It looks like a spaceship in the middle of a yard sale.

I tell him I've got homework and he waves and smiles and sips and watches. I've got to get my homework done so I can talk to Brandy a little before I fall asleep. I don't finish the beer, but I bring it with me.

"Hey, Will?"

I think for a minute he's going to tell me not to bring the beer up. Like he's realized it was a mistake to give it to me.

But all he says is, "Good to have you around, son." He sounds weird; choked up. Like he might cry.

"Good to be here," I tell him, not turning around. I don't really want to know what his face looks like. I feel like he already might know all the shit I was thinking. I wonder what my face looks like at times like that. When I get upstairs I take a piss and then dump the rest of the beer on top of it.

I finish my homework really quickly; when I get upset about shit, I'm like the opposite of most people. I like having something to do, even if it's something stupid like discussion questions for Global Society or the diagram of a camera's parts for Photography. Once it's all done and zipped up in my backpack, I get in bed. I normally sleep in just my underwear, wherever I am, but now I'm rocking these thermal fleece pants and shirt that Jay gave me for Christmas one year; they're like the base layers you wear under your clothes when you climb Mount Everest or whatever. I get under the covers, the light of the phone glowing under the quilts, because it's so cold up here, and I text Brandy to call me. A second later, she does.

"I miss you," she says. "It feels like we barely see each other now that school's started."

"I know," I say. I know I should say I miss you back, but I can't.

"I should quit yearbook. Or the newspaper. All I'm doing is taking photos. No time to develop half of them, either."

"No, don't," I tell her. "I'm going to be at my dad's full time now."

"Really?"

"Yeah. I talked to him today. He's got lots of stuff for me to do. And all the driving back and forth sucks."

I should say it sucks because I want to see her and can't. I don't know why I can't say the things that I know would make her happy. But to say it back just sounds like copying her. Like it wasn't really my idea. Or true.

"Your mom won't care?" She sounds like she wants to be really happy but is nervous about it. She's never met my mom but I've told her a little bit about her. How my mom's suspicious of my dad. I don't have to say she doesn't like my dad; they're divorced, it's obvious.

I tell her it's going to be fine.

Then I tell her that I can't stop thinking about her.

That I wish she was here. In bed with me.

She doesn't say anything. She's just breathing. So am I.

This isn't anything I know how to do. She seems like she's waiting for something.

"You still there?" I say.

"Yeah. Just . . . sleepy."

"Me too."

And then I turn off the light. I'm cold but everything feels sweaty and I want to jerk off. My hand's in my boxers. I am turning into Jack-Off Telios. Since Jack himself is no longer Jack-Off; he's got girls around him all the time lately. Like they are lining up for service now that he's all manly.

I'm thinking I'll tell her good-bye, but then Brandy says she wishes she were older.

The TV downstairs turns off, and some music comes on. My dad has a turntable he found in the trash behind the Laundromat and he took it home and fixed something and now he's got all these records. Scratchy-sounding shit. It's some lady wailing. Blues.

I pull my hand out of my boxers. I ask Brandy why she wishes she were older.

"Because I already know what I want in life," she says. "I'm sick of just waiting to be old enough to have it."

I don't know why but this scares me. I don't say anything. I want to keep her on the phone; I'm imagining her naked in her bed, I can see it perfectly, as if the phone is some kind of magic device that transmits her through it. But I can't jerk off now.

I don't know what I want in life.

Correction: I don't know what *one thing* I want.

I tell her that she is beautiful. I tell her I wish I was under the covers with her. I tell her that I wish I could go over there now and get in bed with her.

"My aunt's home tonight, though," she says.

"I don't care," I tell her.

"I want you so much sometimes," she whispers. "All the time, I want you."

Yes, I think. *So do I,* I think.

"You want to hang out tomorrow?" I ask. "After school."

She has a yearbook meeting, but after that? I tell her yes. I want to make her happy. I want to want only her.

Just as she clicks off, I realize I'm the worst person ever. She thinks about me: *all the time, I want you.* Why can't I figure out how to say it back? It's like I'm being stubborn.

And Brandy? She doesn't deserve this shit. But I can't change it, the truth that I want both of them. Both Brandy and Angus.

When I jerk off, I think about both of them. Together. Apart. With me or alone. I can't help it, though it makes me feel like I'm cheating. I never want them together in real life; I can't stand thinking about us all in one place, like that day after we went swimming at Roy's.

I wish I could figure it out. Choose. Know for sure: Which one is the one?

But neither of them is the one. I want all of it. Both. Together. Apart. I don't want to choose.

TWELVE

IT'S AFTER FIVE in the afternoon in early October when Taylor and Kinney's birthday party packs up all ten insane hollering girls into Jay's car and my mom's SUV. They've been flailing around the house like they have rubber bands instead of skeletons under their skin, so naturally now they're all going to Drop Zone, which is some kind of horror-show place that's nothing but trampolines and dodgeball. After they're all gone and the doors slam and it's quiet, Brandy and me are staring at each other like *holy shit*.

"Whoa," Brandy says.

"Yeah," I agree.

She starts to clean up the paper plates of cake and ice cream, but I grab her.

"Come on," I say.

"Where are we going?" she asks. But she's smiling.

"To my room," I say. "This'll just take a couple minutes."

"Wow, so smooth," she says. I laugh. We are like this about sex now, even though we've only done it exactly six times. I wish it were more, but six (about to be seven!) is good. So good.

We do it in my bedroom, even though I suppose we could do it in any room here, really. Afterward, I flush the condom in the bathroom while she gets dressed. She seems dazed. Out of it. I feel completely opposite: I could go out and run around the block. I feel like doing everything. Like, once I've cleared that main thing out of the way—sex—then my body's, like, rubbing its hands together, going, "All right! Time to get shit *done*!"

I get my clothes on, though only because she's getting her clothes back on. I could roll around with her naked all day; I can't imagine what it would be like to be able to do that. But my mom and Jay are only going to be at Drop Zone for an hour and after that the girls come back here for a slumber party, and Brandy and I definitely have had enough of preteen girls today.

She has me zip up the back of her dress and I do it, and then she gets a text and sits down on the bed again. Her face looks upset.

"What?"

"Nothing." She keeps reading.

I don't want to look over her shoulder—I hate it when people do that—so I just grab her hand and kind of doodle around with it. I feel so goddamn *good*. I want to go get something to eat. Go to the movies. Go anywhere, really.

"We should go to Target," I say. "Saturday night at Target! We've never done that!"

But she pulls her hand away from me to text back so I go into the kitchen. Eat some of the leftover cake, no plate, just my hands. Get some lemonade out of the fridge; see my tacked-up paycheck still on the magnet clip, next to a drawing Taylor made of Santa Claus as a ninja with this giant sword. Taylor is my favorite, for sure, but sometimes I think she's kind of fucked up. I shove the check in my pocket—I need to cash it—Angus found out I was having my mom deposit my checks and give me cash and he gave me shit about it. You have to establish credit, you idiot, Angus said. This isn't your grandma sending you ten bucks for your birthday anymore.

When Brandy finally comes out of my bedroom, she puts her phone in her bag and says she's got to get home. Something's off.

"Your aunt say so?"

"Yeah."

We get in my car and I start it; along with the weird noise when I go too fast, there's a burned smell whenever I start my car lately. I don't want to tell my mom, because I don't want to answer a million questions about what I've done to it; I don't want to tell my dad because it's another thing he can't afford.

The whole drive, Brandy is barely talking. Not that she's super chatty normally, and I appreciate that, being a little shy, myself. Some girls seem hell-bent on filling up every available silence, though, and, I mean, if all you have to say is idiotic shit that no one can think of a response to, that's not any better. Conversations aren't hard for Brandy and me. We don't hang out quietly like we're in a library or anything, but we can talk pretty easily.

When I pull up to her house, she doesn't invite me in.

"What's the deal?" I ask. I'd turned the car off, expecting we'd go in and hang out.

She glances at her house. There are lights on, but I can't see anything beyond that.

"My mom's here," she says. "It's not . . . I don't want you to meet her. Seriously."

"Okay."

"It's not because of you," she says. "There's nothing wrong with you."

"Okay," I repeat, though that's not strictly true. There's plenty wrong with me, but I'm disappointed. After we'd hung out with my mom and Jay, and my mom seemed like she thought Brandy was nice, and my sisters were all show-offy to her, and then we had sex, I felt like the whole night was ahead of us.

"It's because everything's wrong with *her*," she says. "If I don't call you tonight, don't get worried. Usually I get really depressed after I see her. It's not a big deal."

"All right," I say. Though nothing's all right. I feel this little zinging panic running from my ass to my throat.

"Seriously, don't worry," she says. Swipes a tear from her face.

"Will you at least text me? I have to work tomorrow, but I'll be around later."

She nods. She doesn't even kiss me, just opens the door and rushes up inside the house.

Then I don't know what to do. DeKalb's not answering his phone. I'd call Angus, but I was just out in Oak Prairie and don't feel like wasting all the gas to get out there again. Since I'm nearby, I decide to just go to my dad's. The burned smell in my car is getting worse, and no amount of turning up the radio helps me ignore the weird noises, either.

When I get there, Garrett's truck is out front and he's standing beside it. The sun's almost down but I can see he's giving my car the hairy eyeball.

"What in the hell?" he asks when I get out. "You know that there's something wrong with your car?"

I shrug. "It's been making a weird noise lately."

He tells me to open the hood and when he does, he steps back from a big gush of smoke.

"Jesus fucking Christ, Will," he says. "You've blown a coolant line and you're dumping it all over the road."

"Is that a big deal?"

"You see everyone else driving around with this kind of smoke pouring out of the engine?"

I feel like an idiot now, and it sucks, because I kind of liked the idea that Garrett thinks I'm this kid who's on top of shit.

He looks under the hood a little more, waving away smoke, muttering things. I stand there, all useless. The zinging feeling is now ten times stronger.

"Know where your dad is?" he asks.

"Been out at my mom's all day."

"He's not answering my calls or texts," Garrett says. "We were supposed to meet up today at that self-storage place. Says there's some kitchen equipment I might want."

"What kind?"

Garrett shrugs. Like he thinks the whole idea is bullshit, anyway. "Let's go inside," he says. "Want to see how things are going."

I would tell him that things aren't going anywhere. That my dad seems to have shot his load on the remodel with the demolition of the walls. Now all he's doing is acquiring junk. All the people who owed him favors are square with him; there's no asking for more. Roy's at college. It's just me, and I have school and work myself. It gets dark earlier and earlier now too.

But I just follow him inside and help snap on utility lights because I know where they are and he doesn't. The whole place smells bad. Like garbage and beer and dust. And I stand there, watching him look at the walls and the piles of things. The new record player. The box of vinyl records. The Skil Drill on the card table next to a pile of brown bananas. A bunch of empty cans of Nordeast.

Garrett says nothing. He's still wearing his Time to Eat shirt; he looks tired, but his eyes don't stop scanning around. Then he heads to the basement. I follow him, even though I don't want to.

"Jesus fucking Christ," he says after he fumbles for a utility light. I think the same thing. I haven't been down in the basement in a while. But holy fuck; it's unbelievable.

Nothing but shit. Boxes and bags. Piles. You can see tools; you can see building materials, but most of it's just junk. A double sink full of clothing I've never seen before. A stack of flowerpots with little scruffs of dirt around the rims. A bunch of bright-blue shutters stacked against the wall. A cable TV satellite dish. Bookshelves, sagging, lined with boxes and books and lots of other randomness. And buckets. Buckets everywhere. Ice-cream buckets, paint pails, industrial buckets. All of them full of crap. One's full of *Home Handyman* magazines; one's full of beer-can tabs; one is full of, amazingly, quarters. There must be a thousand dollars in quarters in this bucket. I bend over to lift it and can't.

Garrett is quiet. The zinging feeling is now burning in me. I feel like we're going to get caught here. Garrett goes over to a corner and rustles around; it's hard to see from where I'm standing. And I can't move, either. I'm listening for someone coming in. I'm panicking, but I'm immobile. Freeze-framed panicked.

"Jesus fucking Christ," Garrett says again.

I want to ask. But I don't want to know. I notice there's a shopping cart down here. A fucking shopping cart. It's full of firewood. Or what was something wooden but what is now firewood.

"Come on, Will," Garrett says. Tapping my shoulder. I am unfrozen. But the zinging feeling's still there.

I follow him upstairs. "You have any stuff you need here, you should go grab it," he says.

I want to ask him what stuff? All of it? But he gets out his phone and says a few things into it. The main floor smells awful again. I wonder if I should take the garbage out.

I go up to my room. I realize how different it is up in the attic. Not just cold. It's empty. It smells like soap. There's nothing in my room. There's nothing in the hallway. I grab my backpack, make sure all my homework's in it. My laptop. Some clothes. The condoms I bought for Brandy and me. There's not a lot left.

In the bathroom, I stare at the dog sleeping on the bed. It looks so calm. The opposite of my zinging feeling. I think my mom is fucked up for not wanting this picture; I almost want to take it with me, but I don't know where I'm going, really. Probably to Garrett's, but that doesn't mean I'm moving in.

I grab a couple things from the medicine cabinet, but there's nothing to take in the shower. I hadn't asked my dad to re-up anything. I've got an electric toothbrush at my mom's, anyway.

I stare at the sleeping dog once more. Like I'm saying good-bye to it.

Then I go downstairs and Garrett says, "Ready?" And we go.

Kristin is waiting outside when we pull up in Garrett's truck. Folding a man's jacket over herself, like she grabbed the first thing and threw it on.

"You hungry, Will?" she asks. I say yes, but I'm not.

Kristin puts her arm around me and shuffles me to the kitchen. Puts a plate of chicken in front of me, with mashed potatoes and some green beans. A corn-bread muffin. It's the kind of meal you'd get in a movie; it looks American and wholesome. I start eating it like a robot; it's warm and it smells good and they are in the other room, talking about me. About my dad. About the basement full of crap.

I pull my phone out of my pocket. Text my dad, ask where he is. Reply to Angus, who's just texted about some place he and DeKalb are going to play next week. Text Brandy, tell her I'm thinking about her. I sound like a really fucking sappy boyfriend. And I only *wish* I was thinking about her. Because I don't want to think about me.

Kristin comes back in the kitchen, asks if I want more food. I shake my head. She takes my plate. Kristin is nice, and she's got really good hands. That sounds weird but they are beautiful, in a way. The nails are short and there's no polish, just like Brandy keeps hers, but Kristin's look like they are used to working. She has calluses too, like Angus; his are from guitar, though, not work.

She does something at the kitchen counter, asks me some vague questions and I answer her, put a fake smile on my face. She then turns around and hands me a bowl of ice cream that she's put caramel and fudge sauce on.

"This is Garrett's favorite dessert," she says. "You want to watch TV or anything, go right through that hall, okay? I'm going to make up your bed."

Then she leaves again and I'm glad. I feel like crying.

Instead of crying, though, I eat the bowl of ice cream with caramel and fudge. It's very good. Even the swirls in the bowl are beautiful. Like Kristin's hands. Things that shouldn't be beautiful—caramel sauce, a woman's hands—these aren't normal things you think about that way, but they are. Strange kind of beautiful. Weird. I eat until it's all gone. I don't understand why I'm eating. It doesn't feel any better, but it doesn't feel any worse, either.

Kristin comes back and then takes the bowl to the sink. Then

Garrett comes in. He's in his T-shirt, his blue Time to Eat shirt over his wrist. He looks sweaty and he smells like he just had a fresh smoke.

"Will," he says, "I don't mean to upset you."

I stand up.

"But I don't think you can stay with your dad," he says. "Not for a while."

I nod. Because I can't talk or the crying feeling I have will fall out. I put my hands in my pockets to keep myself steady.

"He's got some things he needs to deal with, and I don't think they're things a boy needs to see," he says. "Not close up, anyway."

I keep nodding; my face feels like it might break from holding everything in.

"You can stay here, long as you like," he says. "But I think you need to stick with your mother for a while. Maybe for the rest of the school year."

"But!" I say. Then stop. Because I don't want to explode. I breathe in and out, like my mom taught me. I swallow.

"Don't tell my mom about him," I say. "She just . . . she won't let up about it. About him."

Kristin is now looking at me, folding her arms over her chest, looking like she's so concerned and sorry for me. Her own lips trembling like she's trying not to cry too.

Now it's Garrett's turn to nod. "Okay," he says. "But you've got to promise not to go there. Stay there."

"But . . ." I stop. My throat is aching and full of tears. Tears are coming out, anyway. I feel like the biggest loser of all time.

Kristin is now crying too. I've made her cry. Even after she made me a good dinner and beautiful swirly ice cream for dessert. This makes me feel mad, then. Not at her. Just in general. At myself.

"Won't he . . ." I, clear my throat, take off my glasses, wipe my wrist over my eyes. Pressing my fingers against my eyes like I'm pissed they're being so out of line. "I told him I was staying with him until it was done," I say. "I promised I'd help him." I'm practically whispering.

"I'll talk to him," he says. "He'll get it."

"But not my mom," I say. "She'll just . . . she'll call in lawyers. She'll complain about money. That's her thing. How she keeps digging at him. You know?"

I wipe my wrist over my eyes again. I've got to fucking get it together.

"Will, honey, why don't you get some sleep?" Kristin says. She puts her arm around my shoulders, and the next thing I know, she's steering me to a spare bedroom, where the bedspread looks like an old horse blanket but is actually very soft and I'm sitting down on it and she's handing me a folded towel, with a toothbrush and a little bar of soap on it. Like I'm a guest in a hotel. I thank her and she pats my shoulder and then closes the door, so slowly and softly it barely makes a sound. Like she's worried I'll shatter. Like the noise'll set me off like a bomb.

I put my glasses on the nightstand, take off my clothes, and get into the bed. Put the towel, toothbrush, and soap on the floor. I can't handle the idea of going out again, opening that closed door, running into Kristin or Garrett, hearing them move around. Hearing them talk about me. The room has wallpaper that looks like horseshoes and for a while, I count them. Let all the horseshoes tumble around until I feel a little dizzy. I turn off the light, and realize my phone's still in my jeans when I hear it buzz with a text. I don't get up. Nobody's got anything to say to me about this, and I can't decide if that's a good thing or not.

THIRTEEN

I STAY AT Garrett and Kristin's for the whole next week; Garrett can fix my car but he just needs to find the time. I tell my mom I'm staying at my dad's and I act pissy about it when she pushes for an explanation. I tell her we're working on this, together, and she needs to understand that it's important to me, not just him.

"This is the house I was born in," I remind her, and she shuts up.

Kristin says I can drive their old Toyota, but that the heater is busted, and they only use it in summer. It also gets shit gas mileage, but I can hardly point that out to her when she's being so nice.

It's kind of a normal week. I don't tell anyone that I'm staying at Garrett's, though—it's too hard to explain. And I don't ask one question about my dad or the house or my car; I just go to school and do my stuff and drive the Toyota home (it's also loud and rattly as hell) and Kristin makes really nice dinners and we all eat and talk about everything besides why I'm there. Most of the time Garrett eats and then leaves right away and I don't ask if he's going to Time to Eat or to see my dad, though I really want to. And every night after that, Kristin always gives me a dish of ice cream with that same chocolate and caramel sauce when he leaves and I still swirl and stare at it like I'm on drugs. I wonder if she thinks I'm going crazy, because she doesn't hover or bug me much, so I think maybe I freak her out. Though it's nice that she doesn't hover or anything. It would be pretty hard for me to think of one thing to say to her, so I eat my ice cream and do my homework and watch television and she just kind of does her thing, then. Cleaning up in the kitchen or dealing with the chickens and goats and whatever else. Kristin is always working, just like Garrett, but she doesn't act busy, like my mom, or stressed out and exhausted, like my dad. She's quieter, for one thing. And I don't know if that's because their farm is loud, just by nature: the chickens are noisy, and so are the goats, and the weather on the edge of the cornfield that Garrett leases out is always whipping up wind. The night's full of crickets and buzzing and probably even coyotes. There's some strange sounds out here in the country. Things you don't hear in Oak Prairie or Minneapolis.

But on Friday, when Brandy comes over to me in Photography, like she does every other day, I just feel like she's looking at me funny. Like Kristin looked at me. About to cry. Sad for me.

"What?" I say, jerking away my arm when she touches the sleeve of my shirt.

"Nothing," she says. "Nothing at all. Jesus. Fuck you." And

then she leaves the darkroom, and I can't race after her because people are already looking at us. So that's how easy it is to get in a fight with your girlfriend.

The rest of the day, I'm silent. Jack is hovering around me in Global Society, talking to everyone near me, about stuff he thinks will make me turn around and call him out on it, but I don't.

After school, DeKalb reminds me that he and Angus are playing a show on Saturday and can I help roadie?

I think it's fucking ridiculous that he uses the word *roadie*—as if they have a *band* and will be playing actual *songs* and anyone will even be *listening*—but I tell him fine and that I've got to get to work but that's a lie. Garrett took me off the schedule. I didn't even fight him on that point, either. I feel stupid about that, but I know it's all I can handle.

After school, I drive the rattly Toyota to Garrett's. Kristin and him aren't around. This is the first time that's happened since I've been here. Usually Kristin's there to greet me when I drive up, but today the place feels like they're both gone. Unless Kristin's in the barn or something. I don't really like the barn; it smells awful and I don't want to step in anything gross. Also, I'm a little bit freaked by the goats, even though Kristin told me they're friendly and they have names like Barney and Cliff and Ginger.

I go inside and drink, like, three glasses of water from this glass pitcher Kristin keeps in the fridge. I like that she's got cold water; I don't know why. The water that comes out of my mom's water dispenser in her fridge is cold too, but somehow the pitcher water tastes better.

Then, because I don't want to watch TV or sit in my little spare hotel room—it's less like a hotel now, since I've spread some of my junk around more—I go out back on the porch, where Angus and me slept that one night together.

I sit on the sofa, pull off my boots. It's late October and the wind's kicking up, but the storm windows are over the screens so, while they rattle, it's not cold. And it feels good, the last bit of four-o'clock sunlight heating things up. I'm wearing a flannel and jeans; I'm the perfect temperature. I breathe in and out. Just breathe. Thinking about breathing. The whole day kind of slipping off me like ash falling from one of Garrett's cigarettes. My phone buzzes in my pocket and I toss it on the floor, next to my boots. I just want to stop. I just want to sleep. I just want so many things but right now it seems like the most important thing I want is for people to stop wanting anything out of me.

I've never told anyone about this.

It was summer and I was with my mom and she was pregnant with the twins. Only she didn't know it was twins, which is part of why I was with her in the doctor's office that day.

I was bored that day, because she'd dragged me to the fabric store and the office-supply store and the post office, which, if you are a kid, are the most boring stores to visit, because there are no toys or food you like there.

At the doctor, in the first room, I had to sit on this chair in the corner of the exam room and the nurse gave me a kid's magazine, which was all pictures of tigers and hippos and everything in Africa, except they showed the animals making their kills, like lions with bloody mouths eating antelopes or whatever, which was cool when you thought about it, except then my mom had a blood test and I had to look at the blood in the vial the nurse carried away in her purple gloves and my stomach felt gross. Then we went to the next room and my mom had to lie on her back in a paper shirt and when I asked her for her phone to play games on it, she shushed me and said phones weren't allowed in here because of the special equipment and other rules. So I sat on the floor until the nurse told me to sit on the chair, which was freezing cold on my legs (I was wearing shorts) from the air-conditioning being jacked up.

The nurse came back in and my mom got hooked up to a machine and then the doctor came in and was all between her legs and I thought for a minute that she was going to have the baby, right then, by total accident. Even though her stomach was barely sticking out like a real pregnant lady's.

But then, she just lay there, completely still and calm. Not like ladies having babies on TV acted, which was all screaming and panting. And after a while, the doctor started talking low to her and they were looking at the screen and the nurse was smiling and the doctor was pointing at the screen and she was smiling at my mom too.

But my mom wasn't smiling. She stopped looking at the screen and said. "Oh my." Then she said it a bunch more times: "Oh my. Oh my. Oh my." Not "oh my God" or "oh my goodness" but just: "oh my." Then the doctor said she was printing something out and labeling the head and the feet and the nurse told my mom she could sit up and get dressed and the doctor and nurse left.

My mom didn't look at me. She touched her stomach, lightly. And then she carefully put on her clothes, her back to me, and crumpled up the paper shirt thing. I knew she was upset so I didn't say anything. Even when she told me to go to the bathroom by the waiting room, and I didn't even have to go, because that was one of her things: *Just go to the bathroom, Will, and get it over with!* She hated it when I said I had to go to the bathroom while she was in the middle of something, like at the grocery store or whatever.

So I went to the bathroom and stood there for a minute and then ran my hands under the sink so she'd think I'd gone and she dragged me out of the waiting room, her phone by her ear, her purse flapping behind her. Some people think pregnant ladies are delicate but not my mom. She was pulling me like I was a kite. She seemed stronger than a lion taking down a zebra. Fast like a gazelle about to get its neck snapped by a cheetah.

Once we got to the parking lot, she started crying. Talking to Jay.

"Two of them," she said, opening the driver door of her car and tossing her purse into the passenger seat. I got into the back, automatically, which was the rule. My dad let me sit up front with him, but my mom was strict about that.

She sat, turned on the car, which was good, because it was hot in there. The air-conditioning whooshed over me and I put the burning-hot seat belt over my chest before she could turn her head and say anything about it. She wouldn't put the car in drive until I was buckled up; we'd only had that kind of standoff once or twice before I gave in.

"I know, but Jay!" she yelled. "You're not hearing me! Two. Two of them. Two of everything. How the hell can we afford that?"

Then she started sobbing and sobbing and I could hear Jay on his end, telling her over and over, "Tess. Tess. Come on, honey. Where are you? Tess. Come home. Just drive home. I'll be there as soon as I can. Tess. Tess."

I never told anyone about this because when we got home, Jay hugged her and smiled at me and we ordered pizza and he let me drink two cans of Coke and after that everything was happy. Everything was happy and my mom set out to make arrangements for two of everything, all of it pink, because it was girls she was having, both of them would be girls, I would have sisters. I would be their big brother and there would be two of them. Which was what I told my dad when I went to his house for the week and he nodded and told me congratulations, that I had a very important job and I would be very special to my little sisters. That he had a big brother and he loved him very much, even when he died, which was when he was a lot younger, and it was sad, but he would always remember him.

Then Kinney and Taylor were born. Nothing was the same. Everything double. Everything pink. Everything busy and moving and crazy. I was the big brother. Jay gave me a T-shirt that said so, and a paddleboard and a pile of comic books. My mom was in bed for what seemed like months. And Taylor and Kinney got everything they needed and wanted—everything. Everyone was busy, but everyone was happy. Holding them. Feeding them. Changing their clothes and diapers. Taking their pictures. Tickling their naked, sticky pink feet. Giving them baths in the kitchen sink, then the tub. They both got to stay at my mom's all week; they never went anywhere, like I did. They never had to ask anyone for anything, because it just appeared, in their hands or in their mouths.

And I wasn't mad about that. I wasn't. I was the one putting things into their hands and mouths. Tickling them. Getting them to laugh and smile. Getting them to walk to me before crashing down on their big diaper-padded butts, clapping for them.

I clapped and gave them things, tickled them, because I knew at first that they'd upset my mom. They'd been the wrong thing, like something in a catalog she hadn't meant to order. An extra of something. And I didn't want them to know that I hadn't cared about them that much, either. I didn't want them to worry that someday, there wouldn't be enough. That someday, it could all run out.

I open my eyes. It's like I've been dreaming or sleeping but I haven't. Just remembering. Remembering, because I'm in between places, where it's easier to remember this, when I'm not near either of them.

It's almost dark now, so that's why I see the headlights before I hear the car; it's Garrett pulling up in his truck. I feel more tired than before but I get up, wipe my eyes a little, and meet him at the door.

"Need you back on the road and back on the schedule," he says. "Everardo's got vacation coming up and Carl's due some time off too."

"What's going on with my dad?" I ask. I regret asking the second it comes out.

Garrett shakes his head. "He's not doing what I hoped he would," he says. "But he's not fighting me as much. He's listening now. A little bit."

I don't know what that means. I don't know what my dad fighting sounds like. My mom I remember yelling. My dad's side of it was quieter. Even when they told me about the divorce, my dad was quiet. My mom explained to me her side of things, how she wasn't happy, and how she needed other things in life, and how she would be a better mom if she were happy and got those things. That I was the one who mattered most. My dad just nodded, but he didn't look like he agreed.

One time, I tried to talk to my dad about it, before the papers were signed and the lawyers happened, and the moving back and forth started. I tried to say something I'd seen on a TV show, about how it was a misunderstanding: "It's not anybody's fault," was the thing I remember someone telling the kid in the show. I was trying to be smart. For him to pat me on the head and maybe smile once in a while. I just wanted to make him feel better. For even five minutes.

I said something like, "Dad, you should listen to Mom's side of the story. Then maybe tell her your side? Because it's not anybody's fault."

But he didn't smile. He barely looked at me. He just shook his head and sighed and said, "Everyone's side of the story is just how they sugarcoat their own fault in it. It's just bullshit, Will. Bullshit."

Which was when I understood that my dad was right about one thing: being quiet about what bothered you was probably for the best.

Garrett says he's got the stuff to fix my car now and we head out to do that. I try to focus so Garrett doesn't think I'm a total waste of time. He won't let me pay him back for the part and stuff, either. Just wants me to watch and see how it's fixed, in case it happens again. Even though Angus texted me to come hang out while he and DeKalb practice before tomorrow's show, I don't text back, because I want to pay attention to every step. I know Angus must wonder why I'm blowing him off—like with Brandy, I try to answer all of his calls and texts as soon as possible—but we're not done until it's really late. Like ten o'clock. Which isn't late for teenagers, I know, but I don't feel like it's right to just be like, "Great! Thanks! Bye!" to Garrett and then tear off after he basically fixed my car for free.

We go inside. Kristin's not back yet so I ask him what the deal is.

"She's at her friend's place for the night," he says. "They're working on a website Kristin wants to set up."

"Oh."

I think he'll make us dinner, but then he just pulls out the bucket of vanilla from the freezer. "You want?"

Garrett and me eat ice cream in front of the television. Like we're old people. Or, given the heaping portions he's put in our bowls, like we're old people who've just suffered a breakup. All we need is a rom-com on the television. Instead, we watch *SportsCenter* and then this movie about a little kid who sets things on fire with her mind.

"That's Drew Barrymore," he says, nodding at the TV.

"Who?"

"God, I'm old," he says, shaking his head. "Want more ice cream?"

I'm not really hungry, but I say yes. Mostly I just like how it swirls in the bowl. It's like hypnosis. I like to move it all around with the spoon until the whole thing's just a bowl of brown, no more lines of caramel or chocolate.

I can't finish the next bowl, though. I swirl it to brown, the spoon making little clinks. My teeth feel all gritty, coated with sugar. Like they're rotting in my head. I can't remember the last time I went to the dentist. My mom would know.

I put the bowl on the coffee table and Garrett turns off the TV.

"I'm beat," he says.

"Me too."

"Hey," he says, and his tone is different. Now we're going to talk about things. Talk with a capital *T*. I wonder if that's why he gave me a fuckton of ice cream—just to make me all sluggish and immobile so I'd have to stay and listen to him.

"A couple of things, besides you're back on the schedule," he says. He leans forward toward the coffee table. I lean back into the couch.

"I'm trying to talk your dad into an inpatient rehab," he says.

"What?"

"For alcoholics," he says. "He's not even considering it, don't worry. Or maybe"—he laughs a little—"do worry. It's affecting his health, Will. His judgment. My dad was a drinker. In the same way. Had all the same excuses. Same patterns. Said and did a lot of the same kind of shit your dad's saying now. But my dad never stopped. Wouldn't. Only thing he had left by the end was his job."

"What happened then?"

"Nothing," he says. "Kept his job until he retired. Then he died two years later, from a fall. A fall while he was drunk, of course, but my family didn't call it that. Even my mom, who divorced him, she didn't call it that."

"Oh," I say. I feel very cold, suddenly. And the zinging feeling is back. Flying up and down my back, sinking into my stomach.

"There's kind of a history for me here. And not just with your dad. So I hope you don't think I'm butting into your lives unnecessarily or anything."

"I don't think that."

"Good. But you might not like that I've told your mom what's going on," he adds.

I don't say anything. My stomach clutches up. He's going to have to have this conversation by himself, from here on out. I'm so angry and so close to crying, I can't handle words.

"She's okay with you staying here, but I know she'd prefer you home. Says you've got friends there, says you'll be more comfortable around family."

"Jay's not my family." That just flies out. Louder than I mean. It's not like I even hate Jay. Jay and I barely even bullshit; he stays out of my way. I'm his wife's problem, and he's always understood that. But he's not my family and I can't help but point it out, I guess. Even if I'm arguing against something that's already over.

"Your sisters, she means."

I am quiet.

"She agrees, though, that whatever you decide, you need to give your father some time and space," he says. "He's not thinking clearly and he's not doing well. You really don't need to see him like this."

But I *have* seen him like this, I want to yell. I mean, what the hell is everyone talking about alcoholic shit for? It's not alcohol. It's like no one ever asks *why* he drinks like that. When it's totally fucking obvious to me. It's that he's never gotten over the divorce. He's all by himself. Nobody is helping him. Nobody is there for him. Not even me.

Garrett says more stuff. About patience. About understanding. About support. About coming to terms with our parents' flaws. I nod. I nod and say "yeah" and "okay" and "right" so many times I wonder if he can tell I'm not listening. I am listening; it's just that there's nothing to really hear. Nothing I don't already know. Finally, he asks me what my weekend looks like, because it's one of my last free ones before I have to fill in for Everardo's shifts and I tell him that I'm going to Angus's band's thing tomorrow, and he says, "Good, good. You need to keep doing the stuff you do. Living your life."

When I get in bed, I text Brandy. I'm halfway hoping she's over whatever pissed her off in Photography. **hey what's up**

She texts back: **just say it to my face**

I have no idea what she's talking about, so I call her.

"What," is how she answers.

"Hi," is what I say.

"Just get it over with," she says. "I don't want to be in some long, dragged-out breakup, okay? I've got better things to do."

"What are you talking about?"

"You're not into it anymore," she says. "It's all right. I could tell all week."

"Brandy?"

"Just say it already."

"Okay, I'll just say it: DeKalb and Angus have a band and they're doing a show at this coffee place tomorrow and I have to be there. To help with equipment."

"So?"

"So, after that, do you want to go out?"

She's quiet. I can hear her breathing. Is she crying? I hate this. I wish we were just texting. This feels different from waiting for a text back. Waiting while she breathes. While she withholds. It's terrible.

"What if I don't want to?"

"Brandy, Jesus Christ. What the hell?"

She's quiet. God, I hate people when they're quiet. Or maybe I just hate *her* being quiet.

"I don't even believe you," she says. "You say things, but there's

184

no truth behind them. You don't mean it; you sound like you're totally over it."

"I'm not over it," I say, lowering my voice for no good reason. "I like you. This week kind of sucked, okay? I had to move out of my dad's. It's sort of complicated. He might go to rehab."

"What?" Suddenly, she's back. "What happened?"

I tell her, then. About the basement and about the house being all unfinished and about Garrett telling me I have to stay with my mom and how I don't want to do that, but probably don't have any choice.

"Why don't you want to do that?" she asks.

"My mom'll be all *I told you so* about my dad. She's just kind of, I don't know. A jerk about it. She's never understood him."

"Good they're divorced, then," Brandy says.

"Yeah," I say. "I guess it is." Though it doesn't feel like it. It feels like they're still together and unhappy with each other, but it's just from a bigger distance. Even if she started over. Even if he didn't. It feels like he didn't on purpose, kind of.

"So you'd rather live with your dad, then?"

"I don't know."

"Oak Prairie is so far away," she says.

"We'll figure it out." I tell her how my car broke down, but then got fixed. I tell her, as I'm stripping off my clothes and getting into bed, how I'm back on the schedule. How I'm sorry my fucked-up situation made me an asshole. How it won't happen again. She laughs at me.

"I have you beat in fucked-up family situations," she says.

185

She laughs again. "I can't even talk about it without getting depressed," she says. Her voice lowers.

"You can, though," I say. "Talk about it."

"No," she says. "Because I'm in bed and I just want to fall asleep listening to you. I don't know why I freaked out. I freaked out for nothing. I do that. I get ideas, I hear rumors, I assume the worst. I always assume the worst."

"I missed you," I say. Finally meaning it.

FOURTEEN

IT'S THE NIGHT Angus and DeKalb's band plays, and Brandy's coming. Because her friend Shania is all into DeKalb lately. There's nothing I can do to talk her out of it, because then she'd ask why and I can't explain that, either. And I can't get out of helping my friends.

I can barely eat any dinner. Kristin looks at me sadly. Garrett is preoccupied with something on his phone. I take my plate to the dishwasher pretty quick and thank Kristin for the food that I didn't really eat.

It gets worse, though. Brandy calls to say that she's told her aunt that she's staying at Shania's. She tells me I should tell my mom I'm staying DeKalb's house or something.

"Then we can be together," she says. "All night, even. And Shania knows of a guy whose parents are out of town; DeKalb knows him. Maybe you do too? Just a sec . . ."

I listen to her ask Shania what the guy's name is, even though

I already know. Jack's parents are in San Francisco for the weekend. He's not having a party but has invited some people over later. "A select, specific few," he said, which made me want to kick him in the face.

"Jack Telios," she says. "You know him?"

The coffee place is in a strip mall by an Olive Garden and a bunch of other little shops. A nail place, a dry cleaner, a dollar store, a Radio Shack. The kind of place nobody hangs out at, really; you just run in and do your errands and leave. It's kind of embarrassing—this is where they're playing?

Angus has parked his mom's Escalade out in front of the coffee place when I get there; right away, though I'm not late, I feel a little shitty. DeKalb and him are already unloading their gear.

"It's just this bass and one amp?" I ask. Now I'm pissed; they hardly need any help.

"The keyboards are heavy, though; everyone else isn't here yet," Angus says. He looks at me just a second too long and then DeKalb butts in the way and we start unloading the stuff and dragging it inside the coffee place.

I feel the zinging again. My stomach is growling but I don't feel hungry. I look at Angus, at how his jeans slide low, how his boxers stick up when he bends over. I remember touching him and I feel sick. I feel sick because I like to look at him. I want to touch him. I know him, I think, but then I don't know him, either. It's been a lot of years since we talked about our hopes and dreams, our favorite colors. Not that we have favorite colors. Maybe he does. I just have colors I don't like. Purple and red and yellow. Angus mostly wears black and white. Angus smells like aftershave and deodorant; he uses the same deodorant as me. I want to touch his chest. Angus wants to go to college and major in art; he's been working on applications since last spring. Angus, I don't know why it matters, but I can't stop thinking of what we did and I'm so stupid. Brandy's on her way here and she has no idea. I'm so fucking stupid.

Then this girl and guy show up, park right behind Angus. The girl is wearing pigtails looped with pink ribbons and a black dress and a necklace made of tiny rubber ducks and she's got star tattoos all up and down her forearms. The guy is just a guy; nothing rubber ducks and tattoos about him. The guy has a keyboard thing and the girl opens a violin case—her violin is yellow and has a big duck sticker on it. So this is Andrew and his girlfriend who made him pussy stupid.

Once everything's been heaved into the stage area, there's nothing for me to do. I look around the coffee shop. Just a few people sitting in front of their laptops. I don't know where to sit, though there are plenty of tables. The guy at the counter is squirting whipped cream on top of a giant mug of something for a customer. The zinging feeling is back. Buzzing in my stomach, all the way to my spine. It's the worst. I wish I could curl up and go to sleep.

Brandy and Shania show up then. Shania's a cute girl; she's very tall and smiley. DeKalb thinks she's cute but he says she talks too much shit about people. As if DeKalb doesn't! They come over to me and look around. Shania looks at the place like it's kind of disappointing, but she waves at DeKalb, who waves back, and then she says, "This where we're sitting?" She points to an empty table by me and I just nod and sit down while they go get their drinks.

I'm watching Angus while he sets up a microphone with the rubber ducky–violin girl. She's laughing at something he's saying, he's smiling back. Then he puts his guitar over his head and his shirt rides up over his stomach. The part where he has the little trail of hair down to his dick. Trail to the whale, DeKalb calls it.

Just as they start doing sound checks, Brandy sits down with a cup of coffee and a muffin. She leans into me and says, right into my ear, "I packed like I was going to a sleepover. I brought all my face cream stuff. And pajamas."

"Oh really," I say. I watch Angus tie his bandanna up to get the hair out of his face. See his shirt slide up again, the strip of hair on his stomach.

"They have owls on them," she says. Then she kisses my cheek and Angus makes eye contact with me at just that second. I see, for the first time, something on his face. Like he's disgusted with me. Pissed too.

"Sexy," I say. But it's not sexy. And now Angus is moving out of the way so the pigtail-rubber-duck girl can stand next to him and they don't even say anything about who they are. The girl just says, "Good evening," even though it's only like seven o'clock, and then they start playing a song with no words.

Then it's kind of boring. The zinging/buzzing fades a little, even. Like, I don't know what the hell I was worried about. Angus is just playing his guitar and Brandy is just sitting by me; it's not that big of a deal. It's sort of lame. They don't do anything but play the music, which is nice and everything, but there's no one singing. When I look around, there's really no one paying attention, either. They're like a living version of background music. Except they don't seem to notice this. They're just playing and looking at each other, not the rest of us. Shania's on her phone, texting sometimes, and holding it up other times, clicking away like she's taking pictures. Brandy's just staring. In a way that's natural. Normal. Like she's happy she's here. Like she likes the band. Her face is calm and pretty, and I like how her hair won't stay tucked behind her ear. How it slips out, slowly.

It'd be nice, sitting here next to her. If she weren't looking up at Angus. Angus isn't looking at me anymore. He's just focused. Intense. Looking at the music in his mind, maybe? He doesn't look at me. Only DeKalb, and sometimes the rubber-duck girl, and sometimes the keyboard guy. It's like nobody else is even here. I almost feel jealous of him. Like the music builds a big loud layer between him and people looking.

After a while, the zinging feeling is almost gone. Because the music? It doesn't stop. There's no break. There's no singing. And it's like, what's the point of watching? I go and get a muffin and a thing of Coke, which they only sell in a bottle and it costs, like, three bucks but whatever. I eat the muffin and then I go get another one. Shania is texting, still. People come in and go out of the coffee shop; the guy working the counter looks bored, and when I go up to get a third muffin, I say so.

"I've been here since six, man," he says. He shakes his head.

"That sucks."

"Yeah," he says, pushing the muffin onto a plate across the

counter. "Plus this music? It just makes me want to fall asleep. Not that it's bad. It's good. Seriously."

I laugh and he laughs. The second I think how he's kind of a good-looking dude, it panics me, though. I quick hand him the cash and take the muffin and then neither Brandy or me eats it. It was four bucks and I stare at it like everything's the muffin's fault. I want to leave. I don't want to go to Jack's.

The music: it goes on and on. Shania picks at the third muffin. DeKalb is sweating and looks like he's in pain. He looks like he's going to fall over. Angus is sweating around his pits and neck. The boring guy never looks up. He isn't sweaty. Or hot. Either meaning of "hot," really. I hate that I'm all gay about this. While sitting next to my girlfriend. The counter guy is dumping a big vat of iced tea into the sink when I turn back to look at him and he catches me looking. Great. Now he probably thinks I'm gay too.

Then, just when I feel like I might lose my fucking mind, the rubber-ducky girl sets down her violin. Angus stops playing. DeKalb and the regular guy just maintain a little background tune, though, and after a minute, the rubber-ducky girl steps up to the microphone, the one between her and Angus that nobody has used, and she starts singing.

> *Hush-a-bye, don't you cry,*
> *Go to sleepy little baby.*
> *When you wake, you'll have cake,*
> *And all the pretty little horses.*

It's like a lullaby, but now with the music behind it, DeKalb and the regular guy—it all makes sense. Just when I think they'll go back to instrumental, though, rubber-ducky girl steps away and Angus takes her spot. Then Angus is singing:

Black and bay, dapple and gray,
Coach and six little horses,
Hush-a-bye, don't you cry,
Go to sleepy little baby.
Hush-a-bye, don't you cry,
Go to sleepy little baby,
When you wake, you'll have cake,
And all the pretty little horses.

Angus, singing. Looking at me, I think. Or at Brandy.

Which makes me look at Brandy. And she's crying. Brandy's crying. Then Shania's nudging me, like I need to do something. But I can't do anything. I'm stuck between her and Shania, between her and Angus.

And there's something about him singing that I love. Normally, when dudes sing, like in show choir or whatever at school, I think they sound like freaks. Like, the definition of *gay* is right there, when a guy's belting it out. Especially a young guy. It's not like one of those fat old opera guys with the deep-ass voices, who sound like they could knock down a chandelier if they felt like really going for those low notes. Young guys always sound a little girly, even though they don't want to, and it's all terrible. Embarrassing.

But not Angus. He sounds like a guy. Like a man. But also, you can hear the parts where his voice breaks, and it's not gay. It's not embarrassing. It's just *him*. Like everything about him. Good. Honest. Exactly what he is. And it's not sexual for me, none of this is, but it's this exact minute that Brandy takes my hand and squeezes it, and I know it's because she's crying but I think it's because, right that minute, I know that I love Angus. That I'm in love with him and I'll always love him. I'm as gay as any gay choir boy. As gay as any theater kid. Gay. And holding my girlfriend's hand.

Then rubber-ducky girl comes back to join him at the microphone, and she does the next verse.

> *Way down yonder, down in the meadow*
> *Lies a poor little child*
> *The bees and the flies are pickin' out its eyes*
> *The poor little child crying for its mother*
> *Oh, crying for its mother*
> *Way down yonder, down in the meadow*
> *Lies a poor little child*
> *The bees and the flies are pickin' out its eyes*
> *The poor little child crying for its mother*
> *Oh, crying for its mother*

Brandy lets go of my hand. She blows her nose into a napkin. Angus and the rubber-ducky girl now sing the chorus together. I'm sweating. The whole room's still. Looking. Watching them sing. The counter guy too, leaning against the wall, a bus tub of plates and cups in his arms. I think of all the times I've sat in Angus's garage, listening to him play, drums or guitar or whatever. I've never heard him sing. Not once.

Then Angus and rubber-ducky girl step back from the microphone. She's on her violin, he's on the guitar. They finish out the song, a few extra flourishes, and then it's over. Then Angus steps to the microphone and says, "Thanks a lot. Good night."

To say people are clapping sounds weak. They are standing up and hollering and cheering. One woman, whose head was stuck in a book the whole time, is whistling through her fingers. Brandy is clapping, wiping her face with a makeup-streaked napkin. I stand, along with Shania, who is taking photos. DeKalb looks a little caught off guard. But keyboard guy is smiling and so is Angus. Rubber-ducky girl is crouched down, just calmly putting her violin in its case, when the counter boy comes up to the edge of the stage and says something in her ear. She shrugs, then smiles at him, and he walks off, still carrying the bus tub.

"That was amazing," Brandy says. "Just . . . amazing." She keeps saying that. And apologizing for crying. I tell her it's okay and she kisses me. On the mouth, like she has a million times, in front of other people. But now I can't look at Angus anymore. And I want to just leave. But I have to move equipment. I'm their goddamn "roadie," after all.

There's a line for the one bathroom, otherwise I'd go hide in there. Instead, I clear the shit off our table and bring it to the counter guy's bus tub, who's left it by the register while he refills someone's coffee. People are talking to Angus and DeKalb and regular guy. I go back to Brandy and Shania and they're all hud-dled together and talking and it doesn't look like I should butt in, so I look at my watch. 9:15. Then I pull out my phone. No texts. Because no shit: everyone I'd want to talk to is already here.

I turn toward the door. Rubber-ducky girl is standing by coun-ter guy, and writing something with a black marker on his arm. Her number? Though I assumed she's still with Andrew. Maybe it's Jack Telios's address? Brandy gets in close with Shania and they're whispering and then Shania hugs her, and that's another thing I can't look at.

Back at the stage, Angus is talking to the whistling woman with the book. The keyboard guy's carrying his stuff out; DeKalb's unplugging the amps and microphone. I go up to him, nodding at Angus, who's still talking to the book woman, and ask him what he needs.

"Take this amp." He glances at Angus, who's still talking to the woman. He hasn't even taken his guitar off his body yet. "We got to get going."

"You coming to Jack's?" I ask. We start to make our way out of the place. Brandy and Shania are laughing now, looking at us.

"Hell yeah," he says. "My aunt's in town and we got church in the morning."

"Church?"

"Yeah, we only go when she comes around," he says. "She's a minister."

"That makes no sense," I tell him.

DeKalb stops, grabs my shoulder. Talks into my face like I'm an idiot. "I hate church. My aunt's annoying. Told my parents I'm staying at Angus's house."

"Your dad lets you go out there?"

"Oh, he thinks Angus is fucking golden. His old partner is the high-school cop at Oak Prairie, where Angus goes, so he thinks he has some kind of inside track. Any time I go out there, he's all fine with it."

"Oh." I'm surprised. I guess I just figured I'd know if DeKalb and Angus were hanging out.

"Fucking slow as hell, that kid," DeKalb says, when we load his bass and the amp.

"You want to leave now?" I ask, glancing back at the coffee shop. I want to run away now. Drive away. Leave. I can't go back in there. I can't.

"Why you all huffy?" DeKalb says. "You get into it with Brandy or what?"

"No," I say. "No. Just, you know. Sick of waiting."

The zinging's back. Everything's off. This is what love does to you, then. It changes everything. Takes a house and turns it into a scrap heap. Makes a lullaby into a horror show.

Everything's different.

A pretty girl in tears.

A boy who never sings gets the whole room on its feet.

I made this.

FIFTEEN

I HATE THAT I get all freaked out about nothing. Because we all get to Jack's—me and Brandy and Shania and Angus and DeKalb. Even the rubber-ducky chick and regular guy show up later, with the coffee-shop counter guy. There aren't many people besides us. Maybe ten or fifteen other people. Lots of girls Jack's been hanging out with. And it's all fine.

Once we're all there, and I've called Garrett to tell him I'll be at my mom's tonight, I feel a little better. But the truth is, I'm not up for a big party. I just feel like going home. Going to my mom's. Or Garrett's. Even my dad's, because it's the closest. But I promised Garrett I wouldn't.

Around two in the morning, everyone's pretty fucked up. We're all in Jack's living room and kitchen, drinking a weird mix-match thing of everyone's booze in the fridge and it's just a jumble of cans: whatever anyone could steal from their parents, whatever leftovers they had from the last time they'd got someone to buy for them. Angus is passing around his weed, all generous. And he's not saying much, but I catch him looking at me and Brandy a lot—her hand on my leg, her whispering in my ear, her drinking out of my cup—and it makes me tense. Nobody here knows him how I do.

It's a strange party; there's no music, just the sound of Shania and Jack playing video games. It's one of those old games they reworked so it's new, with better graphics, but they kept the old audio, so you hear all these corny sounds: *s-waannnng! bloooooop! ka-ching! pow!*

I get up to take a piss and see Angus's head bob up, glance at me.

"Where are you going?" Brandy asks. "Can I come with?"

I tell her I'm going to pee and she leans back on the sofa.

Jack's house is fucking huge. The first bathroom I find, the door's locked and someone yells, "We're in here!" but not in a pissed-off way. Like they're doing something naughty and fun inside and want to brag.

I've only been to Jack's a couple of times but I remember there being a bathroom by the garage, and yes, I'm right. I'm not that drunk. Yet.

I unzip and piss. So much piss. It's like I didn't realize how hard I'd been holding it in until now. I feel like all my stress is coming out, in one big bubbly yellow stream. Ridiculous.

I wish Angus wasn't here. I wish Brandy would fall asleep. And I'm so tired.

I wander around Jack's house before going back to everyone

else. Jack's house is old on the outside, all brick and ivy. But the inside is all remodeled and new. Jack's dad is an architect; his mom some kind of city politician lady. Or a lawyer. Or both. Whatever; they make way too much money so it makes zero sense that Jack goes to Franklin.

I keep opening doors. Snooping. There's an exercise room with a wall of mirrors, yoga mats, weights, and a treadmill in front of a flat screen. Next room is another bathroom. Next room is a bedroom that doesn't look like anyone's bedroom. Though it's nice; a bookshelf full of books, a quilt on the bed that's antique, a flat screen on the wall. Next room, an office. I have to stop snooping. Next room is not a room: a closet full of sheets and shampoo and shit.

Next, a staircase going down. I go down and it's colder down there. That chalky Sheetrock smell that reminds me of my dad's house. The wall along the staircase is lined with shelves holding jars and cans: strawberry jam and soup and canned pears and tomatoes. Boxes of mashed potatoes and ramen noodles and spaghetti. A giant jar of popcorn kernels.

At the bottom of the stairs is one of those old moonshiney jugs, with the big cork and a blue stencil with NO. 1 on it and a basket full of *Architectural Digest* magazines.

The basement is not as nice as the upstairs. There's nothing cool down there. Just a washing machine and dryer, and a little drying rack that's got bras and lady's stuff pinned up on it. A tool bench. A long freezer along the wall. An exercise bike.

It's not a great basement but it's normal. It's not full of shit. It's not nice, like Angus's basement, where he sleeps, or my mother's basement, where Kinney and Taylor have this whole huge playroom that they barely ever use. It's just what you'd imagine a basement to be: behind the scenes, storage, nothing great.

I'm so tired.

I go back upstairs then. I need to drink some Coke or just get Brandy to come to bed or whatever. But when I get upstairs, it's like everyone's gone. Not everyone, but it's just Jack and Angus and Brandy, sitting on the couch. No one's playing video games but the same noises keep repeating, softly: *s-waannnng! blooooop! ka-ching! pow!* Over that, Jack's put on some music, which is all spacey sounding and I'm suspicious that it's something he found in Sweden. But I'm not going to say anything; it's his house and he's not being a jerk to me.

I sit down by Brandy and she takes my hand and then whispers in my ear: "DeKalb and Shania." Then she laughs a little. I look up and catch Angus watching us. Jack is telling a story about Sweden.

"So, then it was like, we all had to get off our bicycles and just walk them down the street, because the cop guy didn't want us to get hurt. He was barely a cop, when you think about it. He was more like Mrs. Demarest than like a cop."

Mrs. Demarest is the guidance lady at Franklin. Her voice sounds like something you'd use to talk to a baby with a hangover: all cooing and soft and understanding.

Only Brandy and me laugh; Angus just smiles, having no idea what Mrs. Demarest's deal is.

Jack's story goes on and on and I think he's told me this. Maybe he told other people while I was nearby? It sounds familiar. An old sod barn, a wine cellar. Jack and these three girls, who are all cousins with this one guy, and they drink Russian vodka and eat pineapple from a can and watch the sun come up while the girls sing some song they learned in their Japanese-language class about a samurai fighting an evil merchant. Like a fairy tale from the future.

Brandy's impressed, though. Even if she thinks Jack dresses douchey, she's impressed by his story of life abroad. And maybe his house too.

"I want to go to Argentina," Brandy says. "We saw this movie in Spanish about it and it seems really cool. Like, they've got Italians there? Like a Little Italy? And they eat steak, like, constantly. They have cowboys; their version of cowboys, at least. And the tango? It's kind of crazy."

Angus agrees. "I'd go there," he says. "I'd go anywhere, really, though."

"That's because you live in the suburbs," Jack says, all snobby.

But Angus doesn't flinch. "True," he says. He sparks up his pipe again and passes it out. Jack takes it; I wave it off, but Brandy takes it. I haven't ever seen her smoke pot, but she seems to know how to work a one-hitter all right.

"I don't think it matters where you go," I say. "It's, like, just the scenery changes. You're still the same you."

"Bullshit," Jack says. "Going places makes you different. You see everything different. It's all about the angle of inquiry."

Angus raises an eyebrow at that last thing, and I almost say something about how douchey he sounds, but then Brandy starts up.

"It's not bullshit," she says. "Where you are matters. Like, Franklin? It matters. It's a shit school. The building's old and unloved. Awful. The teachers feel old and unloved and awful too. And you guys? You don't even know."

"That's because public schools aren't valued," Jack says. I can feel him getting all riled; all political. Trying to tell Brandy what's what.

But Brandy keeps on.

"I lived with my mother until I was, like, five. We lived down in Winona, Minnesota? Middle-of-nowhere place. You guys don't even get it. She was crazy. She *is* crazy. And she would live, like, in these shitholes. Like, one room, full of garbage. No food. Or with her mother, my grandmother, who is the biggest, evilest cunt you've ever known."

Well. Now Jack shuts up. Angus puts his one-hitter on the coffee table, softly.

"My mom didn't have a car, she didn't have a job, she didn't have shit. But she had me and she dragged me around and didn't know what to do with me. Everywhere we went was worse than the next place. I didn't go to daycare or preschool; I didn't know any other kids. I had this blanket and I had a crazy mother, who'd leave me alone with my blanket, and then she'd not come home and then I was with her bitchy mother, because my mother got caught stealing steaks from the grocery store. Steaks! Because she was going to sell them to her dealer or something? I mean, crazy, right?"

Angus nods. I just sit there, frozen. Jack is staring away from her.

"So, then my grandmother takes my blanket, that same night. The same night the cops come to my grandmother's and tell us my mom's detoxing in the psych ward and my grandmother slams the door on the face of the lady who wasn't a cop, but who was just trying to help us. And then she tells me to go to bed and I won't, because she's got my blanket, and I cry until she gives it to me and then I wake up in the morning and my blanket's gone. Because my bitch grandmother had set it on fire in her frying pan on the stove. She told me it was time to grow up and stop acting like a spoiled only-child brat. After that, I was screaming and screaming and screaming and she was slapping me to make it stop and I didn't stop and then she put me in my room, which was my mother's room, and I didn't come out, for anything. And then, like a few days later, my aunt Megan came to get me. And we moved from Winona to Minneapolis, just that night. And I had my own room and my nana was there, even if she was my dad's mother, and my dad's a loser too, and I got to go to kindergarten and everything was different. I got to be different, in a new place. And it was better. It *is* better. So. That's why I believe that. Why I want to go to Argentina."

Nobody says anything. It was kind of a big speech. Then the probably Swedish music ends and we're all left with: *s-waannnng! bloooooop! ka-ching! pow!*

Then Brandy leaves the room. Not all upset. She just stands up and walks out. Angus is staring at me.

Jack says, "So. What? Her aunt's awful too? Because, like,

technically, if she still wants to go somewhere else, like Argentina, that would mean—"

"Shut it already, Jack," I say.

Angus smirks, just for a second. Then Jack says, "You gonna leave her on her own, Will?"

I don't know what to say. I ask where everyone else went.

Jack ignores me. "She isn't one of those cutter girls, is she? That carve stuff into their arms when they get all depressed?"

"No," I say. I've seen her naked. I would fucking know. I almost want to say this but I can't because of Angus. "Where'd that rubber-ducky girl go?" I ask.

"She's with the coffee-place guy," Angus says.

"I thought she was with that other guy in the band," I add. Slowly. Because I'm working on suppressing the strangling feelings.

"Andrew," Angus says. I remember him talking about Andrew, that first night we kissed. Pussy-stupid Andrew. We stare at each other for minute, and I swear he's remembering that night too.

"They just kind of all left," Angus adds. He keeps looking at me, like, *They all left and now it's just me and you and Jack and he'll leave and then it'll be me and you. I've waited everyone out. I'm patient. It'll only be me and you, even with your girlfriend in the same house.*

I stand up. I know that's how it could go. I can see it, actually, going that way. I wish it could. Everything's easy with me and Angus. But only when we're alone.

"I'll be right back," I say.

"Sure," Jack says. Laughing. Angus doesn't say anything.

I grab my backpack in the front hall where I left it—that's where the condoms are—and I poke around, looking for where Brandy is, hoping I don't bump into Shania and DeKalb. I find her in the spare bedroom, the one that I snooped in earlier. She's in the bed, the little nightstand light turned on, her boots and bag on the floor. I set down the backpack, pull out a condom from the strip.

When I zip up my backpack, she rolls over and looks at me.

I'm caught. I don't move for a minute, because it's not a look inviting me to anything. Finally, she closes her eyes.

Slowly, I take off my shoes, sit down on the bed, pull back the covers. She's wearing her shirt and just her panties. There's a picture of Jack on the wall, which is sort of creepy. Jack, smiling, as a little kid, looking at both of us. I take off my glasses so he's blurry. Turn off the light so it's like he's finally gone. Just us.

I take off my jeans and hoodie. When I get in the bed, she sniffs like she's been crying again. I transfer the condom from my jeans to underneath the pillow, so the package doesn't crinkle.

I am nothing, then, but all this wanting. Drunk wanting. I know I shouldn't, but I can still feel her bare legs on mine and it flips the lid off every other memory of every other time until I have a boner.

I want everything. But it all seems impossible. I want her to stop crying, I want to get his face—Angus, staring at me—out of my brain. I want to stop being in strange bedrooms all the time.

I'm so tired.

But I need to say something that'll make her feel better. I

breathe into her hair, which always smells nice. I slide a hand over her hip but don't push too close to her. I don't want her to feel my boner. I wish I didn't have it when she's obviously sad.

"I want to go home," she says.

I freeze.

"I wish we hadn't come here," she says.

I run my hands up her back, softly. She kind of leans toward me, like this is what she needs. She's still crying, though. Her spine shudders, which heaps on the guilty feelings. Kills my boner. Though I'm not guilty for what her mother and grandmother did, I'm still guilty. Could easily have been me that made her cry.

I breathe. In and out. One. Two. Three. Four.

S-waannnng! Bloooooop! Ka-ching! Pow!

Everyone's side of the story is just how they sugarcoat their own fault in it.

I feel like I grow up, in those breaths and minutes. Like a hundred years. I am the oldest I've ever been.

"I'm sorry." It's the only thing I can think of. I say it a bunch, over and over. Like I'm singing her a lullaby. I think of Angus, singing with the rubber-ducky girl. I left him to be here, with Brandy, but now I hear his voice in my head. The song, his voice, my words: *I'm sorry. I'm sorry. I'm sorry, baby. Go to sleep my little baby.*

SIXTEEN

NOBODY GETS CAUGHT the next day. Not DeKalb, who said he was at Angus's house. Not Shania, not Brandy, not even Jack. Shania and DeKalb stayed back to help Jack clean up, even, then took the bus back home together. So romantic.

No, the one who gets caught is me. Only me. And it's all because of my dad.

My dad, who showed up at my mom's house last night, asking for me, only to be told by Jay that I was at Garrett's. Then he called Garrett, who was at the restaurant. So my dad went to Time to Eat, drunk out of his mind, and Garrett said I was at my mom's and what the hell's going on, and my dad started yelling. Garrett had Sierra put him at a booth, just to calm him down so Garrett could grab his keys and drive him home. But my dad was all pissed off and knocked over a bus station, whether on purpose or by accident, no one was sure, and he broke a bunch of dishes all over the place. Then Carl went to clean it up and tried to get my dad to his feet, and my dad passed out while trying to lift up a broken glass. Sierra called an ambulance, because she thought my dad had had a heart attack, and then the cops showed up and my dad came to, and then Carl tried to calm him down. Just as the paramedics walked in, my dad punched Carl in the face.

Which is why I'm not busted until after I get back to my mom's later that day, when Garrett finally has a minute to call her from the hospital and tell her that Tom's in detox and does she know where I am.

I'm standing over the sink eating a banana and talking to Taylor when my mom gets the call. The look on her face is something new. A blend of I don't know who to kill, you or your father. Taylor's not afraid; she's used to Mom losing it.

But my mom doesn't lose it. Maybe because Taylor's standing in front of me. A little eight-year-old shield.

"We have to go, Will," she says. "Now. Get your shoes and coat. Now."

"Why, Momma?" Taylor asks.

"Not you," my mom says, looking over her daughter and straight at me. I know I'm busted. But then instead of hustling me to the side to bitch me out, she grabs her purse and her phone and flips into her coat, all in one motion, like a snake. Then she points toward the door, toward her Mercedes wagon.

"Don't come out here! You don't even have a coat on!" she yells as Taylor follows us out. Taylor doesn't listen. She walks to my mom and her lip is trembling.

"Go wake Daddy up," she says to Taylor. She smoothes Taylor's hair. She's trying to pretend it's all fine, but Taylor's not dumb. "He's in the TV room, watching football. Wake him and tell him to call Mommy."

"Are you gonna die? Is Will going to jail?"

"No, everything's fine," my mom says. "Just do what I said."

Having explained, in various tones, from raging to near tears, the whole story of my father bleeding out and falling over and punching Carl in Time to Eat—she seems more mortified that someone she was ever married to would cause such a spectacle: "there were children there!"—by the time we get to the hospital, my mother is out of bullets. Tired.

My mom sighs as we walk through the automatic doors. Garrett's in the lobby, next to the gift shop, which is full of stuffed animals and those tacky-ass sun catchers you hang in the window.

"He's in detox, so you can't visit now," Garrett says.

"You've been here all night, then?" my mom asks. Another thing to blame my dad about—Garrett's obvious exhaustion. I see my mom tallying it all up. How much everyone's paid already for this mistake.

"Pretty much," Garrett says. "They ran a bunch of tests, stitched up a cut on his hand. Gave him a sedative. The detox thing they saw right away but it was a matter of paperwork. He's self-insured, right?" He looks at me.

"I don't know," I say. Garrett looks at my mom.

"Will's on my insurance," my mom says quickly. Like to say, *I'm not a loser without insurance! And neither is my kid!*

"Well, whatever, it's out of my hands," Garrett says, sighing. His shirt is greasy and his breath is awful and I feel completely guilty. Again. Like, I was out drinking and staying out all night and this was the cost. Brandy, crying. Angus, giving me the eye. My dad, crashing around town like a drunk tornado.

"I didn't know it had come to this," my mom says, brushing something invisible off her yoga pants. My mom lives in yoga pants. She has a job in a real company, where she wears business outfits, I know—I see the outfits in the laundry room—but basically, whenever I see her, it's yoga pants. "But I suppose I shouldn't be surprised. Will never said a thing about it, the drinking. I feel like I need an explanation. Of why my son was living with a man who's not sober"—her voice screeches up a few levels now—"and who has just ripped apart his house and filled it with trash, and now is bouncing around town like some kind of lunatic." She reaches up toward my face and for a minute I think she's going to hit me. But she just pushes back a little bit of my hair behind my ear.

I shake away from her. Take off my glasses and wipe them on my hoodie.

Garrett doesn't look down, though. He looks right at her and doesn't flinch. "At this point, it's up to Tom to explain things."

"Not just Tom."

Garrett does this half-laugh thing. "That's between you and Will."

"He lied to both of us," my mom points out.

"Tess. I know. But I think that—"

"I wish we didn't have to do this here," my mom says, super

211

crabby. Looking around at all the old magazines and the people going in and out of the automatic doors and the gift shop. The smell of burned coffee and cafeteria food and floor cleaner.

"Where else did you want to go?" Garrett asks.

My mom sets her mouth in a little line, at that. He's frustrating her, but she knows he's been up all night dealing with her loser ex-husband. She knows he's not the problem. We all sit down in the lobby chairs, as far away from other people as possible.

"Did you call his sister?" she asks.

"I don't have her number."

"Sharon's got her hands full. She's taking care of his mother now, even though she should put her in a nursing home. She's got dementia. She's been a disaster since Tom's brother died, if you ask me. But that family's too cheap to let anyone help out. So Sharon's just getting her life ground out dealing with that woman because of it. Still, she probably ought to know."

Garrett nods and my mom finds my aunt Sharon's phone number for him to put in his phone. I can tell he doesn't want to call my aunt and I wouldn't, either. My grandmother Caynes has been in one medical situation after another since I can remember. My dad didn't really get along with her to start with, and then when his older brother died—I think he's who I'm named after, although nobody really says his name much anymore—she kind of lost it. And there's no Grandfather Caynes. He was never *in the picture*, which was how my aunt Sharon put it.

"So," my mom says, turning to me. As if we're all done with my dad, and now it's my turn. "Where were you last night, Will?"

I look at Garrett, hoping he'll deflect my mom's hard-ass tone.

His mouth tightens in a way that says he's sorry but he can't take up for me. Fuck.

"I was at my friend Jack's."

"Jack who?"

I feel like saying "Jack-Off," just to be an idiot, but there's nothing funny here.

"Jack Telios," I say. "He goes to Franklin."

"And what? You just stayed there all night? You couldn't tell us that?"

"Well, I mean, I could have. But I didn't."

"Why not?" she pushes.

"Because . . ."

"Because, let me guess! Jack Telios's parents weren't home? Is that right?"

I nod. I try not to smile. Nothing about this is funny. My father in detox and my mom reaming me out in the lobby of a hospital, but I have a feeling she's going to say something crazy next. Like, "So! Did you shoot up weed? Have an orgy?" Like some bullshit she read in a magazine for parents. Where everyone gets kidnapped or killed or dies in a meth-lab fire or whatever.

"So, what happened? A party?"

"Not a very big one."

"As if that makes a difference!" she says. "Who was with you? That girl Brandy?"

Garrett presses his hands together, looks down. I can't tell if he's embarrassed for me or what. I'd be embarrassed for me.

"Yes," I say. "Brandy was there and so was Angus, and nothing happened. We just drank beer and . . . that's it. Went to bed."

"Really?" My mom crosses her arms.

"Yeah." Because—it was. We didn't do anything but sleep. Of course, I'm not going to talk about the weed. Or confess about other people having sex. I don't know if anyone else had sex. Brandy and I were the first people out the door; we didn't even really talk to anyone. She told me to drop her a block away from her house and she walked home. She texted me that her aunt Megan had taken her nana to breakfast; they had no idea about anything.

"I think I need to speak to that girl's mother," she says.

"Mom, come on," I say. "Besides, she doesn't live with her mother. Her mother's crazy. Like, seriously."

"Jesus Christ," my mom hisses. She's not a big swearer, so I'm a little caught off guard. "Wonderful. Even better."

"She lives with her aunt and grandmother," I say. "They're good people. They take care of her."

"You're being careful, then," Garrett says. He clears his throat. "You and this girl."

I'm surprised he says this. So is my mom. She sort of sits back in her chair.

"This girl?" she asks. "She's, what? Fourteen years old?"

"Fifteen," I say. "She'll be sixteen in March."

"Jesus Christ," my mom says again. She looks at her phone and then stands up. "I need to call Jay. He's texting and has no idea what's going on . . ." She walks toward the automatic doors and through them, whooshing outside.

Garrett and me sit there, then, quiet.

"So, are you?" he asks. "Being careful?"

There's no reason to lie to him. There's no reason to try to get him to think we're not having sex. It's easier just to tell him, and to tell him that I know what condoms are and we're safe. We're not going to be teenaged parents.

"Yeah," I say. "We're not stupid."

He laughs. "You know how they work, then? Condoms?"

"What?"

"I mean, a lot of young kids, they don't really know what they're doing."

"We know what we're doing."

"Not in the sack, Will," he says. "With the rubber."

I feel like the whole room could be hearing us now and I can't look up. I can't believe he said *rubber*—it's such an old-person word to say.

"No, I know," I say. "I know what to do."

"And every time," he says. "Every single time. The whole time too. Not just at the last minute."

I'm getting a headache, I'm so embarrassed. I see my mom's point, about doing *this* right here.

"I *know*, Garrett."

He sits back, unclenches his hands. "Okay, okay," he says. "I just think you'd rather hear it from me than your mom. Or Jay."

"Ugh."

"You know it's not your choice," he says. "Whether you become a father. It's always the girl's choice."

"What?"

"I mean, you get her pregnant, it's no longer your call what she does with it. She can have an abortion, she can make you a daddy. You have to do the thinking way ahead of time. That's all I'm saying."

"I don't think she wants to make me a daddy. Or anyone else, either, Garrett."

"I get that, Will," he says, glancing over at my mom, who's just walked back inside and is gesturing while she's on the phone with Jay, slapping her hand against her hip, as if he can see her.

"But once you let it loose that way"—he clears his throat again, and I wish I could be buried alive, the embarrassment's so bad— "it's not your decision. It's hers and hers alone. So if you don't want any kids and she does? Or she doesn't go get an abortion in time? Say she waits too long, deciding, and then can't? Well, then, there you go. Now you're someone's dad. Until you die. Until they die."

"Garrett, I don't—"

"That's what I mean," he says. "On the front end. On this side of things—that's where your thinking's got to be. Not in crisis mode." He glances again at my mom, who's struggling to keep her voice down but not doing a great job of it.

"Look, we're on top of it, it's okay," I say. "Really. We're being safe. We haven't even really . . . It's not like we're doing it every goddamn day or anything. It's not like we've got a lot of time. That was why . . ."

"Why you lied."

"Well, yeah. I mean, and the way it turned out, she got kind of drunk and then didn't feel so good, so we just kind of went to bed. Nothing happened. It wasn't even worth it."

He looks up at the ceiling, smiles a little. But he looks so tired. It's like he's gotten more wrinkly since I've been around him. And gray too.

"Look, this thing with your dad," he says. "I know he'll want to see you. And you'll want to see him. But I don't know if that's anything you want to rush into."

My mom is back, slipping her phone into her purse. "Why not?" She doesn't sit down, just stands there, staring down at Garrett.

"Well, it's not just me saying this," Garrett adds. "I mean, my own dad, he was a drunk, but he never did anything about it. No detox. No treatment. But I was talking to Roy last night. He was the first person I thought of to call."

"Why?"

"Well, Roy had said something to me in passing this summer and I was glad he did. Kept me on the lookout. Roy, it turns out, has some experience with this. With addiction and getting sober and everything. More experience than anyone his age should have, actually. And so I called him last night, while they were processing everything, and he kind of gave me his take on detox and what the family should do."

I look at my mom. She's not really *the family* anymore, is she? Not as far as my dad is concerned.

Still, she doesn't say anything. Just stands there, listening.

"Your dad, he just doesn't get it, you know? And he's not looking that hot. I mean, that's the truth. Physically and mentally. He's being kind of, I don't know."

"An asshole?" my mom supplies.

Garrett nods. "Roy says that detox is different for everyone, but generally, the staff recommends no visitors. Limited phone calls. There can be issues … manipulation. The pressure on families can be intense. There are lots of medical things they need to monitor and it's better if family stays out; it can be difficult to witness."

My mom puts her hand on my shoulder. It doesn't feel like she's comforting me but more the other way around.

"And also, he's not going to be ready to talk about behavior or programs or anything. He might want to just focus on getting out. The hospital staff can advise on this, I guess. He's made it clear he's done with me, that's for sure. So it's your decision: if you want to visit, if you want to stay back. Maybe you want to give Roy a call?"

"Yeah."

He asks if I have his number and I say yes. And then there's nothing left for us to do. We just leave and walk to our separate cars in the parking lot. I want to go with Garrett, a little, just because I know that he'll leave me alone, let me go lie down in the hotel bedroom, but my mom is steering me toward her car and I can't say no.

We get in the car and instead of driving home, she makes a few stops. I kind of can't believe that she does, but it's like she can't stop getting things accomplished. She's even got a list in her purse. Walgreens, the vitamin store, SuperTarget—I go with her, like some kind of robot. Walking behind her. Pushing the cart. Watching her fill it up with stuff: shampoo, granola bars, fruit cups, trash bags.

I carry everything out, I wait for her to click open the hatch on the back, I load all the bags. Like her butler, or just a really nice husband. Like Jay does.

She doesn't say much to me, beyond directions, this whole time. She stops at a gas station when we're almost to Oak Prairie and asks me to pump until the tank's full while she goes inside. She comes back with a Diet Coke and a regular Coke, both from the fountain-drink area. Hers is small, mine is giant; they are 99 cents here, for fountain drinks, any size. My mom is the only person in the world who probably gets the small, though.

I thank her, put the drinks in the cup holder. We buckle up and she starts the car and we drive home, listening to the news on the radio.

It's not until she pulls into the driveway and garage that she says anything.

"You're here now, Will. With us. With me. I should have done this long ago. I should have done something about your father. I didn't. But I could have. I just didn't want to."

It's something she's admitting. But she's not emotional about it, and neither am I. I'm not angry, like I normally am when it comes to her talking about my dad; she's not weepy, either, considering she's admitting a fault.

I say, "yeah" or "okay" or something. I don't want to say anything, but I know she needs acknowledgment, or we'll sit in the garage all afternoon until she gets it.

"We're going to have a nice Thanksgiving. A nice Christmas," she says. "All of us together. It'll be very good. Fun too. Your sisters will love it. And your father, well. He's in the best place he can be now. He really is."

I think of the house. The shit in the basement. The way everything smelled. The hot water coming and going. The power surging and blowing fuses. The cold.

"Yeah, Mom," I say. "He really is."

SEVENTEEN

AND JUST LIKE my mom declares, they are nice, the holidays. At least from the top, everything seems nice. But I don't get any flashes of happy. Underneath everything, I feel bad. We have Thanksgiving at one of Jay's brother's houses over in Minnetonka, and Kinney and Taylor go bananas with all their cousins from their dad's side and I sit there and eat a lot and try to seem normal and then watch football a little, but it's weird, because I don't know any of these guys and nobody talks shit about Joe Buck or whatever.

My mom gets hovery. It's December and she's in full shopping mode. It would be fine if I couldn't tell how stressed she is. She's always putting her fingers at the sides of her head and breathing slowly. Making lists. One thing she's determined about is my graduation party. She's planning it. Asking me about the cake and what kind of food we should have. If I want a certain theme.

"A theme? What?"

She lists off ideas: it could be a pool party, or a barbecue, or something traditional, like fried chicken. I have no idea what she's talking about. I tell her that I like chocolate cake, but whatever else she wants is fine.

I text Brandy. We text a lot. She got grounded until New Year's; her aunt found the picture she took of me that one night when we first had sex. I didn't even know she'd developed it; she took it with old-school film and I didn't think she'd ever bothered to process it.

I had to go over there and sit in the living room and talk to Brandy with her aunt Megan right there. We had to talk about our decisions and plans and how much younger Brandy is than me and did I know Brandy's mother had her when she was very young?

"Too young," Megan said. "Way too young to be a mother."

"She'll never be old enough to be a mother, if you ask me," Brandy said. Megan didn't dispute this but she didn't let it distract her from the point.

"I trust you both, but I wanted to get this out in the open. I don't want any more secrets, or lying. You wouldn't want that between the two of you, would you?"

"No," me and Brandy both said, together.

"Then be clear with me," Megan said. "I'm not a prude and I'm not an idiot, but this is something that's a big deal. You need to be sure that you can handle it, that your relationship can handle it, and that you understand the consequences. I'm not saying you guys can't see each other. I'm just saying, I need you to really stop and be aware of how sex changes the game."

In terms of wishing the earth would open up and swallow me

whole for the rest of human time, this experience with Brandy and her aunt would rate as a top number-one thing. It was only maybe ten minutes that we talked about the consequences of our game-changing sex, but it felt like thousands of years. And in the end, Brandy was still grounded, which didn't make sense to me. Hadn't she said we could still see each other?

At least we could text. Which wasn't the same, even if Brandy started sending me dirty texts, and once, a picture of her with no shirt. Which, I have to say, was pretty fucking cool. And even though she told me not to send it to anyone else, ever, I was like, *relax already*. Why the fuck would I ever send a picture of her boobs to someone else? I mean, it was like they were *my* boobs too. Nobody else got to see them but me. Which was why we were together, right? Even if I had to mail her my Christmas present, which was this necklace that she'd told Shania she liked once, only not with an orange charm on it, but a green one, and two packages of Gummi Worms and a photo book that cost almost seventy-five bucks but that she kept checking out from the library every second, which was just a bunch of selfies this woman took back in the fifties or whatever, and which nobody ever knew about until some guy bought a box of negatives at a rummage sale.

"My girl Vivian," she called the selfie woman. I guess that was her name, the lady who was in all the pictures the guy bought. It was sort of depressing, that book, considering how much it cost. But I wanted to make her happy. We'd had a few phone conversations that involved Brandy crying a little, so I was feeling extra bad.

One night when his family's having this Christmas-party thing, I go over to the Racklers' and find out that Angus got into that college in Chicago he liked. Arty, musical place. Very small. He was pretty happy about it too, and he shows me all the crap they'd mailed him and everything.

"There's like a train downtown," he says, shoving the glossy catalog at me. "And you live in these apartments too. Like pods. You have more than one roommate. So, that's cool. In case you don't like one person, odds are good you'll like another."

I guess that's one way of putting it. I mean, Angus is made of statements like this. Like, he hated his boss at the nursery place he worked this summer. *Hated.* But he liked the other people on his crew so he didn't quit. And he told me once, *just once*, that he hated his boss. Which was pretty amazing, considering the reason he hated his boss was because the boss called people fags all the time. Yet, Angus kept working there, because the other people were cool, he said. None of that made sense. Angus didn't need money like I did; he could up and quit that shit if it offended him. I mean, it offended me, and it wasn't even my goddamn job.

But that's Angus. Like, everything is just cool and ironed out. Add a little pot and he's just fine. He's, like, the only gay person I know who is super calm and happy about his gayness. About everything else too, seems like.

I look through the catalog while he goes upstairs to get us food from the Christmas party. There's a stupid movie on TV where the kids save Christmas with Santa Claus and get the parents back together by the power of the magical season or whatever and

I want to change the channel, but I can't find the remote.

While I'm tearing around the sofa cushions looking for the remote, Angus comes down carrying a bag of chips, two plates loaded with snacks, and a two-liter bottle of Mountain Dew.

Then he finds the remote (under the coffee table) and hands it to me.

Why is everything so easy with Angus?

We sit down and eat and he finds a movie we both haven't seen but want to see (again, a miracle, and not anything that happens easily most of the time) and then I feel kind of weird. Nervous. There's an adult party going on above us; my mom might even stop over with Jay, and Angus's sisters are home visiting, one with her husband and she's pregnant too. They're all upstairs; they all said hi to me when I came in.

But here we are, in the basement, with the lights low, eating and watching a movie and I wonder if his family knows. Does Angus tell them this shit? I used to tell my dad more about what I did, especially when I was a younger. I thought that was just because he was mostly cool about it and because I didn't have any older siblings to ask. Maybe you don't do that, when you're a guy, with your sisters. Who does Angus tell, then?

Another thing: both of us are sober. I don't know if Angus has any weed; if he does, he hasn't made moves to dig it out. There's plenty of booze we could swipe upstairs, but he hasn't said anything about that, either. We haven't done anything sexual since summer, and I know getting fucked up might have led to it happening in the first place, but that makes it sound like an excuse.

Once is a fluke. But more than that is not. And it's not just sex, either. It's not. It's like, he's *Angus*. He's like my brother.

Well, not that. Maybe I don't know what a brother is really like. But it's not because I'm just fucking horny and need to get off. Obviously, I don't. I shouldn't. I have a goddamn girlfriend.

We watch the movie and drink the Mountain Dew and Angus gets us two more rounds of food that doesn't seem to go together—lasagna, steak on skewers, egg-roll wraps, cheese dip and chips, pasta salad with pepperoni slices, sugar cookies shaped like wreaths. It's all good.

Between Brandy and him, Brandy's the one who'd be crushed if she knew what was going on. Angus knows about Brandy but I know he's handling it okay. I wonder if maybe this shit happens sometimes, with guys who are friends. Maybe it does and maybe I just need to relax about it. Maybe it doesn't have to mean anything.

That night I give off a vibe or something. Probably because we don't drink. Because Angus's sister, the nonmarried one, comes down and hangs out. But we don't do anything physical that night. And it kind of sets the tone for the rest of Christmas vacation, which is good, I guess, because we hang out a ton, Angus and me, almost every day. Watching TV, playing video games, going out to get food. We even mix our friends together: Angus's friends from his school and his job, and me introducing him to people at Time to Eat, including Carl, whose roommate happened to have some weed that Angus wanted to buy.

"Carl's weird," Angus says the day before Christmas Eve, when we're leaving Carl's apartment after settling up on the weed and watching a little basketball. "But he's cool."

"Yeah," I say. I'm embarrassed around Carl a little, still. I haven't been on the schedule regularly in a while. Garrett asked me to come in a couple of shifts for Carl and everyone looked at me like they felt sorry for me for having an insane drunk-ass dad. Carl's face is still bruised under the eye. It makes him look kind of badass, except it was my drunk dad who did it, so I just feel mostly shitty when I look at him. I don't know why it hasn't gone away; Garrett says sometimes bruises are like that.

Being Carl, though, he never brought it up. He just watched basketball and did bong hits and let his roommate who sells the weed talk. The roommate was a blabbermouth, which I suppose is a good thing, when you're essentially in sales. When you sell pot, you can't just be all, *fucking bitches, making money*, like Carl is. Though Carl laughs a lot more after he does bong hits. It's not like he's slow in the head or anything. He just doesn't produce a lot of verbal stuff unless he needs to. I mean, he knows how to cook, he's taught me lots of stuff. He just isn't a big talker. The world does need that other half to do the listening and everything.

"You want to smoke?" Angus asks as we get into his car.

I do, but I say no. I have to visit my dad soon; he's in the day treatment program at the hospital and I'm meeting him there with Garrett. I could have visited him before, but I haven't. I know Garrett's sick of me putting it off.

Angus smokes out quick, then drops me at my mom's. He tells

me I can come over later if I want. There's a part of me that's tempted.

I'm in the house like five minutes when Taylor is showing me this sign she's making for Santa Claus, which is like a checklist questions and reminders:

Do you like our cookies? Do you really like milk? Be honest. I hate milk. You can hate it if you want it's not like you can get in trouble it's just feelings.

Make sure you rest your reindeer because animals get tired too.

The doorbell rings and Jay's like, "Who the hell could that be?"

"Daddy, you swore," Kinney says. Jay apologizes and wipes his hands off on a dish towel as he goes to the door. He's been off all week and he's wearing the same workout crap he had on for the gym but now he's making hot pretzels with Kinney, so he's all covered in flour.

"Oh, yeah. Hey," he says. "Come in."

It's Garrett. I'm sitting at the counter with Taylor and her list and Garrett's standing there, in my mom's house, looking very out of place. It's like if my dad himself were here, sort of. My dad has never been inside my mom's house. Not even to run in and pee or compare calendars or any of that stuff. They did all that scheduling over the phone and email, and he's only seen the house from the driveway. It was like he couldn't accept that she lived here.

Garrett says hi to the twins, who stare at him like he just fell to

Earth from space, and I quick get my shoes on. There's something about him seeing this house that embarrasses me more than my dad's house. Everything here—the plum-colored walls and the lavender sofa no one sits on and the rugs on the floors—green, purple, red—and the Christmas decorations on every goddamn surface. It's just so fakey. Unreal. A place that I had nothing to do with. A place that has room for me to stay, but that isn't anything about me. Isn't for me.

While I put on my coat, Jay and Kinney go back into the kitchen to roll out their pretzels on the granite-topped counter. Garrett's watching them. I feel embarrassed to be here, embarrassed for Jay. I don't know why I didn't see it before but there it is: whatever his faults, my dad is a real man. My dad isn't macho, but he isn't making pretzels from *Martha Stewart's Holidays with Kids* cookbook, either. I know there's nothing wrong about making pretzels; Kinney loves to make things with her dad. Taylor's all too happy to eat them too. But seeing Jay and my sisters in this giant kitchen, this overly decorated house, with its wood floors that are obviously fake laminate and not real wood, and Jay's gym body in his high-tech fabric wind pants, I can hear my dad laughing about it. Saying Jay's neutered. Boring. Pussy whipped, even.

I can't imagine Garrett saying it, though. Not to me, at least.

We get into Garrett's truck and the whole way to the hospital, we talk about the stupid weather. It's snowing out; it's been snowing on and off for the last few days, but finally it looks like it might accumulate. Kinney and Taylor take snowboarding lessons so it's the kind of thing that everyone's always focused on lately.

Talking about weather's better than discussing my dad and where he is and why I haven't visited him. Garrett hasn't said a word about it but this is worse, I think, than being yelled at. I've had teachers like that too, who just look at you and instantly your shitty actions begin to throb inside you like a heat ray until you have to fix it or just combust.

We get there, and I follow Garrett. Up the elevators, twisting and turning through different floors. We get to a desk full of nurses and Garrett tells one we're here to visit Thomas Caynes, and then we're buzzed in.

I don't know what I expected a drug-treatment place to look like, but it's not this. This is just a bunch of hospital rooms, with fluorescent lights and people wearing scrubs and it smells just like the regular hospital. Except they must have had dinner, because it smells specifically like mashed potatoes and gravy. Garrett scans the rooms for the number the nurse at the desk gave us and it occurs to me that everyone here sees my dad as sick. Like he has a disease. And this place is going to cure him. I think of the basement full of crap, the bucket full of quarters, the recycling crammed with beer cans. The way the cold slips through all the cracks in the siding. How can they fix any of that from here?

Garrett pauses, then knocks on a door. We hear a "Come in," and Garrett opens the door. I'm afraid to follow him. I'm fucking frozen again. I wait until I hear Garrett speak. And then I only go in because of what he says:

"Tom? Are you leaving already?"

In the room, my dad is packing stuff into a plastic bag. He's wearing normal clothes, but he's got a hospital wristlet on and he looks like he hasn't showered in a while.

"I'm just heading out," he says. He looks at me, doesn't smile. "Hey, kid."

"But it's not even been the whole stay . . ." Garrett stops.

"The whole thing is voluntary," my dad says. "And I'm done volunteering." He shrugs, like it's no big deal.

Garrett looks at me quick, then back to my dad.

"I don't know about this, Tom," he says. "Have you talked to the doctors?"

"I've talked to everyone here, trust me," he says, laughing a little. "The doctors. The nurses. Everyone, including the janitors and the lady who brings me Jell-O, and I've come to the conclusion that I'm done. They've done their tests, we've talked it all out, and I know what I need to do."

"What's that, then?" Garrett says.

"I need to get back to work," he says. "I've got things to finish and things to take care of and I don't have time to sit here any longer, letting it pile up."

I'm sweating, standing there in my coat. No one says anything for a couple of minutes.

My dad puts on a hoodie I've never seen before. I wonder if the hospital gave it to him. I wonder how he's getting home.

I wonder if I will ever say anything. It doesn't seem like a conversation I am old enough to have yet.

"You know this better than anyone, Garrett," my dad says,

zipping up the hoodie and pulling the little cinch-rope on the plastic sack. "Or you should."

"I talked to Roy, though, and he said he'd be able to—"

"Not the same," my dad cuts him off.

"It's Christmastime," Garrett says. "I'm sure you could just wait another—"

"Holidays don't count for you and me," my dad says. "Jesus, Garrett. You know this shit, man. I would have thought of all people, you'd get it." He stops, like he wants to say more. Then he looks at me. Points at me. Grabs his plastic bag by the rope cord.

"And you?" he says. Shakes his head. Stops, like he's trying to bite back words. "I've never been anything but honest with you, Will. That was our deal. Telling each other the truth. Being good to each other. And then you go and tell lies to me, and your mom, and who knows who else. You're responsible for that." His voice sounds off. I can see his hands are shaking a little too.

I just stand there. Take it. Don't say anything.

His voice gets louder: "I put that on you, even if your mother won't. She'll just blame me, since it's easier. But you've not been straight with people. And I don't want you to forget about it."

"Tom, I don't think—"

"No." My dad cuts Garrett off again. "Don't tell me about how to deal with my kid. You have your own kids? Then you deal with them in your own way. But you don't have any and you don't have any idea what this is like, either."

Garrett looks down at the white bedsheet. He's gnawing on his thumbnail like that's the only way to keep quiet.

My dad starts pulling at his hospital bracelet to rip it off, finally chewing on the snap at the end of it. He looks crazy but I don't say anything until he tosses the bracelet on the bed.

"Dad, I'm sorry. I didn't mean—"

"I'm not interested right now, Will," he says. "And I'm not interested in you staying with me any longer. You say one thing, you do another, you get Tess all up in my business, the fucking county is on my ass, again, which I can only guess is your mother's doing as well."

I take off my glasses, wipe them on my shirt. My eyes are watering. I can't look at him.

"You know, I'm doing all this stuff because it's *our* house, Will. You and me. I just want to make it nice for you. I want it to be better. For you always to live in, to be comfortable in. I wanted to always welcome you, for you to come back to live here, for you to bring your friends over and one day, maybe your own wife and kids. Your own family. But now I see that you're a self-absorbed teenager, just like any other. You don't give a shit about me or what I'm doing. You have no respect, no skin in the game. You can always go live out in Oak Prairie, in that big bland beige monstrosity of your mother's, that lifeless neighborhood where everything looks the same. God forbid you drink too much and end up in someone else's garage, someone else's bed. I could see that happening, no question. So. You go soak all that up, son. When you're ready to be your own man, and take some responsibility, you come see me. Then we can talk."

He grabs his bag, then, and brushes past me. He smells a little gross, even in passing. Unshowered. Garrett rushes behind him, but I just stand in the empty room like a fucking idiot. Listening to them in the hallway.

"Jesus Christ, Tom—"

"Hands off me, Garrett. I mean it."

"How are you going to get home, even? Have you thought about this at all?"

"I've already called a cab," he says.

Another voice. "Is there a problem here?"

I hear Garrett sigh. My dad says no, that he's signing out, and then I hear the nurse say, "You need to come with me, then, Mr. Caynes," and then Garrett's standing behind me, his hand on my shoulder.

"Time to go, Will," he says.

By the time Garrett drops me off, I'm sick of talking about it. I feel like I might throw up. Garrett's said it a dozen different ways: *I'm sorry. Your dad's sick. He'll come around. This isn't easy. Things like this take time. He didn't mean what he said. He's angry, that's all.*

He's trying to be nice. But I don't want to deal with it anymore.

I go inside, brush past my sisters, past Jay, past the hot pretzels on the dining-room table, past my mom, who Garrett intercepts and says, "Can we talk for a minute?"

In my bedroom, I take off my boots, They're wet and muddy from the snow. I've probably tracked up the carpets but I don't

234

care. I take off my coat and hoodie and toss them on the floor. Pull my phone out of my pocket, and because it's almost dead, plug it into the charger.

I can hear Garrett saying to my mom (and probably Jay too, who tells the girls to get their pajamas on, in a stricter voice than normal) all the crap he told me on the way home: "He's hurting; he doesn't mean it; he's leaving treatment; he's stubborn."

My mom says stuff back but I can't hear it. Her knowing this is just fuel on the fire, really. Lighting her up even more about how my dad sucks.

"So, you're not pressing charges?" Jay asks. His voice is louder than my mom's.

Charges? I sit up, stand by my door to hear better, but then the TV goes on in the living room—a cartoon for Kinney and Taylor—and I can't hear shit.

I take off my clothes, turn off the light, get in bed. I want to be asleep if my mom comes in here. Garrett hasn't left; I'd feel the front door close. I go to take off my glasses but then my phone beeps that I've got a text.

In the dark, I check it. Brandy. Wondering why I didn't call earlier.

I call her; it's easier than texting. I tell her a little bit of the story; I can't say much because I'm trying not to cry. And I'm trying to be quiet so they won't come in here. I want them to think I'm asleep and not bother me.

Brandy's got it together, for someone who's had the fucked-up shit happen to her that she has. She tells me nice things. She tells me it's not about me, it's his deal. That I need to block it out and remember the people who love me and care about me. Remember that he doesn't mean it, anyway. A lot of it what Garrett said. It's like I get it, in my brain, but I still feel broken. Shitty. And like I've aged again. Like, another ten years, at least. At this rate, I'll be an older old man than my dad.

I feel the door thud closed from the other room; I don't know if Garrett slams it or if it's just this house, looking like a mansion but built from shit materials, like my dad always says about new houses.

Now Brandy's telling me about her day; they're not going anywhere for Christmas. Her uncle's coming to town, her dad's other brother. It's like her dad's the shitty one of Brandy's family. Megan and her uncle are very cool.

I tell her I miss her. I can't wait to see her. She says she's got something for me. She says she's going to hang up and send it.

So I hang up. I hear my mom and Jay getting Taylor and Kinney to bed, turning off the TV, my sisters yelling in protest. Hear them going upstairs, the toilet flushing, the sink going, lots of stomping around. Usual Kinney-and-Taylor shit. I'm glad I've always been here, on the main floor. Apart from the rest of them.

Then my phone dings with a text. A photo. Brandy's naked tits, her hand going down her panties. I can't see her head but I can tell she's in her room from the wallpaper. Instantly, I'm hard.

do you like she texts next.

fuck yeah I text back.

lol thought you might

god yr awesome

just took it bc i miss u so much!!!

me too

send me one back

srsly?

yeah

I've never done a dick pic before. Is that what she wants? Or just me in no shirt?

I can barely figure it out, the phone and my dick and only one hand and do I turn on the lights? Yes, I have to, the flash makes everything look terrible. I send her the same thing she's sent me; my chest, my hand down my boxers, where I hope she can see what's going on there.

nIce she texts.

Is she playing with herself? Do real girls do that or just older women? Or women in porn? I'm full on jerking it; I can't help it. I can't stop. I've got the phone in one hand, my dick in the other. I can practically see it, her in her room, the flower-candle smell, everything.

pretend im there she texts.

I don't text back. I don't have to pretend.

cuz im pretending yr here she adds.

One second after that text beeps, I come all over my stomach, my head twisting into the pillow so I don't make any noise. My glasses get crooked. I never jerk it with my glasses on, really. I'm glad she can't see me.

I wipe my hands off on a towel hanging over my desk chair and then she texts back.

got yr present today she texts. THANK YOU!!!!!!

do you lIke It

yeah but wish I sent you something im so broke its not even
   funny

don't care I text back. don't need anything but you

8 more days b4 im off house arrest!!!

8 more LONG days I add.

shit megans home gtg merry xmas baby!! have sexy dreams
   abt me!!!

always do, I text.

I turn off the light. The house is quiet now; I can hear some footsteps back and forth upstairs but it sounds just like Jay and my mom, probably brushing their teeth or whatever. There's nothing left in me. It's the season of giving and I've spent everything and I want everything and tomorrow we'll have Christmas Eve dinner. Go to the church by our house that we never attend except on holidays. Kinney and Taylor will open a few gifts and then rush off to bed like angels, the only night of the year there's no stomping and whining and bullshit. We'll wake up and open presents. My mom will make coffee cake or cinnamon pull-aparts. I'll eat a ton of that, get all sorts of things. Clothes. Gadgets. Maybe a snowboard—Taylor all but told me that's my big present, since she loves snowboarding and can barely keep in big secrets like that. It'll all be nice stuff. Good stuff.

And my dad? Who knows what he'll be doing. Alone in the cold, ruined, dirty-smelling house. *Our* house, he says. Makes me sick to think of, makes me sad. It's just like he said: I am selfish. I don't want to be with him. Not in that house. Maybe not in any house.

What I want for Christmas is what Brandy just gave me. Something I didn't even know I wanted until she gave it. Something that disappeared when I turned off the phone but still have inside me. The feeling. That flash of happiness. She can't ask for it back or hem it in to fit some rules or take it away like other people can. I can have it once the flash is over too; remembering it, how good it felt, how surprised I was, how easy she made it. How it costs nothing. Is worth everything.

EIGHTEEN

THE WORST DAY of school is not the first day in September. Or any of the days you have big tests. The worst day of school is after Christmas break. It's cold. It's fucking January. There's only maybe one day off in January. Even if sitting around the house being snowed in is boring, which it was, since it blizzarded like twelve times after actual Christmas, the idea of another half a year of school sounds like a death sentence.

After the first few weeks, the drive from Oak Prairie to Minneapolis was killing me. Not just in terms of gas, which my mom and Jay agreed to help with. But the roads would suck and I'd end up leaving at six thirty only to barely make it to class on time.

I didn't complain about living full time at my mom's, though. Brandy thought it was bad enough that she couldn't just hop on a bus to the Vances' and see me. We got in the habit of comparing schedules in Photography, mine with work and hers with the Vances, plus if her aunt was scheduled to work and whether her nana would be taking her nap or possibly watching her afternoon shows or had a doctor appointment and if the bus would be there or if I could drop her off or what. I almost wanted to put everything in Excel and just map it out, since we were doing all that kind of thing in my Econ class anyway, forecasting and planning inventory for our fake businesses. But that was a little too nerdy for me to do. Even for sex.

When it worked out that I could drop her off or pick her up at the Vances', then I had an excuse to drive by my dad's house. She never said anything about it. And I didn't drive slow or anything. I just wanted to see what he was doing. All the work he said he wanted to get done.

Some things had changed. That was for sure.

My dad no longer just had his truck. He had some creepy rapist van too. White and rusty, with lettering from someone else's business painted over.

There was snow in five-foot-high drifts up and down the block, which all his neighbors had blown or shoveled into even higher piles. But the last time I'd driven past, my dad's driveway just had more packed-down snow, two ruts of ice down the center. When I'd go down the alley, I couldn't see much but snow-covered piles. There'd been a lot of wood back there before. I doubted he'd used it yet, either.

Garrett put me back on the schedule. I mainly work weekends. One Friday after school, I go into work and spend the first half of my shift prepping and filling in for the servers, delivering dish racks, clearing tables, taking out trash. After my dinner break, when I punch back in, I go behind the line where Carl's setting up a row of burgers. That's usually a Friday special—burger and fries and a shake for $6.99—because it keeps drunks from ordering complicated crap late at night. Plus it's cheap enough and easy to fire out for the servers.

"Can you get me some more pepperjack? And pull up those rings?" He nods at the fryer and I pull up the basket.

"You need regular fries?"

"Yep."

I take care of the next round of fries and go grab another cambro of cheese portions, along with some extra cheddar and lettuce and tomato. As far as I know, Garrett didn't press any charges against my dad, and it doesn't seem like Carl holds a grudge about it. I don't understand why he doesn't. I mean, what in the hell? I'd be pissed as fuck if I were him. But he's his same, "making money, fucking bitches" self. Like getting clocked in a dining room full of customers isn't anything surprising.

Sierra appears at the window.

"Is there no more strawberry ice cream in the walk-in, Will?"

"Dunno."

"Well, how the fuck can I offer strawberry shakes?" she asks while loading up the burgers Carl just pushed through the window onto her giant tray.

Carl's not looking at her, just flipping through the order wheel.

"Just add that strawberry syrup for the sundaes to the vanilla," he says.

"Tastes like shit; people hate that," Sierra says.

"Then tell 'em we only have the chocolate and vanilla," he mumbles.

"But the menu says strawberry." Carl's turned to get some more eggs out of the reach-in.

"I'll go check the walk-in again," I tell her. Which is what Sierra wants, to start with. Carl always acts like he doesn't like to move from the line. But I know there might be a tub of strawberry ice cream back there; it's really popular for some reason and I know Garrett always orders extra.

"Need more pickles, while you're back there," Carl adds.

I find the strawberry—it's the last tub—so I carry it up to the beverage station for Sierra and then grab the pickles, and give them to Carl. Then I pull up the fries, salt them, and dunk another load.

"God, veggie burgers are just gross," Carl says, digging out a pale peach-colored veggie burger from the freezer-burned stack in his reach-in.

"You probably get sick of salad all the time if you're a vegetarian, though," I say, portioning out fries to his plated burgers and buffalo chicken breast.

"Whatever," Carl says. "Those kinda vegetarians? First ones to slobber down french fries. They just *avoid* meat; they're not really into eating *vegetables*."

"Potatoes are technically a vegetable," I say, pulling up the next round of fries and sinking another.

"Potatoes being such a healthy vegetable," Carl huffs. You wouldn't think Carl gives a shit about nutrition, given what he serves up for a living. But he doesn't ever eat fries, actually. When he eats at work, it's always a club sandwich. I don't know if it's work that makes him like this—like he's had a reaction to all the grease and fat and can't bear it—or if he's always been that way.

I think about that until Carl and me punch out later that night. How I can't go anywhere anymore and just buy something or eat something without thinking about how all these people— workers, who used to be background people—have their own specific lives. Nothing to do with their jobs; but they're there, working, earning, waiting for the end of their shifts so they can punch out, take off their name tags and gross, dirty uniforms, and be themselves.

Like, Carl, who used to skateboard to work, now in winter gets a ride from his weed-dealing roommate. Carl used to live with his brother until his brother died from some weird cancer. Then Carl had to live in a group home until he turned eighteen. That's why he doesn't drive; he's never had the money to learn how, never mind a car. Not that he told me; Garrett did. What Carl doesn't have to tell anyone about, though, is his obvious crush on Sierra. You know because he never says one thing to Sierra that's gross. Never anything about bitches and making money. He can barely look at her without getting a little red faced.

Knowing stuff like that: it just makes the world seem even bigger. Or denser. More compact, more crammed full of stuff. A store like Target: it's not just a place I go sometimes when Brandy's in a weird mood. It's stuffed with things to buy and people who endure all sorts of checklists and strange little rules and procedures, who deal with their coworkers' possibly dumb jokes. Who maybe like their bosses, like I like Garrett. Who have crushes on cute girls and never say anything about it. Who get fired for saying things about it, like the last night-shift cook Garrett hired, who couldn't shut the fuck up to the servers about how *fine* he thought they were.

"I knew that guy was a fucking drooler," Carl says as we stand out in the cold waiting for his roommate. He's smoking a cigarette and stamping his feet. "Now I got extra nights coming. Fucking asshole."

I wait with Carl until his roommate shows up, wave at them as I clean off the new snow from my windshield. It's after midnight and snow's blowing everywhere across the road.

I'm in that amped-up mood again. I always get it after work, even though that's stupid. I wish I got it *before* work. And what's weird is that my mom's the same way as me. She comes home from work and you'd think she'd be wanting to relax. But instead, she's in her yoga pants, in a tizzy with dinner and lists and driving the twins places and yelling for Jay to do this or that. Laying eyes on me and reporting a list of the graduation-party things she's got set up: "So, the tent, the menu, invitations are ordered, I need to set up your senior portraits, that reminds me!" And she's back to scribbling something on her list. Winding herself up like a fucking supernova about to blow.

I drive home in silence. I don't listen to music after work. Nothing. I just like thinking, I guess. About what happened. Or didn't happen. I feel like I don't make sense, like if anyone knew how much I liked being at work, how I wished I had that to do all the time, they'd probably laugh. Carl's probably drinking a beer in the shower, then he'll rip a couple bong hits and watch TV until he falls asleep on the couch. Sierra's probably lighting some incense and reading some book about psychic shit, or walking around in her panties doing weird hot-girl witchy stuff, invoking the four elements or whatever. Counting her tips and doing money spells. Either way, their jobs are things to endure and live through.

But lately, work's really the only thing I like. School is boring and full of possible shittiness, like Brandy getting upset for something I didn't do but I still have to help her with (losing a camera bag one day, or getting yelled at by her gym teacher another) or getting called to guidance to talk about my living situation; since the county declared my dad's house unfit for habitation, minors cannot live there, never mind adults. That shit I can't get used to.

But work? Work makes sense.

Get me another cambro of mushroom sauce, can you?

Pull up those fries for me, please?

The wheel's pink, can I get a hand in plating these things?

I'm slammed out here; help me clear out some booths quick, Will?

All that shit, I know how to do. I can do it really quick too. And the second it's done, there's the next thing, the next request, the next ticket on the order wheel, the next load of dishes to rack, the next orders up to fire through the window. Then, downtime where me and Carl'll go in the back and sharpen knives and bitch about shit and I'll try to bring up Sierra but he won't crack. Just keeps scraping his blade down the honing steel and not biting on any of it.

When I get home, the house is quiet. The dishwasher's humming, the kitchen is all tidy. I take off my shoes and coat, head toward my room. But my mom is asleep on the couch in the TV room, a book over her chest.

"Where've you been?" my mom asks, sitting up.

"Work," I say.

She marks the place in her book, pulls the sofa blanket off her. "I knew that," she says. "It was on the calendar."

Since everything with my dad, she's become a little more into me. Not strict or anything. Just interested in knowing where I am, when I have to work. She wants to make dinner for me when I'm around; she wants to make sure we all eat together on those nights when there's no snowboarding or dance lessons, when Jay's home, when she doesn't have yoga. There's this huge laminated calendar on the side of the fridge. It's color-coded, explains who is where and when. I don't know what to think about it, except that it's like a work schedule that Garrett makes. But with things like "pick up snowboarding" or "pizza night" or whatever. I'm supposed to fill in too, for those times when she can't pick up Kinney and Taylor at their after-school care place, or whatever. Take Kinney to dance (Taylor hates dance and won't do it), take them both to the snowboarding practice, that kind of shit.

"Angus came by," she says, folding the blanket into a square and setting it over the arm of the couch. "Did he call you?"

"I didn't check."

"Well, I told him I'd tell you," she says. "Listen, Jay and I are going out of town tomorrow. I'd like you to be in charge of the girls. Two nights. Take them to snowboarding on Saturday night; there's a party in the ski place with one of their friends."

"What?"

"I know you're not scheduled to work. I checked with Garrett, in case. Your sisters don't know yet, because I wasn't sure, but I think they'll be very excited."

"Mom."

"It wasn't on the calendar," she says quickly, like she's apologizing. "Jay wasn't sure if he was going to have to travel for work but he doesn't. So, we're going to Wisconsin for the long weekend. Just until Monday. The girls don't have school that day. Plus, Jay has to catch a flight out Monday night to New Jersey."

"Okay."

"Will, here's the thing." She's all calm, her book on her lap. I feel weird, standing there, looking down at her. Like she's begging or something.

"I know you have a girlfriend," she says. "And she's welcome here. Always. But not while we're gone. Not with your sisters here. You understand why, right?"

"Well, obviously, Mom."

"I mean, I like her very much. It's just that, I can't take that responsibility. And neither can you. I know you can handle Taylor and Kinney. You know the drill when it comes to them. But

I think you need to just deal with them without your girlfriend. Focus on them."

"But—"

"Listen to me. I've talked to the Everetts."

"Mom!" The Everetts are the neighbors across the street, this old couple that are always into everyone's business. Taylor and Kinney suck up to Mrs. Everett like whoa; Mrs. Everett has a cookie and popsicle stash just for them. They pretend to rake her yard or shovel snow with Mr. Everett. They're the kind of old people who don't just grow old and frail but who walk their little cocker spaniel three times a day, keeping themselves healthy and vital in their retirement.

"They'll be watching out for the house," she continues. "Any strange cars, any weird traffic, anyone but you and the girls coming in the door and I'll know about it. They've got my cell number. Jay's too."

I nod. I don't know why I'm fighting this. Except it's kind of annoying and babyish.

"Jay and I . . . we just haven't had much time to ourselves in . . . well. A long time." She laughs a little; an old, tired laugh.

I'm annoyed. Not because I wanted to bring Brandy here; I'd never get a second alone with her with my little sisters hanging around, anyway.

"And I know things have been very difficult with you and your father and everything," she adds. "So leaving you alone wasn't anything I want to do. I've been trying to make that not happen, in fact."

I nod. Because, duh: the calendar. But also: how am I alone with Taylor and Kinney climbing up my leg?

"Jay doesn't think we should go," she says. "He thinks it's not good to leave you on your own. But I decided it would be okay. Every kid needs some experience with that and if there's no other opportunity for you to make good choices after we've seen you make bad ones, I don't know how I expect you to learn anything."

"So, Jay doesn't trust me in his house. With his kids."

"No! Not at all!" she says. "This is your house too, Will! Don't you forget that! Jay knows you can handle Kinney and Taylor. He just thinks, well. He thinks you've been on your own too much, with your dad and everything. He thinks you've had enough of that already. He thinks . . . well, never mind what else he thinks. The fact is, we're going, and I'm going to be positive about it, because it'll be positive for Jay and me. For the girls too."

She stands up. Puts a hand on my shoulder.

"So, here is me, trusting you," she says. "Trusting that you can take care of your sisters. Trusting that you're okay to be on your own for two nights. That you won't do anything to endanger yourself or anyone else and you'll respect this house and the things in it."

God, it sounds like something she read in a magazine. Like she clipped it out and memorized it.

"All right, Mom."

"Trusting that you can handle this."

Jesus. Will she ever stop?

"It'll be fine, Mom. It's no big deal."

"And I have Garrett and Kristin looped into what's going on," she adds. "So they can drop by at any time and check on you."

Fuck. Has she notified the local police too? Ms. Demarest, the guidance counselor?

"Right."

Then she hugs me. Tighter than I want to hug her, but whatever.

"I love you," she says. "Go take a shower. You smell like a hamburger and fries."

"Thanks."

"I'll touch base with you in the morning," she says. "Just wanted to have this talk before tomorrow, when everything'll be crazy."

They leave the next day, packing up Jay's car with suitcases and duffel bags. Kissing Kinney and Taylor a million times, telling them to be good, telling them "Your brother will call us if you're not behaving"—like I want to do that! Interrupt their little love weekend because Kinney refuses to watch anything besides the goddamn Disney Channel.

Then they're waving good-bye to me as I stand in the doorway in my T-shirt and boxers, shivering, and holding the printout of directions and emergency numbers and crap my mom went over ten times while I yawned. The second they leave, Kinney and Taylor run upstairs to their rooms and I can hear them jumping on the bed. Kinney turns on some music and turns the volume way up, higher than my mom would ever allow, and yells, "Party time!"

I go to the kitchen and pull out the milk from the fridge.

Taylor bombs down the stairs, still in her nightie. "Woo-hoo, Will!"

"Easy," I say as she whips past me to the cupboard.

"You don't have to worry about us," Taylor says. "Not at all. Me: I'm gonna eat cereal three meals a day. Plus snacks. There's nothing to it, really!"

She pours a mountain of Cinnamon Chex in a bowl. I hand her the milk.

I watch her snarf down the cereal. If they weren't here, Brandy and me could have sex in every room in this house. This isn't a great thing to think, given the lockdown surveillance my mom's got, but still. It's worth a minute of consideration. A moment of silence for what could have been.

But then my phone beeps. And it's Angus: **you around?**

And it's like Brandy is gone. Was never in my head.

Because no one minds Angus coming over. Angus, who Taylor and Kinney love. Angus, who could be here all night. And doesn't even need an excuse.

I pour myself a big bowl of cereal too, and sit down by Taylor.

I text him back: **come over**

"Nothing to it," I repeat, and Taylor and me clink spoons in the way she likes, because she saw it on a commercial. "Nothing to it at all."

NINETEEN

I CAN'T THINK about it. About what I'm doing. About Brandy. Because my sisters are insane. One minute, Angus and me are sitting in the kitchen playing Texas Hold'em, the next Kinney is screaming and Taylor is slamming a door and laughing.

Angus thinks it's all funny. Angus tickles Kinney and she runs away from him, hides in the TV room watching her show on Disney that no one can stand but her, the one where the family dog talks and runs a bowling alley or whatever. Which is fine. Taylor is being a giant show-off for Angus. She has him listen to music she likes, she sits at the table beside us, drawing in her diary with the shitty plastic-chrome lock, and making a big deal of how we can't see what she's drawing and writing.

Around four, we all go to the park where Taylor and Kinney snowboard, where the birthday party they're invited to is. I bring them to the chalet and check them in with the mom of the party and Taylor wants to introduce me and for once, Kinney is nice and holds my hand, because suddenly she's shy and doesn't want me to leave.

"Can we call my mom, please?" she asks, whispering.

I think of our mom and Jay, probably in some hot tub drinking champagne.

"After the party, we'll call them," I say. "It's too loud here." I hand her the gift and tell the mom of the kid that I'll be here, snowboarding, and here's my cell number, like my mom instructed me to do, and she's all, "Right, Tess gave me your cell already," and I feel extra responsible and weird.

Then, after I disentangle from Kinney, Angus tries to give me a lesson. Because just like I predicted, I got a snowboard for Christmas and I've only been out on it once. I really didn't get much of a chance, because the hill iced over in freezing rain that day and we had to go home early. Doing something that my sisters are automatically better at than me isn't on the top of my list, but Angus convinces me it's not that hard and so we go out on the baby hill to try it again.

I pretty much suck, is the thing. And I don't have snow pants; haven't had them since I was a kid, so I'm wearing a pair of Angus's sister's, which actually fit me. At least they're black.

It's not that easy, but it's not that hard, either. I've never skateboarded much, a fact I need to remind Angus of a bunch, because he keeps talking in those terms. After about an hour, though, I start to feel it. The rhythm that Angus keeps referring to; you get the rhythm of where and when, he keeps saying.

It turns out to be a good day. The sun comes out for the first time in a long time and I get it, why people like to spend a lot of money on a thing like this. Snowboarding is expensive as hell—the equipment, the lift tickets—but it feels fucking good to be outside and in the sun and moving moving moving. Moving so fast. Only thing on my mind is the next thing I'm gonna do, the next thing I have to avoid, the next feeling that might tip me over or send me off the trail into the trees. Angus is laughing. His hair bobbling up under his blue bandanna and sunglasses. Sunglasses that must have cost a lot of money, but don't look douchey out here in the snow, because there's a point to them. Unlike all of Jay's equipment. The Helly Hansen shit I've got on under my jacket—there's a point to that, now. Here.

So many flashes of happy. Me, spraying Angus with snow. Angus, laughing at me when I wipe out in the worst way. Me, sailing down the snow hill, loving the scraping noise of the board on the icy edge. Angus, seeing me smile on the chairlift, squeezing my thigh and pretending it's nothing.

Looking away like it's nothing. I know, right then. That he'll stay over.

At seven we pick up Kinney and Taylor. They're eating cake at the chalet but Kinney's being an asshole and won't eat the pizza the birthday girl's mom is serving everyone. I know she's probably starving—I'm eyeing the pizza myself after a few hours of being out and about—but her dickishness is driving me nuts. I leave Angus to deal with her because he seems concerned about solving all her little problems. ("My coat is too tight! The zips on my snow pants are full of ice!" etc.)

Taylor and me drag most of the equipment back to Angus's car—he's got his mom's SUV, which fits more stuff than mine—while Angus carries Kinney on his shoulders. Taylor's peeved at her sister, I can tell, but she doesn't say anything so I let her sit up front with Angus, which unleashes another fit of bitching from Kinney.

"Too bad," I say to her.

"Next time," Angus says.

"There won't be any next time!" Kinney says. She's crying. God, I want to smack her.

"What do you want to do, Will?" Angus says, looking at me in the rearview mirror. He looks upset, but his voice sounds casual.

"Let's go get some food," I say.

So we go to a place where they serve pizza and plain butter noodles and chicken fingers, which are Kinney's main favorite foods in life (and which makes me crazy, because, butter and noodles, who wants to spend actual money on that shit?). But Angus is trying to make her happy. He keeps asking her what she wants, and I let him handle the ordering, because we like the same crap on pizza and because him asking her all these questions at least minimizes her complaining. The only time I step in is to order a pitcher of Sprite instead of Coke.

"They'll be up all night with the caffeine," I explain.

"Even after snowboarding all day?"

"It was a few hours, not all day," I say, staring at Kinney, who's giving me her evil glare. "Trust me."

After the food comes, sure enough, Kinney stops acting like a pain in the ass. The twins bubble their pop with their straws and twirl butter noodles and pizza cheese around their fingers and pretend the chicken fingers are cigars and it's dorky but Angus laughs. Which the twins think is totally hot shit; they are crazy and showing off more.

After we get home, Taylor and Kinney want to play video games, so we do that, even though it's annoying because Kinney keeps making us pause it so she can sneak more snacks into the TV room and I let her but after a while I bust her and say no and then she's bitchy again. Then I'm not sure if I should make them take a bath or what, because I don't know the rules of that. I mean, how gross can you get when your sweat doesn't stink yet?

So, they watch a movie they've seen a thousand times, about this time-traveling orphan girl. Taylor looks half asleep, slumped on the other side of Angus, under her ducky blanket. But I'm worried that if I tell them it's time for bed, they'll revolt and freak out. That's how they usually roll with my mom and Jay.

Brandy's texted me a couple times. I don't text back. I click the phone off and put it on the bookshelf behind me.

"All right," Angus says, the second the credits wrap. "That was super good, but we should get you guys to bed." Taylor is asleep. Kinney is pretending, but I don't know if Angus can tell. I pick up Taylor, ducky blanket and all, and carry her. She farts as I lift her up, which is funny, but she doesn't even wake up from that.

It's kind of miraculous, how we get them into Taylor's bed. They have to sleep in the same room, even though they each have their own room, but they each have a double bed, because they've always slept with someone else and can't go to sleep on their own. Taylor is pretty much comatose and barely moves once I lay her down. Kinney I'm not sure about, though her eyes are closed. But it's pretty much the easiest bedtime I can remember for my sisters.

Angus slips downstairs, his feet in socks light and silent. I turn on Taylor's green swirling pinwheel lamp that they use for a night-light. They both have the same one. If Kinney wakes up without it, she screams. The second I do, though, Kinney wakes up.

Fuck.

"Will?"

"Yeah?" I almost don't want to answer.

"Is Angus staying over too?"

"Yes," I say. Though we've not talked about this.

"Oh good," she says. "Let's have pancakes with him tomorrow, okay?"

"Okay," I say. And she curls up toward her sister and shuts her eyes. I stand there for a couple more minutes. Worried any move I make will make her eyes flip open again.

I listen to the whir of the pinwheel light. My sisters' breathing. Angus turning on the sink in the kitchen. I wait a long time, breathing slow like they are. Like I want to fall asleep standing up. It feels like forever but I want to make sure.

When I get down to the TV room, Angus is on the couch, flipping through the channels, trying to switch the TV from the DVD player, which no one really knows how to do but me and Taylor and Kinney. Jay usually just quietly asks Kinney to fix it for him so he can watch his own channel, or slips upstairs to the bedroom to watch his own simple TV. My mom thinks TV is terrible and never bothers with it until she wants my sisters out of her hair.

"What do you want to watch?" I say, taking the remote from him and sitting down on the other side of the couch and hitting the right buttons to make it go back to being regular TV. My mom and Jay have about three trillion choices of regular channels, plus every sports pass, plus a million pay-per-view things. We could watch an entire show in the time it takes just to scroll through the menu of options. It's fucking annoying as hell.

Plus I'm annoyed too. With myself. Because we're alone and I know what I want. But I don't know how to make it happen.

"Hey," he says.

"What."

"Jay got any beer?"

"Probably. But I wouldn't bother with it."

"Why?"

I explain how my mom talked to me before they left. Not that Jay counted his beers or anything, but I just didn't want to deal with it.

"All right."

"You out of weed?"

"No."

"Did you bring it with you?"

He looks at me like I'm an idiot, this *well, yeaaaahh* look on his face.

"So," I say. "Let's smoke out."

"There's not much left."

"But you just bought a bunch from Carl's roommate?"

He shrugs. I think for the first time, that unless he shared that bag he just bought, that he smokes kind of a lot of weed.

"It's kind of shit weed," he says. "Plus, I just don't feel like it. I feel like drinking. Do you have any popcorn?"

"Yeah," I say. We go into the kitchen and I do a couple of bags in the microwave while he looks through cupboards.

"Look!" he says. "Boxed wine!"

"God," I say.

"Ah, who gives a damn," he says. He gets out two plastic cups, the kind Kinney and Taylor use for their milk at dinnertime, and fills them up.

"Easy on that," I say.

He hefts the box. "There's a shit ton in there. They'll never notice."

"Want to play cards?" I ask.

I don't want to go back into the dark TV room again. So we play a few rounds of hearts, but it's boring with two people.

He gets up for more wine.

"You know the guy who's living at your dad's now? That guy whose house we went swimming at?"

"What?"

"Roy," he says, handing me a full plastic cup again. "What's his deal, anyway?"

"He's living at my dad's?"

260

"That's what he said," Angus says. "Ran into him at this coffee shop in Uptown. I was trying to get a gig there but the guy was a dick. Roy was there, getting coffee or whatever. Told me he was back in town. Helping your dad out. Staying at the house too. His parents are pissed that he bailed on college, I guess."

"Whoa," I say. "I mean, I can see why they'd be pissed." Then I fill Angus in on Roy, the whole secondhand story he told me, about the drugs and the jail and the dead baby and how he's a lot older and everything.

"He's twenty-five?" Angus asks. "He's as old as Carl."

"Carl's twenty-five? He seems so much younger. Or older. I can't decide with him."

"Roy seems older to me," Angus says. "But I think that's only because he has, like, a decent family. Money and stuff. Carl's had a fucked-up life. Did you know his mom used to make him and his brother eat cat food? And she would beat the shit out of them too. He said she'd hold his hands to the stove fire until he'd blister."

"What?"

"I know," he says. "He told me he was happy when she died, because then it was just him and his brother."

"But didn't his brother die too?"

"Yeah," Angus says. "I mean, talk about shit luck. He lived in, like, seven foster homes too. And that was in only two years, before he turned eighteen."

"How do you know all that shit?"

"His roommate told me," he says. "I went over there last week."

I'm surprised he went over there for more pot, especially if it's crap. But I'm also surprised he'd just go over there alone, without me. Not that I want to supervise his pot deals, but I wouldn't have done that. I'd have felt shy and weird about it. And anyway, how much fucking weed is he smoking lately?

"Where'd Garrett dig him up, I wonder."

"Maybe he just applied for a job."

"Huh," I say. Swigging more wine. It seems like Carl's been working at Time to Eat his whole life. Like, if Time to Eat were a box that you open up, like a kit you assemble, Carl would just come with the whole set.

But Roy? At my dad's? What the hell is that?

We play another round of cards. It seems like every game we get sick of even one time: Gin, Gin Rummy, Crazy Eights. Next thing I know we're playing Go Fish, which is stupid, but I'm feeling a little buzzed.

"So," Angus says, laying down a match of two sixes. "I went out on a date with a girl last week."

TWENTY

"WHO?" I ASK. I'm trying not to be shocked.

"You know her," he says. "She's in the band."

"Rubber-ducky girl?"

"Her name is Cora." He laughs. "Used to be Andrew's girl-friend, way back."

"The pussy-stupid guy?"

He laughs again. "Not anymore," he says.

"So? What the hell? And what about the coffee-shop dude?" I don't even know what to ask first.

He shrugs. "Who knows. She was the one who asked me," he says. "So we went. Saw a movie. Then we ate pie at this shithole place in Minneapolis."

"Okay."

"Then we went to her house and made out for a while. Her parents were home the whole time."

"Really."

"Yeah," he says. "She didn't seem to give a shit, either. I told her I was gay a million times. But she didn't seem to care, or think it mattered. Was, like, stuffing my hand down her pants, and her parents were downstairs. Watching TV. It was kind of crazy."

"Whoa."

"Yeah. Fucking insane. I don't think Andrew's missing anything."

"Dude, what are you doing with her, anyway? What the fuck?"

"I just wanted to see," he says. "You have that one girl. I've never done that. Never even occurred to me. But I figured, she asked, and then she went for it, and then I thought, why not give it a chance."

"So, did you like it?" I am so embarrassed to ask but I do because I'm tired of fucking waiting for him to get to the goddamn point.

"No," he says. "But then again, I've never liked Cora. So that was working against it, probably."

I wonder if he got hard with Cora. Even half hard? A quarter hard? Does it matter if you don't like the person? I can get hard just thinking about touching Brandy like he said he touched Cora. But then, I'm weird. There's something beyond wrong with me, beyond gay, beyond anything else. I'm addicted or something. To lying. I'm as bad as my dad. Selfish. Bad as my mom too.

"What do you want to play next?" he asks. "Are we down to War? Slapjack?"

He's waiting me out again. Just like at Jack's party. If he's not waiting for me to do it, then I don't know what he's doing.

"I'm going to bed, man," I say, like it's nothing.

"Okay," he says.

I take a piss. Brush my teeth—my mouth is red and winey, like I've been drinking blood. When I go to my room, Angus is lying on the couch in the TV room, flipping through the channels.

Whatever. This is so fucked up. I'm embarrassed at myself for wanting it. For being so sure of it on the ski lift.

I get in bed and feel like I'm going to be there a thousand years. But I do fall asleep, the TV noise from the other room like some kind of hypnotizing static.

It's almost like the first time I was at his house. I wake up because Angus is beside me. "Will," he whispers.

I've been dreaming sex stuff. Not with him, or with Brandy, either. Just me, feeling it, hard. Me, looking for it. In a way I've never been looking for it in my life: on purpose, walking around, stalking it like some kind of animal.

"Shove over a little," he says.

And I do, I roll to the inside of the bed until I'm next to the wall. His breath is hot on my neck. I know why he's here and I'm hard and he knows it, because it's the second thing he touches, after he touches me right between my shoulder blades, his hand running up my back smooth and quick, pulling my shirt off. And then I roll over and I kiss him. I kiss him so hard. I suck on his tongue.

I say, into his mouth, "I want you to fuck me so bad." I can't believe I say it but it comes out and I'm kind of happy about it.

One of us should be clear about this, for once.

He smiles, but keeps kissing me. His mouth is sloppy. Wet. Tastes like wine.

Then he says, "No."

I'm quiet. I shouldn't have said that. It's something I would say to Brandy. I think he's going to leave for a minute, but then he's standing up, taking off his shirt, undoing his belt, dropping his jeans. Pushing down his boxer briefs. His dick is huge and hard. I can see it in the Christmas lights from the outside of the house blinking in through the window.

"You're not ready," he says. "And it kind of hurts."

I don't want to know how he knows this. He could have this whole other secret life—he probably has this whole other secret life. But there's no way I can be jealous.

"How do you know?"

"Because I love you, Will," he says, and gets back in the bed with me. And then, even though this doesn't answer the question, I don't care how he knows what he knows. All I know is I have his dick in my hand, and then in my mouth and then it's both of us doing that, back and forth. There's no more waiting around. No more television, no more card games, no more boxed wine. I could laugh out loud I'm so happy to be here, on the other side of all that wondering and waiting.

But I don't laugh out loud. We have to be quiet, I tell him. He understands. And we are: so quiet. I see his face in the light from the window. A big mess of us sucking and rubbing and rolling over onto each other. I have done things like this, in this same bed, with Brandy, but they are so different. The things Brandy can do are different. The things Angus can do are different. Both different. Both good.

My whole body's tense and open and shivering and I'm nervous too, for some reason, but at the same time, I'm happy. So happy.

Because I love you, Will.

I come so hard I don't even know where I am for a while.

When I finally open my eyes, he's not in the bed. I freak a little: he's gone? Did I dream it? But then he's there, again, a blur against the Christmas lights from the window, where the sky is lightening, just by a shade though. I'm lying on my back, stark naked, looking up at him as he wipes me down with a towel from the bathroom. I'm nervous, imagining him naked, in the house. My sisters could have seen him.

"Are they still asleep?" I ask.

"Must be," he says. His hair is curly and shaggy, a lot longer; it looks like he's gotten taller. Bigger somehow.

I feel fucking amazing.

I should not feel this good.

Then he bends over and kisses me. Soft, then rough. Tongues. Stubble against stubble. I want him to get back into bed with me and fall asleep. I want it so hard that it almost hurts me. I wonder if he can tell, if he can feel it coming off me, how much I want him to stay.

I'm embarrassed of how much I want to have them both, Brandy and Angus, forever, separately, but forever, always. I can't stop it, can't stand it: the way I have to tuck that inside myself so no one sees how much I want. How much I always, always want.

But then he pulls back and wipes himself off with the towel before dropping it on the floor and finding his clothes again. I roll on my stomach as he puts his clothes back on. And then he's gone. Back on the couch to sleep. Where Kinney and Taylor find him first thing in the morning, like some kind of living Christmas present, and we're all having pancakes together, pretending everything is normal.

He stays over the second day too. It's not weird, given the history of us hanging out and how it's been; a text to his mom and she's fine with it. I can't tell him not to. And Taylor and Kinney love it, I swear, because it's like having new parents, except neither of us ever get that mad at them.

He goes home to change clothes after breakfast, brings back the same box of wine that we swiped from my mom, slips it into the fridge.

"What'd you do that for?" I ask, my eye on the TV room where Kinney and Taylor are glued to the TV in their pajamas.

"I kind of finished it off last night after you went to bed." He grins.

"Where did you get it?" I nod toward the new box. He's wrapping the old one in a plastic bag and tying it up. He'll probably stuff it at the bottom of the trash, which gets picked up tomorrow morning. We've been doing this sneaking-around shit for a long time, me and Angus. We could write a book on how to get away with shit.

"Must have been on sale," he says. "We had a bunch of it left over from Christmas."

I think about what my dad said about where my mom lives, how everything's the same, how you could drive up to the wrong house if you were drunk and not realize it wasn't yours until you got into bed.

Brandy texts me again; she also called while Angus stepped out, but I didn't pick up. She wants me to call her but I can't make myself do that. She's upset (**are u mad at me? are we breaking up?**) so I need to come up with an explanation. Because she'll probably have called Time to Eat by now. And I'm not the kind of idiot who forgets to charge his phone.

I text her quick that I got stuck watching my sisters. Text her that I'm sorry I didn't reply. Say that Kinney got sick, which is a lie, but I don't want Brandy to feel shitty.

She texts back immediately, saying that sucks and that she's been stuck at home all weekend, the snow's been terrible and there aren't any plows on the roads and she's so bored. I tell her I can call her later. I hope that's okay.

Angus comes up behind me, where I'm sitting at the table, staring at my phone, and he reaches around my chest and squeezes, then says, soft into my ear, "What do you want to do today, then?"

I don't think it's fair that something like that would make me get hard so fast and it almost makes me angry, him doing that. But he moves back, before I can push him away, and goes into the TV room, laughing, asking the girls what they want to do today?

"We can do anything you want," he says to them. But I feel like he's saying it to me too.

We go snowboarding. My mom left some spare cash, so I take that for me and Angus's lift tickets; Kinney and Taylor have season passes. It's not as sunny today, but just as warm, and I'm sore from yesterday, but I don't care.

Today, we all go out together. My sisters tease me for being slower, for wiping out. For having Angus rebuckle my boot for me like a dummy. They seem to think this is the best thing ever, like their brother has a brother kind of now too. A brother would have been nice. One thing about being the only kid my parents had? It's pretty easy to guess that there was a reason for only having one, and that reason is you. You're the standard they didn't want to duplicate. You're why they shut off the tap.

We're out on the hill for almost the whole day. When the sun goes down, we eat hamburgers and french fries in the chalet. Angus buys it all and brings it to us on a tray. Angus never thinks about money. He hasn't worked since summer but somehow his wallet's full.

Kinney and Taylor eat like starving animals and suck down pop (orange, because there's no Sprite) and I start feeling worried they won't go to sleep tonight. I wonder if we've worn them out enough. Because there's nothing else to do with them, and while I'm fiddling with the radio, the forecast says we might get up to a foot of additional snow. And that's just tonight.

"Do you think we'll get a snow day?" Kinney asks.

"You don't have school tomorrow," I remind her.

"I know, but couldn't they just write a rain check on that? We could get the next day off?"

Angus laughs. I tell her that's not how it works.

"It should, though," she says.

"No fair to get a blizzard day when there's already no school," Taylor echoes. Then yawns.

We pass Target and I tell Angus to stop, but he doesn't get it. "What for?"

"Oh, you know," I say. "If you need anything?"

He looks at me like I'm crazy. Like he doesn't understand the code I'm talking in.

"We should go look at toys!" Taylor says.

"We've got to get home," Angus says. "This weather's shit."

"Swearing!" Kinney yells. "Angus, I'm telling your mom."

I laugh. Kinney is fascist about swearing.

"Please don't tell her," he says. "She'll get so mad."

"Will she take your snowboard away? Ground you?" Kinney asks.

"Probably," he says, glancing at me. I swear, I get all freaked out, him just looking at me like that. All secret and sneaky.

"Then I won't tell her," Kinney promises. "Because when my mom and dad get back? I'm going to tell them that we all need to go snowboarding every weekend like this weekend because it was so fun and Angus is the best babysitter we've ever had."

"Hey!" I say, getting fake offended. "What about me?"

"*I* like you, Will," Taylor says, trying to make me feel better.

"Angus is nicer, though," Kinney says.

"And you're already our brother," Taylor adds, a rare moment of aligning with Kinney's bitchiness. "We're *used* to you."

Angus makes the turn toward my house and he glances at me, smirking again.

This time, bedtime is a little harder, like I figured it'd be. Kinney argues that they should sleep in her room and Taylor doesn't want to and I make them take a shower, which turns out to be a disaster, even though I think it'll relax them and be faster than a bath. But Kinney's secretly afraid to have water go over her face and that's why they still take dumb baths even though they're eight years old. After seeing my sisters swoop all over the hills today on their boards like pros, it fucking kills me that they take baths, with floaty toys and shit like that.

Once they holler down that they're finally in their pajamas, I come upstairs and they bitch because they want Angus to put them to bed but I'm a firm bastard on that score. Angus will just make them hyper and now they're all ragged and yelling and assholey from being tired. So I put them in Kinney's bed and turn on the pinwheel lamp and shut off the light but I don't leave. I sit on the floor by the bed and tell them a story, in the slowest, calmest voice I can, about a time-traveling orphan girl.

"I know this story already," Taylor says.

"No you don't," I say. "This is a different story."

I have no idea what this story is, except that I'm ripping it off from that movie we saw the night before. And in this version, the time-traveling orphan is a girl named Brandy ("like your girl-friend!" Kinney yells, and I have to shush her) who meets a boy named Carl with a magic rock.

"A *rock*?" Taylor says. "A rock's a pretty dumb thing to be magic."

I tell her it's not. Because *this* rock can make anything become a perfect place to stay for the night. When you're tired and worn out from all your traveling, you kiss the rock and say, "Take me home," and it transforms into the place you've been wishing for. Everything you need. Like, if you want a hammock, you get that. Or a big fluffy bed, with a canopy and feather pillows, that's what would appear.

"I'd want a big fluffy one," Kinney says, yawning.

"I'd want bunk beds," Taylor says. "But not to share. I'd get both."

"Hogger," Kinney says.

"Shhhh," I tell them. Then I keep up the story, which really doesn't go anywhere. Carl and Brandy meet people who are nice and set up a place to stay with their magic rock and they have a good time. Or Carl and Brandy meet people who are horrible and mean and they run away just as Carl wishes and kisses the rock and then they are saved, escaping into a castle with a drawbridge slamming shut, and the moat full of alligators gets the horrible people. Carl and Brandy don't get anywhere or do anything, but repeating the same formula seems to make my sisters happy. Or bored. They fall asleep as I'm describing Carl's wing of the house, which has its own skateboarding ramp and movie theater. Again, I wait, superstitiously, for a long time to make sure they're all the way asleep.

It's kind of nice, sitting on the floor, listening to the pinwheel light whir. I like knowing Angus is downstairs. It's not even eleven o'clock.

I get up slowly. Turn to look at my sisters. They are asleep, their heads turned in opposite directions, their hair tangling together on their pillows. Taylor's mouth is partway open. I don't stare at my sisters much and I don't admire them, really. They're always driving me nuts. At least Kinney is. But now I can see a little how they'll look when they're older. My age. They'll look like my mom, mostly, and a little bit of Jay. They'll be cute. Pretty.

I back out of the room, pick up a couple towels that got left in the hallway after the screaming shower disaster, and hang them on the rack.

When I go downstairs, the lights are off. I can't hear the TV. No Angus.

I go into the bathroom, smiling to myself. I brush my teeth, take a piss. My dick's already getting hard, just thinking.

In my bedroom, he's there. The nightstand light's on and he's already in bed. Reading a book. One of Jay's, about climbing Mount Everest, a true story. He's not wearing a shirt. Probably nothing else.

Taking off my clothes like this feels strange but I pretend it doesn't. I strip down to my boxers, and kind of fiddle around at the last minute. Pull my wallet out of my jeans, charge my phone. I can avoid Brandy all I want, but I have to make sure my mom can still reach me. With it snowing like it is, they could be delayed awhile.

I look at Angus. But his eyes are intent on his book.

I could have another night of this, maybe.

If I was gay, I could have this every night. Not every night. But you know. We could move out, get our own place. How hard would it be, me and Angus, to do that? Carl seems to manage it okay being a dishwasher.

Except Angus is going to college. In Chicago.

And then there's Brandy. She's got two more years after this.

"You going to get in bed or what?" Angus says. He doesn't look up from his book.

I turn around, fiddle with my phone again. I get into bed and he turns off the light, drops his book to the floor. Wraps himself all around me and we stay like that for a long time before we do anything else, and I can't stand it, how good it feels, this thing that I shouldn't be doing.

In the middle of the night, I think I hear Kinney. I get up and put on my boxers and glasses and listen at the bottom of the stairs. Nothing. I go into the kitchen and get a glass of water. It's 3:28 a.m. I shut off the drying sequence on the dishwasher and listen some more. Nothing.

Then I go back to my room. Angus is in a heap under the covers. Naked. One of his feet is sticking off the edge of the bed. He's kind of a covers hog, it turns out. Or else we need a bigger bed. It's not easy, with two guys of our size; his bed is actually better.

My phone is fully charged on the nightstand, the little blue light blinking. I unplug it and turn on the light. Then Angus rolls over.

"What are you doing, Will," he says. His voice is low and scratchy.

"Nothing," I say. I open the camera app and start to frame him in the shot.

"Are you taking my fucking picture?" he says. Sounding more awake now.

"What if I am?"

"Make sure my dick's not in it," he says. "It'll ruin the composition."

I laugh and snap one picture of him sitting up, his arm over his eyes. No dick, but the covers are so low you can see hip bones, his hair.

"Let me do one of you."

"Not on my phone," I say. "I don't need a naked pic of me on my fucking phone."

"On mine then," he says. He gets up and grabs his from his jeans on the floor. I stand there, holding my phone over my dick.

"Move your hand," he says, laughing.

"What the fuck," I say.

He takes the picture and the flash is blinding. I'm blinking and seeing spots. I take off my glasses and press my hands into my eyes before I get back into bed. A little horrified, a little thrilled. Angus is still bent over his phone. He's smiling.

"Delete it," I say.

He gets into bed and slips all around me, his hands over my chest, his dick hard on my leg.

"Not a chance," he says.

TWENTY-ONE

I FEEL SO guilty about the weekend I ignored Brandy for Angus that I go a little nuts trying to make it up to her. We are together whenever I can swing it. She skips her study hall to eat lunch with me. I go with her to take pictures of the debate team and the Mathletes for the yearbook. She goes with me to get my senior pictures done, which is awful, because the photographer lady keeps making me take off my glasses and that makes Brandy laugh for some reason. Plus I think I must look like I'm lying; I have glasses—why put a picture in the yearbook that pretends I don't?

She gives me head once in my car when I skip gym. We have sex once at her house when her aunt and nana are downstairs and once at the Vances' when the kids are outside playing in the snow. But she gets upset with me about the time at the Vances': "What if one of them got hurt?"

I apologize. I apologize a lot. I actually feel sorry, though; it's not bullshit.

It's like, I see her: Brandy, her hair and her flannel shirt and her skirt and tights and the way she dresses, which isn't sexy but isn't not sexy, either, and I just *want*. There's no brain in my head. Just me and her and what I want. I watch her look over photos she's taken for the yearbook, her face all wired up like she's making a decision about which one's best, and I wish I could feel that intensely about any of the dumb homework I do. I wish there was something specifically shitty about her, or annoying, or that she was even a little bit mean, but she's not. That would make it easier for me to do what I'm doing.

And Brandy likes me even though she knows all this crap about me. What my dad's house looks like. How I look naked. How I look when I take my glasses off—"you look kind of surprised by everything, like you just came out of a cave." How looking at her, being around her, even if we're doing nothing, even if we're not touching, is just so good.

The thing is, I think this is how all cheating people must feel.

One Thursday, after school, I take her with me to spy on my dad. I haven't been in a long time. It's the week after Valentine's Day. (I gave her a bunch of flowers and all day, her face was all blushy red and smiling, looking down, like she didn't want anyone to know how good she felt. It was pretty fucking cute, actually.)

Anyway, that Thursday, she doesn't have to go to the Vances' and we have to do the laundry—Thursdays are laundry days at her house, so we usually hit my dad's Laundromat. He hadn't been at the Laundromat when I went with Brandy a few times, and I was disappointed about that in a way. I wanted to remind him that I was still alive, even if he didn't want to see. And when I thought of the shitty things he said to me at the hospital, I wanted to go past his house and see that nothing has changed. Even with Roy's car parked out front, nothing looks different.

"Why do you do this?" Brandy asks. She's got her camera on her lap, the real one with the big huge bulky lens that she uses for the yearbook.

"What."

"Spy on him," she says. "Obsess over him. It's not going to make you feel better."

"I don't obsess over him."

"It's like you want him to keep doing shitty things to you," she says. "Like you can't get enough."

"I don't want that," I say. Wishing I'd never told her all the crap he said to me back at the hospital rehab. I start the car and don't look back at the house as we drive away.

"I think you want to hurt him back," she says. I don't answer her.

Once we're at the Laundromat, I get hypnotized watching Brandy's system of sorting. She never explains it, but she separates lights and darks and then household stuff, like blankets and towels. She has separate detergents for certain things. I watch her do it and then just carry her piles to open machines. I like doing what I'm told when someone has a good system. When I can see the point to it.

After we get everything running, we sit down and do our homework.

It's weird, I guess, being in this place my dad owns. I notice one of the machines is out of order and there's no dryer sheets left in the vending machine, and the floor needs to be mopped pretty bad. But there's a dude that I've seen around last few weeks. He's got a tattoo on his neck that looks like flames. He goes out and smokes in the parking lot and texts on his phone and part of me thinks he's running the place. Like my dad's hired him or something? But then I see him sitting in the corner doing Sudoku, so maybe he's just got a lot of laundry. Who the fuck knows. He could be dead, my dad. Dead for weeks. How long could this place keep running until anyone did anything?

"I kind of obsess over my mom too," Brandy says, looking up from her algebra textbook. "Just so you know. I mean, she's pregnant, did I tell you? She's pregnant. The baby's due in August or something."

"Whoa."

"I know," she says. "She shouldn't have had me to start with. She couldn't handle me. My aunt's freaking out. She's not sure she can handle a baby."

"No shit she can't."

"No, I mean, *Megan*'s not sure she can handle a baby," Brandy says. "Because they'll come to her first, probably, ask if we'll take it."

"But who's the dad? It can't be your dad, right?"

"No, he's still in prison," Brandy says, and it kills me, how easily she can say that. How it doesn't hurt her. She's tapping her pencil to her chin. Thinking.

"Then it's not Megan's problem, really."

"It would be my sibling, though," Brandy says.

"Half sibling."

"The dad's probably crazy too," she says. "Because she's in a psychiatric ward now. Did I tell you that? She got kicked out of the residential place she was in. They couldn't handle her. But I don't know if she got pregnant there or somewhere else. Whoever it is, he can't have much good stuff going on, either. Getting with my mom; it's not like she's super picky." Brandy laughs.

I don't know how to say how terrible I think this is without making Brandy feel more shitty about her mom and her unborn sibling. Plus I feel kind of terrible for Brandy too. She doesn't know it but she could have better luck than with me.

But then she changes the subject. We talk about her aunt Megan's new car and Kinney's dance recital that's coming up and the show Angus and DeKalb are doing at Miller Grill. We talk about how DeKalb's dogging Shania and how she's not into him anymore and why that is. We talk about Jack Telios hanging around with these two girls in my grade, Loretta and Isabella, who are actually hot girls, and who also happen to be cousins.

"Bad enough all three of them are together," Brandy says. "But it's like incest on top of that."

I'm not even sure Jack's fucking Loretta and Isabella, him being all high-minded about his Swedish chicks and everything. He's all beyond calling people his girlfriends or talking about actual sex, either. He's not into definitions or possessions, he says. Doesn't like labels. I think it could all be bullshit but he never specifically says anything that's going on with Loretta and Isabella. So it could be real too. The only thing I know about Jack is that he's for sure dyeing his hair to be that white-blond he's got it and that he has some weird thing about never wearing a jacket, just these heavy wool sweaters all the time, which make him smell like a wet dog when it's snowing and everything's melting on his shoulders.

We go back to our homework, then, because despite everything, Brandy and I are those kind of students. I do my homework so I don't have teachers crawling up my ass, mainly; Brandy is trying to get on the honor roll so she can qualify for reduced insurance rates. She's in drivers' ed now, so that's all she thinks about. My mom pays my insurance—I know that. My dad used to but then he let it lapse and I got a ticket for going through a stop sign and my mom freaked out because it involved all these fines and fees and paperwork with the court. She doesn't trust him for shit like that anymore.

After we finish our laundry, I drop Brandy off. I don't go inside, because while I've seen Megan since our big sex talk, I still feel awkward about being around her. And then, even though Brandy says I'm being obsessive about it, I drive back to my dad's house, just to see if anyone's around. It's a split-second decision, really. An impulse.

But this time, just as I roll past, Roy comes out and sees me. He's standing still, about to light a cigarette. He doesn't look thrilled, but I pull over and park anyway.

When I get out, he's walking toward me, cigarette lit. He's cut all his hair off; you can see his scalp, and his ears are pink from the cold. They're pierced way up and down too, but there's nothing in there, just holes. I never noticed that before, when his hair was long.

"What's going on, William?" he asks. It's half-friendly, half-suspicious.

"Nothing," I say. "Just was in the neighborhood."

"You're in the neighborhood a lot."

Shit.

"My girlfriend, I drop her off at the house where she babysits sometimes."

"Don't they live on the other side of the block?"

I don't feel like defending myself. He's a dick if he can't accept that I'd be a little curious.

He sucks in his cigarette, then blows it out over his shoulder.

"Hey, you're not alone. This whole street is up in your dad's business lately. What he's doing. What he's not doing. It's kind of become a big problem. For your dad at least."

"Why?"

Roy shakes his head, like it's too much to explain. "Listen, I want you to know that I'm helping out again, living here, and things *are* happening. On the inside, at least. It's getting there. It's just, the snow is making it hard to do anything beyond that."

"I thought the county ruled the house unfit for people to live in?"

Roy shrugs. "Your dad's not in agreement, obviously. He's kind of stubborn."

"No shit."

"It's not like he's a jerk, but he certainly could be softer about dealing with neighbors. That might make them not want to call in the county with little complaints all the time."

I don't know what to say. I feel so angry, I'm afraid my glasses will steam up. I take them off and wipe them on my coat, even though I know it's a wool blend and will probably scratch the coating on the lenses.

"Is he home?" I ask.

"Not right now," he says. Takes another drag of the cigarette. "He bought another Laundromat over in St. Paul; he's over there getting that place going."

"What the hell?"

Roy scratches his head, feels around in his pocket, and pulls out a hat, puts it on his baldness. "Yeah, that happened before I got here."

"When'd you get here?"

"January," he says. "I withdrew from school."

He looks a little ashamed about it, but also like he wants me to tell him it's okay, as long as he's helping my dad. I look at him, sucking at his cigarette, his fingers all dirty and callused. I wonder if he's back on drugs. Like he's not really helping, but staying here because that's all he's got left now.

"Sorry," I say.

He blows out more smoke, which he tries to exhale away from me, but the wind sends it into my face anyway.

"I'll go back probably," he says. "Just not right now." He's not looking at me, but at a FedEx truck stopping at a house down the street.

"Can I come inside and see?" I ask.

Roy steps back. Steps on his cigarette and kicks snow over it. Shakes his head.

"I don't think that's a good idea, man."

"Why? My dad still hate me?"

"Your dad doesn't hate you, Will," he says. "I know he mouthed off and said a bunch of shit he regrets. He's told me that. But I know what he's doing right now. And what he's doing is to make up for it. He's dead set on having your graduation party here. That's his goal, that's his timeline . . ."

"Then what the fuck is he buying more businesses for?"

"Cash-flow issues, I guess," he says. "I'm not making excuses; I wish to hell he hadn't done that either. But the point is, he's focused on making it up to you. And I'm trying to keep him focused too. He won't let anyone in that easily. That friend of his, Garrett? He won't speak to him anymore. I'm like the last tenuous link here."

"Is he still drinking?"

"Not at the house," Roy says. "That was my limit. I can't be around that."

"But he's still drinking."

"I think so," Roy says. "He doesn't like the idea of meetings, though I've tried to get him to come."

"He's not going to stand for that shit."

"He thinks that, now," Roy says. "There'll come a day where it just gets too tiring, though. Where you'll do anything to reverse the direction you're headed."

"So, what? You work on the house and try to get him to be sober?"

"Not in that way," Roy says. "Just, I don't know. I'm trying to listen to him. Be supportive. Remind him, through example, that recovery's possible."

"I hope you don't say it like that," I say. *"Recovery's possible."*

Roy laughs. "Oh, no," he says. "I said that once and he pointed to me smoking and asked what the fuck I thought that smoking was. He's pretty guarded."

"So . . . you're not going to let me see the house."

"I promised him," Roy says. "He's seen you too. Driving past. And he doesn't want you to see the house until he's ready for you to see it."

I say okay and his phone beeps and he looks at it and smiles.

"Another girlfriend?" I ask. It's the first time I've ever acknowledged that part of his life.

He kind of smirks.

"Sex and cigarettes," he says, shoving the phone in his pocket. "My last vices." He slaps my shoulder and lights another cigarette and then I get back into the car.

I'm wishing I had a shift, but I normally have weekdays off. The sky is the color of cement; there's snow and dirt and slush everywhere. It'll be spring in a couple months, at least according to the calendar. The last day of school is May 30 and graduation is two days after that. I'm passing all my classes, nothing great, but I've got C's and some B's. My mom has all these things for college for me to look at. It's like she won't acknowledge that I've done nothing to apply for school in the fall.

There are a lot of good things happening in my life now, but they're all happening to other people. Angus is leaving for spring break to go tour around Chicago. Kinney and Taylor's snowboard team is going to some championship. Jay just got a raise at work. Kristin's goat is pregnant. Garrett just bought a new car. And my dad is building the house up, as a present. For me. I should feel better. I should be happy Roy's there, with my dad. I should feel good that I can stay with my mom. That I have Brandy. That I have Angus. I should feel good about these things. I should.

But I just feel cold and hard inside. Like, I'm a million years older again. It makes me want to check the mirror for gray hair. Because hearing Roy talk about the house being finished, for me, like he believes it? It just makes me tired. It's exhausting, hoping for the best.

TWENTY-TWO

THE SNOW FINALLY fucking stops. But not until the end
of April. Then, the days suddenly get hotter and sunnier and
being in school is torture. One day they call off school because
Franklin isn't air-conditioned and the temperatures in the class-
rooms, even with the windows open, is over ninety-eight degrees.
I don't know why they even bother. Most of the seniors don't give
a shit anymore and with all the fans the teachers constantly have
running, you can't hear anything anyone says.

Now that the sun's out, Jack Telios has taken to unbuttoning
his shirts even more. DeKalb and him have some game going
with Isabella and Loretta, the cousins. And now Jack's the main
roadie for Angus and DeKalb's band, because they're playing
more shows—that same first coffee shop has them regularly on
Saturdays now, along with a couple more places like it. Little gigs,
but Angus is very proud of them. I usually have to work Saturdays so I don't see them all. Plus Brandy likes the band and she

wants to go with Shania, but I can't deal with her and Angus in the same zip code so I always say I'm busy. Even if I'm just staying up late at my mom's, waiting for Angus to call me when he gets home. Which he always does. He's always in the mood to hook up with me after he plays a show.

Except for the weather, everything's the same. Work, me picking up some extra shifts for Carl. Me, with Angus, stolen minutes in his garage practice room here and there; once in his basement on the couch after everyone was asleep. Me, with Brandy, at her house after school when her nana's asleep and her aunt's still at work. There is something about getting sex all the time that just makes you crazy. It's like you're sick. And the only cure for it is more sex. My dial is stuck at *go go go yes yes yes* all the time. It freaks me out to think that maybe I want it exactly like that.

I don't want to like it, though. I never thought of myself as a cheater. Cheating at first seemed mainly like lying. Which is nothing great. But why do liars lie? Because they're greedy. They want everything without admitting it.

But when you're greedy, everyone can see how desperate you are. There's no dignity in it. That's why I can only stand it when no one can see. I can't think about it too much or I'll fucking go crazy myself.

I think I'm going to end up like my mom.

"Tess settled for the suburbs," my dad would tell his friends, when he was drunk and thought I was asleep. Or "Tess can't sit still. Always striving for something." I think they both sound right. But it seems wrong. How can she be both those things, even?

*   *   *

My eighteenth birthday is May 9, but it's on a Monday. Brandy does nice things for me all week: brings me lunch, gives me presents (a new watch, a pair of flip-flops, since I always wear my boots, even with my shorts, which she says is weird). Then, after school, she gives me a blow job in the bathroom at her house while her nana's downstairs in front of her afternoon talk show.

Afterward, I tell her it's not the kind of birthday stuff I'm used to. For her birthday, all I did was buy her a gift card for Target and a new bracelet Shania helped me pick out.

"I'm not used to it, either," she says as I'm buttoning up and feeling a little light-headed. I can hear the TV downstairs; Nana keeps the volume jacked, even with the closed captions on, for some unknown reason. "But I think it's how birthdays should be. We have a lot to celebrate, I think."

She wipes her mouth with the back of her hand and flips her hair out of her face.

I kiss her a bunch. I swear, I cannot even taste myself on her mouth. She must have some magic trick, something in the magazines she and Shania always pass back and forth. Because I always taste it in Angus's mouth. Maybe there's some difference in saliva for girls and guys? I feel guiltier than usual when she gives me head because that is a thing with Angus that I always give back to him. It's impossible not to think of him while she's doing it, actually. For my birthday, my mom bought an ice-cream cake from Dairy Queen and we're going to have steak—that was my request—and she even invited Angus. But Angus is gone overnight for his class campout, so he'll miss it. So I won't see him at all on my birthday, which would have been a good gift in itself. Not that I expected a blow job. Though, lately, when we manage to hang out, that's usually what happens, anyway. Birthday or not.

The next Thursday, I'm at the Laundromat with Brandy and I'm not doing homework but I'm looking over college-application stuff. Brandy keeps looking up at me from her yellowy copy of *Jane Eyre*.

"I hated that book," I say.

She doesn't say anything. Just gets up to go to the coffee shop. She doesn't ask if I want anything, either, which is also weird. She comes back a minute later with a Snapple and sits back down with her book. I don't want to make this into a big deal, like the other times we've fought, which seemed like fighting about air or wind or something invisible. So I take off my glasses and clean them on my shirt and act like nothing's wrong.

Until my dad walks in.

I know it's him, even without my glasses. Can tell, just by how he moves.

I put my glasses on. The three of us all stare at each other. It feels like everything's completely transparent between us, and I'm embarrassed. I know he knows I've told Brandy everything. And I know this is why he's mad.

My mom has been emailing him. Texting. Calling. All about the graduation party. We have invitations with my senior picture—I made her pick the picture where I'm wearing glasses, even though she and Brandy both liked the ones without them better—but the time and place are blank. She's trying to work with him, she says. He's stopped calling her back. Answering.

Now I'm here. In his place of business. Which is as dirty and unloved as ever. I wonder if he's going to throw us out. Or just me.

"Hello," he says. He says it to Brandy. She says hi back in the softest voice ever.

"Hi, Dad," I say. My voice sounds like I scraped it up from my guts.

"Everything working okay?" he asks, nodding toward the bank of washers and dryers.

"Yeah, great," Brandy says.

"Good, good," he says, nodding, like we're customers and nothing more. He gets out his keys and goes into his office. I can hear the lock click after he shuts the door.

I go back to looking at the college stuff. Brandy is staring at me now in a way that annoys me. I don't want to talk about any of this.

"Should we leave?" Brandy whispers.

God. Like he can hear her, from inside his office, with all the fucking racket of the washing and drying!

"No," I say. "Your stuff isn't done."

"Yeah, but—"

"No," I say. "You paid and you get to finish what you paid for."

"Maybe we should leave once everything's done in the washers. Go somewhere else and dry them?"

I try to stay calm. I do. I stack all the college crap into a pile. Breathe in, out.

"Brandy," I say, leaning toward her. "Just because he's my dad doesn't mean you don't have the right to wash and dry your clothes. I mean, fuck. You have nothing to do with me and him. And there's no fucking way I'm going to make you haul all your wet shit out—"

"We could line dry it," she says. "My aunt has a thing in the backyard—"

"No," I say. "That's ridiculous. He's ridiculous. You have every fucking right to be here. And I'm going to be here too. If he wants me to leave, he can call the fucking cops. Neither of us is doing anything wrong."

"Okay."

She blinks. Smiles. I can't help it; there's something about seeing her face soften like it does right now. It kills me. I lean over and kiss her, quick.

I think that'll be it, but then she leans back and we kiss some more. I take off my glasses and I'm hard and we're kissing in a goddamn Laundromat. What the hell, I think. How long do we have together, Brandy and me? As long as Angus and me have, probably. Which is to say, a couple more months. If I go anywhere. And my ticket to going somewhere is sitting in a pile between us while we kiss like idiots.

Later, after we bring back all the washed and dried laundry (and my father never once leaves his office, the door stays almost self-consciously closed), I help her put it away while Megan makes dinner, which we all eat on the patio, even Brandy's nana, whose eyes seem wrong. I guess she's got some eye problems too, in addition to being deaf. God, if she goes blind, what the hell will she have left?

But Nana chews and smiles and occasionally yells some comment that's way off track of the main dinner conversation. It's bright and sunny out. Megan is being normal, like she always is, polite and nice to me, but I still feel dumb around her. Like all she sees when she sees me is that picture of me naked in her niece's bed.

We sit out on the patio after Megan brings Nana inside to watch her evening shows. I ask Brandy about her eyes—is she going blind—and Brandy blinks, shrugs. She seems to think of her nana as a quirky pet more than an actual person.

The wind kicks up and she comes to sit closer to me and I can't keep my hands off her. I am feeling her up, everywhere. Tits and ass and even trying to stick my hand down her shorts. She twists away.

"Not here," she says. "Let's go for a walk."

Brandy's house isn't cruddy but there's not a lot around it in terms of places to go. So we walk for a while, holding hands. I feel like I could run; I'm practically dragging her behind me. She doesn't complain, just scrambles to keep up.

"There," she says. Points. A little brown building that says Public Water Works #7 on the outside. It's got a door and weeds growing out of the sidewalk, and I don't know what she's thinking but then we're behind the building, between two bushes and there's nothing behind us but the back of a tires place and there's no going back to where we were. I barely kiss her. I just undo her shorts and kneel down and pull her pussy into my face and she says, "Jesus, Will," but leans back against the brick wall and lets me lick her there. Everywhere.

I've done this before but never like this. Never with the sun still up, though it's fading. Never outside. Never standing up. Never like this.

I expect her to stop me. To say no. To say, "Not here." But she never does. She holds my head between her legs, her hands in my hair. She sighs. I never take my glasses off but I'm closing my eyes. I imagine her face, flashed with happy. I'm grinning myself. All over her. She's wet so I know it's okay.

She doesn't even have her purse; we don't have condoms, and I don't even take off her clothes or my clothes. It doesn't matter. I undo my belt and jeans and we fuck, right there, standing up against the wall. It happens quick, and she never stops me. She's making perfect sounds, even. Brilliant sounds. I'm lifting her up to get a better angle, to get deeper, to keep the branches of the bushes from scratching her skin where I've pushed up her shirt. Knocking straight into her, fast, then slow, then all over, in and out, no rhythm. With no condom, it's unbelievable. Over faster than normal, though.

Just as I'm pulling out, it hits me what we've done. What I've done. I expect her to get mad. Start crying. Yell at me. Hit me, even.

And I'll take all of that. I totally deserve it. I didn't even ask. I didn't even stop. She should be so fucking mad.

Instead, what she does is kiss me. Kiss me with her shorts and panties still at her ankles. Kiss me and run her fingertips along my shoulders and collarbone, dipping her hands in and out of the collar of my T-shirt. Kiss me and kiss me, like we didn't just fuck, like we're leading up to it instead. Like she didn't get what she wanted yet. Like she thinks there's still a chance I could give her something more.

"Come on," I say, pulling up my jeans. "Let's get out of here."

She is dazed, and I am guilty. I don't think she came or anything, but maybe? I never know with her. It's the one thing about sex with Brandy that I don't like. At least with Angus I always know for sure. With Angus, it's always clear; we're always heading to the same destination and we both know, by sound, by sight, by feel, how close the other is to arriving there.

Brandy, I don't know. It's not that she's silent or apathetic. I know it feels good. But it's not the same.

This time? If she didn't come, I think she might have come close, at least. She's definitely acting different than usual. Which could also be the other fact of what we've just done too.

I pull her clothes up. Button her shorts. Feel a little sorry for how this leaves her—the puddle in her panties, the panic of what we have done burning in me now, that same zinging feeling but worse, because it's such a steep drop from how good it just felt—and that's when she puts her hand in mine and says it.

"I love you, Will," she says. "I love you so much."

TWENTY-THREE

I FILL OUT my forms for graduation. I turn in my textbooks for most of my classes. I sign people's yearbooks, though I don't even buy a yearbook for myself. There's something about Brandy still being a sophomore in my senior yearbook that I don't like. All those pictures in there are ones she took, her pictures, and she only gets the one little square in the whole fucking book. I'd rather spend twenty-eight bucks on *her* than that fucking book.

There's a weird feeling, though, like I'm floating and so are all my friends. Jack is floating, DeKalb is floating. They're hanging around people they've never hung around with, beyond the basketball team and the band, beyond Isabella and Loretta, beyond people who take AP classes or who even go to Franklin. DeKalb has people from Little Caesar's he hangs out with; Jack goes out with Cora the rubber-ducky girl and the barista from the coffee shop of the first show they played. It's like everyone's hovering for just a little while before they take off into flight.

All I'm doing is waiting, counting down the days until Brandy gets her period.

I've been driving by my dad's house. And it's like a miracle. Like the snow melted and underneath the house was new. I couldn't go inside, but it seemed like everything Roy said. There's new siding. A front porch is built, the frame is up, with empty holes for windows. The stacks in the driveway are disappearing. I tell this to Garrett one night when I come in for work and he nods.

"Just heard from him the other day, in fact," he says. "Can't believe he even called me. Sounds like things are getting better."

I don't ask if he's drinking. Or if Roy's still there, because I don't see his car as much as I did. Maybe once a week now? I don't tell Brandy I go there to spy, though. She's not worried about getting pregnant. Not at all.

"I would *know*, if I were," she says. "I would feel different. I wish you'd stop freaking out about this."

"We can't ever do that again, though."

"I know."

"Ever again," I say. And we haven't even had sex, really, since that time. I'm not up for it. I'm too nervous. And even when she tells me she's taken a test—two of them, with Shania—and it said "not pregnant." I feel better but still burned by it. Nervous.

I go pick up Taylor and Kinney from their after-school thing and when I get home, my mom's there. Not in her yoga pants, but still wearing her work suit and heels. She's on the phone. Smiling her face off. Nodding, gesturing, though no one can see her.

"Yes, yes," she says, holding her finger out to shush my sisters and me. "No, absolutely. That'll work perfect. I think the tent will fit just fine, in that case. Okay. Yes. Sure . . . No, not a problem, Tom. I've got all that under control. If you can handle that side of it, I'll handle the rest. Right. Right. All right. Talk to you soon, then. 'Bye."

She clicks off the phone. Clicks over to us, her heels on the wood floor.

"Well, it's official," she says. "Good news!"

Kinney says, "We're going to Disney World?"

Taylor says, "We get candy for dinner?"

My mom ignores them, shakes her head and says, "The party. Your dad's agreed to host it. We can send out the invites now, with his address."

I nod. Press my lips together. I'm not sure what to say. He must be done hating me. And hating my mom too.

"Three weeks beforehand is plenty of notice," she says. "I was going to worry if he didn't call today, but he did. He came through." She looks up, crosses her fingers, shakes her head, like she's thanking God. It's a strange gesture. My mom acting religious is a new development I can't quite accept.

Then, under her breath, while she's opening the fridge and pulling out a bag of carrots. "I can't believe it. My therapist was right."

My mom has a therapist?

Kinney, who has lost interest, is mauling the fruit bowl on the dining-room table, looking for a banana that is perfectly yellow, with no spots. Even one spot's a deal breaker for her. Taylor is lying on the floor, looking at an issue of one of the kids' magazines she and Kinney get.

"So, okay," I say. "The house is ready?"

"He says it will be."

"Have you seen it lately?"

"No. Have you?"

"No." I don't want to tell her that I have. That I know. That it all could be true. I want it to be true too much. I didn't realize it until this minute. I wanted to see what I'm seeing—her believing him, her being happy about something he did, her being thankful and relieved. I wish I could have videoed it for him, actually.

But then Kinney starts complaining about something and my mom's dealing with that. It would have been a five-second video. I'd have been lucky to even snap a picture.

The last bit of school stretches out everything so slow, then. Everything feeling abnormal, unusual. Off kilter. Finals. Locker clean outs. The class trip on a riverboat down the St. Croix where me and Jack and DeKalb get so high, we can barely move without wanting to puke over the side of the damn boat. A bunch of house parties that I attend with Brandy and they're boring except she gets the hiccups a lot when she drinks. The last one is at Jack's house, the day before commencement, but now the house is packed with people, all grades and ages, and shit's kind of crazy, but I'm not smoking or drinking, because the riverboat experience has me spooked.

I'm sitting on the back porch with Jack, who is telling Isabella and Loretta about a nude beach he went to in Sweden, when Shania drags me to a bathroom and shoves me inside. Brandy's in there, drunk and sitting on the toilet.

"I could have sworn I was getting it!" She's yelling, holding a tampon in one hand. "I'm probably making my baby brain damaged!" she says. "Why the fuck am I so stupid!"

Her panties are around her knees and she's staring at the crotch, which I guess she had hoped would be bloody. I don't know what to say. I'm staring at her panties like I'm expecting some kind of answer to appear there. A message on the wall, the face of Jesus. Or Elvis. Some sign from God. I don't even believe in God. Never have. Maybe I should start.

"Brandy, what . . . ?"

Someone starts banging on the door.

"It's almost June," she says, wiping her tears on toilet paper. "It should be here by now. It should."

"I thought you took those two tests and they said you weren't—"

"That was probably too early to take them," she says. "I called the hotline on the box."

"You never told me that!"

She's crying now, fully. Sobbing. Her head in a pile over her knees, her panties. It might be the worst thing I've ever seen, actually.

"Open up, Will!" Shania at the door.

I kneel down in front of Brandy. Lift her head up. Wipe her tears. Push her hair out of her face.

"Brandy, come on," I say. "Put your stuff on, okay." She's still clutching the tampon.

She just sits there. Eyes closed tight. Like she's praying. Like if she wills it hard enough, she'll bleed right this second.

"Come on," I say. I pull up her panties, her skirt. Then I pull her up to stand. She's wobbly. I smooth her shirt over her skirt. She's breathing like she's still crying.

"I'm gonna take you home."

"No, I'm too drunk. Not yet."

"I'll take you somewhere else, then, okay?"

"Just not home. Megan's home. And my nana. Not there."

"Fine. I'll think of something."

I lean her against the sink counter. Her face is terrible right now—red eyes, stark white skin, black mascara smeared all over all of it. A chunk of her hair is stuck to her cheek. I look at myself in the mirror behind her and what I see is worse. The lighting in here is fluorescent, intense. My hair's sticking up in the back and I'm pitting out my T-shirt and I look extra hairy for some reason. My arm hair, the hair on my chest sticking out of top of my T-shirt collar. Even my hands are hairy. Plus I've got stubble.

I look at us in the mirror, my hairy front and her wobbling back. We could be someone's parents. Right now. Look at us. We're a disaster in the bathroom. A disaster inside a beautiful house. A disaster inside her body. I want to get out of here but I don't want to take her with me. I wish Shania would deal with it.

But when I let her into the bathroom, Shania's face is all tilted to the side and slamming the door. So Shania knows. Probably everyone else knows too.

"Oh, girl," Shania says to Brandy, hugging her right away. "What's this? Oh. Here," she says, handing me the tampon Brandy was holding.

I have no idea what Shania expects me to do with the tampon. Put it back in Brandy's purse? Is there some other place to put it? Do girls just leave tampons loose like that? I suppose that's why they have purses, not wallets. The thing barely fits in my pocket.

But Brandy doesn't have a purse in here, anyway. I don't want to ask where it is, because she and Shania are having a little talk, their heads together, Shania talking quietly in this murmur, which is not normal Shania—she's usually loud and laughing. I feel useless, like a taxi Shania called so I can take Brandy somewhere.

Finally, Brandy wipes her tears and Shania turns to me and says, "Are you parked close by?"

We all leave the bathroom together, with people staring at us, girls mostly. Brandy looks down, with me and Shania on either side of her as we go through the house, like she's some wasted movie star and everyone's trying to get pictures of her. I don't know if she's being dramatic or drunk. Both, probably.

We're on our way out and DeKalb stops us.

"Hey," he says. "What's this?" He motions to Brandy.

"Brandy's not feeling so great."

"Yeah, tequila will do that," he says.

"Shut it," Shania says to him. "Don't be piling on."

"I'm not, just joking . . ."

Shania says something to Brandy in her ear and then she steps away and links arms with DeKalb. Are they together again? Or maybe just together for tonight? DeKalb looks like he's happy.

"Make sure you take her home," she says to me.

"No!" Brandy looks up. "No, Will, I can't go home yet! I can't—"

"I know!" I say. "I won't."

"Will..."

"I know what to do, already," I say. "Jesus."

It's still warm out, though it's after nine at night. A couple of people, probably Jack's neighbors, are talking in the street with a bored dog on a leash between them, looking at his house. The place is going to get busted soon, if they're hip to what's going on. Jack's gotten a little lazy about parties at his place. He'd been so unpopular before that it didn't matter. Now, with Loretta and Isabella all over his shit, inviting all their friends, people are getting stupid.

I get Brandy into the car and drive careful, slow. Don't need to give the neighbors any more reason to get suspicious. Not all teenagers drive like hell. Not all teenagers are dumbasses and irresponsible.

Except me. I am. I am an idiot with a knocked-up girlfriend and a tampon poking out of my pocket and I'm not wearing the flip-flops my girlfriend bought me, but my boots like normal, because I'm used to them. Because at my dad's, it seemed like that was safer. You could step on a nail; you could knock into a pile of boards and bash the shit out of your toe. I wear them to work too.

They've been splattered with grease and hot water and ice cream and melted butter and ranch dressing and pancake batter. I hose them off with the dish-room sprayer every night, because that's what Carl does. The leather's cracking and they smell like hell, which was Brandy's main point, I think, but I don't care.

I don't know where to take her. She says she's not hungry. She says she doesn't want to go anywhere. She says she feels carsick. I have only one idea of where to go and when I get there, she asks me what the hell my problem is.

"Why do you keep doing this to yourself?" she asks as I shut the car off. Roy's car isn't parked out front, where he normally parks. Neither the truck or the van are there. There's no lights on, either.

"I don't know where else to go. Want to go inside?"

"No."

"Brandy, come on. What do you want me to do? Drive around all night? You said you were feeling carsick."

"But he told you that you couldn't come until he invited you back."

"But we're having the graduation party here. He called my mom. We sent out the invites."

"I know," she says. "I got mine yesterday. Megan wants to come."

"Don't you want to see it, then?"

"Maybe he wants to surprise you?"

"Come on, let's," I say. "Just for a second."

She doesn't say yes. Just unbuckles her seat belt. We hold hands all the way up to the back door, where the outside light shows that there's not much left in the backyard in terms of piles and materials. The big-top tent folded up in a big white square, the metal poles zip-tied together on the ground.

When I open the door, it's dark. I reach around for a utility light but my hands slip over a light plate. I flick on the switch.

It's crazy. It's beautiful.

The whole main floor is open and finished. There's a new sofa. A new television on the wall. The floors are refinished wood. Smooth and empty. There's some trim along the edges that's undone; I can see the tools and the stack of molding on the floor. Like whoever was working got interrupted for a minute.

The kitchen has all brand-new appliances, with the stickers from the showroom still on them. And the island is a big rough slab of marble, slate black and rough cut; probably some weird salvage thing my dad got on Craigslist. An orange pendant lamp hangs over it, shaped like a flame or a teardrop.

"Wow," Brandy says.

"Yeah," I say. I look up the stairs. The carpet is gone, replaced by wood steps, which are black, with white risers. The handrail is silver. The walls are fresh and white and the whole place smells like Sheetrock. It's amazing. I almost feel like I might cry. And I feel like I should have listened to Brandy too. I'm ruining this, the surprise, by looking too soon. By not being patient. I don't want to go further. Don't want to get caught.

"We should go," I say.

Brandy nods and we slip out and to my car, silent. Brandy doesn't say anything for a few more blocks.

"I can't believe it," she says. "I didn't think he'd do it."

"Me either," I say.

I stop at a gas station to fill up and then go in and get us some coffee and a pack of mint gum. I don't like coffee and don't think Brandy does, either, but I figure it'll help with her breath and sobriety, maybe.

When I come out, she's on her phone, texting.

"Shania," she says, explaining. "Back with DeKalb."

"Yeah, what's that about?"

"I don't know," she says. "Who am I to judge, really."

I don't care about Shania and DeKalb. Because my dad really did it. It's almost like there was a reason for throwing me out. I just didn't believe in him, not in the way I should have. I feel like a terrible son. Roy has been more faithful than me.

We drink our coffee for a minute. No talking. I just want her to feel better. Or really, just feel good enough so I can get her home. She just needs to sleep. This will be okay. It can't be what she thinks. And if it is, well. We'll handle it. We'll . . .

No. It's not going to happen. My dad finished the house. He did it. It's a sign. It's a sign of something changing.

But not changing that way. Not in a-baby's-coming way. Brandy's mom had her when she was a teenager. Brandy's mom is knocked up right now. It's so fucking perfectly obvious that this would be what happens to her, that she wouldn't escape this. That I went along with it makes me feel even more guilty.

Because I can fucking walk away. Even if I don't want to, I can.

"It's going to be all right," I say, driving toward her house.

"How do you even know?"

"I just do," I say.

"Well, I don't," she says. "And it's my body. I don't see how you can know that."

I don't point out how she told me before that it was her body, how she said she would've known then.

"Just don't worry about it," I say. "It'll be okay. Both of us; we'll be okay."

She puts down her coffee in the cup holder. I've barely touched mine. First off, it's hot. Second, it tastes horrible.

"No, we're not. We're not okay. You're almost done with school. We're exactly like DeKalb and Shania. Exactly. And look at them! DeKalb's leaving the day after graduation. Shania's just like me. Another two years."

"DeKalb's just doing Habitat for Humanity in Georgia," I say. "He'll be back to start at the U in August."

"You know what I mean."

"Not really," I say.

"It's just, we can't last forever," she says. "You've got a totally different thing going in your life. You're on a different schedule."

"I haven't even applied to college," I say. "I'm not going anywhere."

She doesn't say anything. My words hanging there sound awful. Because I'm filling them in: *I'm going to be the father of her baby. I'm not going anywhere.*

I pull up to her house. I don't shut the car off.

"Sometimes I wish we'd never done this," she says. "But then, I don't know. God. I don't fucking know."

"Brandy, don't say stuff like that."

She's crying again, but it's quiet. Just big huge drippy tears. I know what I could say right now to make her stop crying. I can feel the words sticking in my throat. But they don't want to roll out. I want her to stop crying, I want her to stop worrying, I want her to stop feeling so shitty about me and her—us—but not enough to say the words.

"Come on, Brandy," I say. "Please?"

I don't know what I'm asking, exactly. And neither does she. Her lips get real tight, then, and she wrenches open the door, slamming it, and stomping up the path to her house. And then I feel nothing but hate. And relief. And like I've done nothing but made everything worse.

TWENTY-FOUR

WHEN I GET back to Oak Prairie everyone's in bed at my mom's, so I walk to Angus's house. His car is out front, but he's not in the garage when I head back there. I go into the side door and the kitchen is dark, the dishwasher humming, the light above the stove on.

The house feels empty and I wonder if that bothers him. Being the only one around. Maybe that's why we get along so well? We're both always the only one.

"Angus?" I call down the stairs.

Nothing.

I go down and he's there, in the dark, the only light from the television. He's got his headphones on and he's playing a game. I stand in front of the screen and wave.

He pulls them off right away when he sees me, and I can hear the sound gushing through them. He pauses the game. Smiles.

"Hey," we both say at once.

Then I laugh, ask where his family is.

"Some party," he says.

"No gig tonight?"

"Not until next week."

I nod. Then I reach over to where he's holding the game controller. Chuck it away from him until it yanks out of the game box. Then I grab him and we just hold each other for a minute.

I want to say lots of things.

Like, *I'm so fucked.*

Like, *how do I fix this?*

Like, *I'm not going to college but I cannot have a baby with Brandy.*

Like, *how much can an abortion cost? And can a sixteen-year-old girl get one without an adult knowing?*

Instead, I kiss him. Kiss him and kiss him and kiss him.

Say, "I fucking need this so bad." Undo his belt, his shorts. Pull them down.

He laughs. I slide between his knees.

He laughs a little more.

I put him in my mouth. He sucks in a breath and I feel his stomach tense up under my hands.

A few hours later, we're watching a movie. We've both seen it before. I have my head in his lap; his forearm is around my neck. It's comfortable, but I'm glad no one can see us. There's no way we don't look like two gay guys like this.

When the movie ends, he gets up to hit the bathroom and I

call my mom, tell her I'm at Angus's, and she yawns and she's like, *Will, I'm asleep, but just come home in the morning so you can help me move some furniture*—she's bought new dressers for the twins and Jay needs help carrying them upstairs. We've got to get that done before the graduation ceremony, for some reason. I say all right and stretch on the sofa. I'm still worried about things with Brandy, but I feel better. Safe, somehow.

I hear movement upstairs. Angus's parents have come home. His mother hollers down the stairs.

"He's in the bathroom," I holler up.

"Is that Will?" Angus's mom hollers back.

"Yeah."

"Tell him we're home," she says.

"And we're going to bed," his dad yells. "*Now*, Gina." I hear her giggle. I wonder if they're kind of drunk or something; they make a lot of noise, knocking around upstairs.

Angus comes back, and I tell him they're home. He nods, runs upstairs, and is gone for a while. I get up and go into his room. Take my shirt off. We never bother with one of us sleeping on the sofa anymore. His parents never come down here, anyway.

I turn on the nightstand lamp. Angus's room is a mess, clothes everywhere, bed unmade. It always seems sort of alarming, seeing his room a mess. My mom never allows that—she always makes me make my bed, clean off the floor. And my dad, well. I just felt like I had to keep my stuff together, packed properly. Every week, I was somewhere new. I couldn't just toss my shit everywhere like I was staying on permanently.

My phone's almost dead; I plug it into Angus's charger—we have the same kind of phone. I think about how weird that is. I think about how if we lived together, that'd be easy, our phones. And our clothes. There's nothing Angus wears that I wouldn't wear. It's not that I mind, really. I like all of it, just like I like the girl things about Brandy. Her candles, the way she smells, the jewelry she wears, the stickers she puts on her cell-phone case. I take off my glasses. I can't think about her while I'm here. I just can't. Or I'll never be able to stand it, the guilt. I'd have to tell him everything.

I'm sitting on the bed, undoing my boots, when Angus comes in.

"My mom's tipsy," he says. Laughs. "Can't unbuckle her sandals. My dad and I were making fun of her."

"Jesus," I say. I've never seen my mom drunk.

"Yeah, she's nuts," he says. "I think she can't wait for me to move out. I wonder if they'll just walk around naked when I'm gone."

"Wouldn't you?"

"Probably," he says. Then he takes off his shirt and his shorts. Dumps his phone and wallet on the nightstand next to mine.

"He fucking did it, Angus. It's all finished. Just like Roy said."

"I got the invitation to the party," he says, coming close to me. Sitting beside me. I see our big knobby boy knees next to each other, and I unlace my other boot. Brandy's knees are tiny, in comparison. Just one round bump, then her thigh. While Angus and me seem to have big old lump knee knuckles practically. And way more hair, for sure, than Brandy's smooth legs. One thing

314

I've always liked is that feeling. Her smooth legs on mine. Soft and slippery. Like a bar of soap.

I take off my socks, chuck them next to my boots. Angus starts touching me. I can tell he's already hard. I'm already hard too. But I keep talking about my dad and the house. I explain how I wasn't sure. How I had been spying, checking in. What Roy had said. And now, it's done. The kitchen, the floors, the walls. A new sofa, a new TV. Cabinets, counters, a sink, all new appliances. A beautiful open room, kitchen and living room on the main floor. The bathroom now a bathroom again, closed up with fresh painted walls, a new pocket door. Just like he's planned.

"It's great timing," he says, kissing around my neck.

"It's a fucking miracle is what it is," I say. Then I kiss him on the mouth. I love kissing Angus. His mouth is so soft but I don't give him stubble-burn like I give Brandy. And he's smooth, for a guy. He doesn't have chest hair like me. He's a good mix of both things.

His hands skim around my belt.

"What the hell's this?" he asks.

I look up. He's holding the tampon that was in my pocket.

I want to laugh. I want to tell him. But there's no way I can tell him.

"Brandy made me hold it," I say. "She . . . it's a long story."

He chucks it on the floor. "God, I'm glad I'm gay," he says, pushing me on my back, onto the bed. This time it'll be my turn, because Angus understands what this is, what sex is for.

He sucks me off and I swear, he means it to last forever. Like, he stops and goes and stops and goes and I want to kill him.

I can't stand it. And just when I think, I'll never come, my balls are about blue from waiting, then he just sucks harder and I swear, when I come, it's so good, I don't know how I'll live when he goes to Chicago.

"I wish you were too," he says, while we're falling asleep a little bit later. His hands are on my back, running up my shoulder blades.

"What?"

"I wish you were glad you were gay too," he says. "Or just would admit it."

There's nowhere to go now, otherwise I might leave. He wraps an arm around me, his wrist hanging around my hip. I'm exhausted. I just want to sleep. Just want to stop thinking.

At five a.m., a phone rings. Angus is closer to the nightstand so he reaches for his phone first—we have the same ringtone, the boring one the factory gives you—but he says, "It's yours."

"What?"

He sits up. "Oh," I hear him say. "It's . . . her."

I open my eyes. He hands me my phone. The room's half light, because the sun's just starting to come up through the window well.

He can't say her name. Which is probably for the best. The way he says *her* is bad enough.

I sit up.

"Brandy?" I say, as low as I can.

"It's okay, Will," she says. "Just like you said it would be."

"What?"

"I got it," she says. She's almost yelling; it's like she's in Angus's room with us. "Started bleeding just now. My period. I pretty much woke up in a puddle. It's so gross. But I'm so happy. You just don't even know!" She laughs. I look up. Angus is across from me. Blurry.

"So, we're not pregnant," she says. "No baby! It's okay. We can just . . . I don't know. We can just be together. Normal. And you're right: I'll never let you do that again. We can't go through this again. I've been totally messed up. Not sleeping. Looking at how much diapers cost in Target. And cribs? And car seats? Everything's so expensive! And you need so much shit, Will. And an abortion is like four hundred bucks too. None of it's cheap. God. I was going insane. But now?" She breathes out. Laughs. "Now I don't have to. Oh man."

"That's great, Brandy," I say. I look up again. Feel across the nightstand for my glasses. Put them on. Angus is staring at me. The expression on his face is clear; I know he can hear everything. Has heard everything.

"I want to celebrate or something! Don't you?"

"Well, yeah, but Brandy, it's like five in the morning," I say. "I'm not even awake."

"Sorry!" she says. "I couldn't help it! I figured you'd want to know the second I did, though."

"Well, yeah," I say. "Thanks for calling. I'm glad you did. Thanks."

I hang up. Angus leaves the room. I hear the bathroom door close. And then I sit there for so long, waiting for him to come back, to explain, that I realize he's the one waiting, not me. He's waiting for me to fucking leave his bed and his house.

When he said he wished I was glad I was gay, or that I'd just admit I was, that was a test. I failed. And now I've failed again.

I get dressed, put my feet into my boots without lacing them up, and head out into the weak sunlight, where the heat already feels vicious and hot. Today is my commencement. I have to be there at noon, so they can line us all up and congratulate us for what we've done.

Commencement's outside on the football field, and the day is perfect and sunny. Not a cloud in the sky.

Everyone is here too. My mom, Jay, my aunt and uncle from Duluth, Kinney and Taylor. Brandy and her aunt Megan. Garrett and Kristin. Even Roy's here. All of them in the same section of the bleachers.

Everyone, including my dad. I see him coming in just after we're seated for the official ceremony. I have a perfect view of him, because he's not in the bleachers, but standing off to the side.

He's even wearing a nice shirt, a plaid button-down with a collar. Same shitty Carhartts, but still. He looks clean. He's wearing sunglasses and fanning himself with his program.

I don't know what to do with myself, I'm thinking so many things. I'm nervous about seeing him; I don't want him to know that I've seen the house, don't want to ruin the surprise. And I'm worried he'll still be mad at me. Or some other thing could go wrong. He and my mom could fight in front of everyone. They never have done that before, but that doesn't mean it couldn't happen.

I try not to look at him for the whole ceremony but it's hard. I guess I can't quite believe it. It doesn't seem right that I'm here, that I'm getting this. My entire family is here, the house is done and it's beautiful, and there's going to be a party for it next weekend. Everything's ordered, and organized. My mom and dad have worked together, talking on the phone, figuring things out. Roy and I will help set things up; my mom's put together all sorts of old photos of me.

It's so cheesy of me, but I'm sitting at my graduation, trying not to look at my dad and listening to the speeches and I'm feeling, like, a sense of accomplishment. Just like the speeches say: the girl talking about going after our dreams, the teacher telling us how hard we've all worked to get here, how proud we should be.

I haven't worked hard at school; a lot of people have worked harder. And I'm not proud of my grades. I mean, they're not horrible, but even if they were, I wouldn't feel too bad about it. Getting good grades has never been something that I really cared about. I mainly did my schoolwork so I could avoid the hassle that not doing it would bring.

But I feel like something did happen, something got done, and after all these years of bullshit, back and forth, and not saying what everyone obviously could feel, that now we're all here and it's turned out fine. It's a strange feeling. Seeing my dad off to the side. Knowing my mom and everyone's behind me. It's a good feeling, a flash of happy that lasts all through the ceremony, through the speeches, through the walk up to get the diploma, through the photographs and hugging and handshakes afterward, the shouts of congratulations as we all turn in our caps and gowns and board the bus to the senior party at the bowling-alley place where we're to celebrate all night without alcohol or drugs. I don't even care about that; about not being wasted to celebrate. I feel high as it is, just from that two hours on the football field, me sitting in a chair, waiting my turn. My mom and my dad and my family, and Brandy, everyone there for me. We've all made it. And it's not just about me, it's not just my graduation. It's unbelievable, how good it feels.

And I'm not waiting for my diploma, or for the principal to say my name. I'm waiting for my dad to see me on the field. To see me and hug me and say, "You did it, Will. I'm so proud of you. You did it." I want it to happen so bad that I can barely let him go when it does. I can barely look at his face when it does, because his smile is so big and proud. I stand beside him and people take pictures of us and I like that position better, next to him, his hand strong on my shoulder. Looking at him is so unbelievable and good that it's like looking into the sun. I tell him thanks, and he tells me he knew I could do it and I know no one has to say they're sorry or explain. It's all okay. It's a fucking miracle.

Two days later, I'm still a little out of it. Staying up all night playing laser tag with the entire senior class at Franklin screwed with my system in a way I didn't expect. It's like I'm hungover.

I'm at my mom's, in bed and slowly waking up. I'd woken up in the middle of night, totally awake to the point where I just got up and watched TV and texted with Brandy—who was also awake for some lucky reason. But finally, I crashed out and now my alarm clock says 2:47 p.m., which is pretty goddamn late. My sisters have tried to wake me up twice, but I just growled at them and they finally gave up, when my mom called them for some other thing they had to do: soccer or dance, who knows. I heard the door open and close; heard the garage door go up, the car start. I don't know where Jay is but the house feeling empty again makes me fall back asleep.

I'm having a dream about Angus; we're in a car, going somewhere, and we're not sure how to get off the highway, and I have to take a piss but there's no exits or places to pull over. That's when the door opens. More like explodes open; it's like Jay doesn't even use the doorknob but just kicks it open.

"Your mother needs to talk to you," he says. "Right now."

I sit up. He looks at my bare chest, makes a face.

"Get some clothes on. And come out here right now."

It's darker now; the sun looks like it's going down. I have no idea how long I've been asleep, but the piss boner I'm rocking is uncomfortable. Jay never tells me to do anything. Barely even talks to me. And he's never come in my room, never mind come in without knocking.

I get dressed fast, take a quick piss. In the bathroom, I can hear my mom trying to talk quietly. One of my sisters is crying. Jay is *not* trying to talk quieter. I hear him say, "goddammit" a whole bunch. And: "Who the fuck does shit like that?"

My skin's tightening all over my body. I don't know what the fuck is going on but I think it's got to be my dad. He's turned the whole graduation miracle into shit again. He has to have. Did he cancel the party? Jay doesn't swear like that, and never in front of his daughters. My mom sounds like she's crying. Pretty much I never want to come out of the bathroom ever again. But then my mom says, in a shaky voice, "Will? Will, can you please come into the kitchen?"

I go into the kitchen, trying to be casual. Trying to be strong. Trying to keep my chin up, for my dad's sake. It occurs to me for a minute that he's dead. That maybe he's killed himself. I imagine him swinging from a rope, hanging. I don't know why; the image just pops into my brain.

Jay's standing at the counter, his hands pressed over the granite. Then he pushes back, stands up, scoops up the crying Taylor, who's lying on the floor at his feet. He stomps upstairs with Taylor crying in his arms like a little child bride, and his face is hard the entire time.

"Mom?"

She's at the counter too. Next to where Jay was. I wonder if Kinney's on the floor. I ask where she is.

"Dance," she says. She's staring down at the counter and then I see it. My phone. My phone is sitting on the counter, in the space where Jay's hands were.

"What's going on?" I say, again, trying for casual. I know exactly what's going on. The photos on my phone. Of Brandy, but most of those are back farther in the gallery. The most recent ones are of Angus. And me; he sent me the ones of me because he wanted to tell me that I don't understand how good-looking I am. And it's like ten pictures, all in motion. You can see my dick, especially in the fifth one. Which is his favorite, incidentally. Or was. We haven't spoken since that night I stayed at his house and Brandy got her period.

I could throw up all over the granite countertop and fake-wood floor right now.

"Will, there's something I need to talk to you about."

"Who found them? Was it Jay? Or you?"

She looks undeniably guilty. She looks like I must look. I take off my glasses and wipe them on my T-shirt.

"It wasn't me or Jay," she says. "Though Jay is obviously . . . upset." She says that last word and I know Jay's furious.

"Taylor?"

She nods.

Fucking Christ. "Mom, what in the hell . . . ?"

"You left that phone out on the sofa," she says, her voice getting louder. "Where anyone could have found it. And someone did." She starts to cry again.

Here is how I come out, I think. My mom's crying, my stepdad's pissed, my little sister's scarred for life. Angus wants me to come out of the closet so bad; well, here I go. I'm going to tell my family I'm gay, when I'm not really even gay. All because my sister wanted to play Fruit Ninja or some other dumb game she could have easily gotten on her iPad.

"You did that shit in my house. With my kids upstairs."

Jay, behind me. Standing there, across the living room.

Taylor must be in her room with commands to stay put. I wonder if she will.

"Jay . . . ," my mom says.

"In my fucking house," he continues. He looks like he's about to cry, and like he doesn't know what to do with his hands. They're just shaking by his sides. "We left you in charge of our girls, and what the fuck do you do?" He shakes his head, looks down. "I mean, you just better thank God that they never caught you doing that shit right here. Right underneath where they sleep! Jesus Christ, what is your problem?"

I can't look at him. I can't tell him that I didn't do anything wrong; that my mom never said anything about Angus. That it was only Brandy she asked not to stay over. And that the pictures aren't proof of anything. I could say that—that it was a joke, just us fooling around, no big deal.

But those sound like lies even in my head. I'm just as guilty as if the whole family, including my dad and Garrett and Kristin and the Everetts from across the street too, had found us in bed, fucking each other up the ass.

Which we've never done. But we might as well have, given how Jay's face is turning red. He looks like something invisible is choking him.

"Will," my mom starts again, but Jay cuts her off again.

"There's no trust," Jay says. "None. This has wiped away my trust in you. Both of you," he adds, pointing. I look at my mom, because I don't want him to include her in the no-trust thing, but then I wonder if he's talking about Angus too.

"Honey, we're not upset with you about it being . . . Angus," my mom says.

"Speak for yourself!" Jay yells.

"It's not about being gay," my mom tries again. "It's about—"

"It's about trust!" Jay yells again. "I mean, you've been living here all these years and all of a sudden, this happens! We've got zero reason to expect you'd abuse our trust, that you'd do something so irresponsible! And boom! Out of the blue, there it is!"

There *what* is, I wonder? He's acting like gayness is some kind of tumor. Or a wild animal ready to pounce.

"It's just that, we need you to be honest with us," my mom says. "Because—"

"We need you to be a person who doesn't take sleazy pictures on his phone and leave them out where children can find them!"

This pisses me off. "It's my fucking phone!" I yell at Jay. "Taylor had no right to look at it."

"That's beside the point!" Jay yells. "You did it and you weren't even careful with it!"

Again: it. The gayness object.

"You left it out where anyone could come across it! Never mind who the hell does that to start with. You're probably breaking a whole ton of laws taking those pictures, as it is!"

"I'm eighteen," I say. "I'm not a fucking minor."

"That girl isn't, though," Jay says, pointing at me again. "And yeah, I found those too. Of course, Taylor found the other ones, not the ones with the girl. Do you have any idea how goddamn confused that kid is? Talk about loss of trust."

Jay screaming isn't helping Taylor, I think. I'm getting pissed just thinking about how he keeps talking about it like it's hurting the kids. It's not my fucking fault Jay and my mom apparently have never explained what being gay is to their kids. I'm not their parent. If she's shocked about that shit, then that's their fault.

"To think," my mom says, "how much fun they'd had, the girls. With both of you. And how we thought nothing of it. That's what it is, Will. That's the part I don't appreciate. The *lying*. Why couldn't you just have told us—"

"Why couldn't you do that somewhere else?" Jay interrupts. "If you had to do it at all!"

"Jay, you are out of control!" my mom suddenly yells. "Let me handle this!"

Jay's lips pinch into themselves and he looks like he wants to yell back. But my mom's fierce stare keeps him quiet. He steps back, reaches into the side pocket of his all-terrain cargo pants, and pulls out his keys.

"I'm going out for a bit," he says. "If you don't mind, Tess."

They stare at each other some more. Like they are sending silent messages between them via their eyeballs. My mom's lip trembles a little, but she doesn't look away or give in until Jay turns and goes out the door.

We don't look at each other, then. It's mother-son time and I feel a little more at ease, knowing Jay isn't here. Jay, who's apparently more homophobic than anyone knew. Even my mom. I know my mom is trying to understand and be progressive and whatever. I know she's got to balance her kid dealing with sex shit and her husband being pissed and the shock of realizing that me and Angus are homos under the brand-new quilt she bought for my bedroom, but she's going to pull it together. She's going to back me. What choice does she have?

"I think you need to find another place to stay tonight, Will," she says.

TWENTY-FIVE

I GO TO Carl's. I know he's not at work. He's not even surprised when I call. Just meets me at the front entrance of his apartment, barefoot, holding an unlit cigarette.

"They kick you out or what?" he asks, lighting the cigarette. We sit down on the front cement stoop of the building. I set down my backpack between my feet; I've got a change of clothes, my phone charger, and that's it. It's like we're having a sleepover. I wish I could be excited about it. It's actually not a bad day, as June goes. Sun's out. It's not too hot.

"For the night, at least," I say.

"Did you call Garrett?" he asks, exhaling smoke. I notice even his toes have red hair on them. It's sort of funny but I have no way to explain this.

"I will," I say. I don't bother bringing up my dad, and not just because he punched Carl in the face. I know my mom will call my dad and probably tell him everything and I just can't fucking do it.

I don't have to tell Carl why I need a place to stay tonight. He doesn't flinch at the idea that the world is full of people who fuck you over and don't take care of you. He finishes his cigarette and we go inside and he says he's making tacos, do I want any?

I sit on the couch. I eat Carl's tacos. They're pretty fucking good tacos. I don't know why I'm surprised. Carl's a goddamn cook. I never cook outside of work. I don't do anything like that if I'm not getting paid. But Carl's got no choice.

"You want to go do something? I was just gonna stay in and chill," he says, after we finish eating. He lights another cigarette, sits down on the couch beside me. "My roommate went to a wedding in Des Moines, so it's pretty quiet right now."

I can't decide if I feel shitty for invading his quiet or good because he sounds lonely. It's hard to tell with Carl. His mood is always pretty much the same.

My phone beeps a bunch with texts.

Brandy. As usual. She's going into text-panic mode because I haven't responded.

One from Angus, though, gets me all tense: wanna talk to you if yr around

"No, I don't need to go anywhere," I say. Carl nods and turns on the television. I get up and clear my plate and do the dishes. Carl doesn't have a dishwasher, which depresses me. It's like his job is everywhere and he can never avoid it. I do all the dishes by hand, laying them on a towel on the tiny counter because I don't know where to put them away. When he tells me there's beer in the fridge, I go grab two and sit back down. He's watching a movie that

I've seen; there's a bank robbery that goes wrong and the money is flying everywhere. There's a woman who's got a big rack who's holding a machine gun. She kind of looks like Sierra and I say so.

"Sierra's way hotter than that dumb chick," Carl says. "And she'd never touch a goddamn gun."

"If you jacked her tips, she might."

"Sierra's pretty relaxed about money," Carl says. "I mean, for a waitress. She told me she makes these candles, with pennies in the bottom of them, and covered in mint oil. Mint brings money to you or something. And when her bills get too much, and she's not getting the tips she needs, she lights one of them until the tips pop back up."

I keep thinking he's saying *tits* instead of *tips*.

"You got her number?" I say.

"It's on the call list for work," he says.

"No, I mean, you should call her," I say. "Have her come over."

"Are you fucking kidding me? There's no way I'm doing that."

I think for a minute about this; he changes the channel. I'm surprised he's talked to Sierra that much but I'm also surprised he's that sure about not calling her. I mean, his apartment's crappy, but it's not that bad. It's sort of clean. There's a dinky little balcony. And nobody's around right now. I mean, I could leave and he and Sierra could do whatever they wanted. Drink beer, smoke pot, watch shitty movies. They're adults and they've got money—and she's even got magic candles—so why he's just sitting here is a mystery to me. But then I look at his toes, with their little gingery hairs on them, curled over the edge of the coffee table, the giant ashtray that's shaped like the state of Minnesota, full of crushed butts. Carl doesn't even have good cable.

What we end up doing is he sets up his bong and we rip a couple tubes, but I'm not used to bongs and get so high I'm paralyzed. It's kind of the worst. Carl doesn't seem to blink at it. He seems to be unaffected. He puts away the bong after we're done and he goes out on the balcony and smokes and looks at the sky. Or the stars. Whatever. I think about the texts on my phone, beeping in my pocket.

I've made a fucking mess of my fucking stupid life.

"You want a pillow or something?" Carl, standing over me. I tell him no. I can barely keep my eyes open.

"I'm going to bed, then," he says.

I pull my phone out of my pocket. Twenty-four new texts. One from my dad. Did my mom tell him about Angus? I turn the whole thing off, chuck it on the coffee table and it clanks against the full ashtray.

"Easy, dude," Carl says.

"I gotta work tomorrow."

"I'll wake you up," he says. He kind of nudges my leg on the sofa with his leg and then walks back to where his room is. I wonder if it's a dump. If he makes his bed. If he's ever fucked anyone in it. Poor sad Carl. Fucking bitches, making money, sleeping alone.

Nobody's there when it happens. Not Roy, not my dad. But nobody knows this at first.

I'm in Carl's shower getting ready for a morning shift at Time to Eat when I get the first calls, though I haven't turned on my phone to hear them. Carl's shower isn't gross, like you'd think. I'm sort of embarrassed about how I assumed his whole life outside of work was pretty much shitty.

Once I'm dressed, though, and turn my phone on, I know I can't avoid it. There are eight missed calls. And the second the phone powers all the way on, Brandy calls again. She's the one who tells me; she's at the Vances' babysitting, which is how she knows. I can barely tell Carl what she says, I'm in such a hurry.

"Go, man," he says. "Just go. I'll tell Garrett what's up."

All the way to my dad's, I'm on the phone. To Roy and Garrett, who don't answer. To Kristin, who tells me to call the restaurant, and that she's so sorry, and to keep her updated.

I refuse to call my mom. Or my dad. If his phone goes to voice mail, I'll lose it.

I have to park on the end of the street and Brandy runs toward me. She's telling me the whole thing, as if it's already not clear: how she showed up early to work at the Vances', expecting them to be in their morning shuffle off to work, only to find them out in the street with all the other neighbors. The alley was blocked by the firefighters and cops.

I run ahead of her, and she trails me, until we get to the police line. The entire house isn't burned, just the attic. But you can see the smoke, still. The Vances, like the other neighbors, are worried the fire would jump, spread to their house, since everyone's houses in this neighborhood are built so close together. The firefighters are already preemptively watering down the neighbors on either side of my dad's place.

A mob of people watch my dad's house smoke away in the already steaming-hot June morning. I stand by Brandy and stare at them, my dad's neighbors, the ones who called the county on him, the ones he pissed off over and over with his endless sloppy remodeling. I hate them in their pajamas and bathrobes and yoga pants and khakis-for-work and heels and briefcases. I hate them staring at the burned house. The miracle house, now smoking and ruined.

Brandy puts her hand in the corner of my elbow, clamping to me, and I don't jerk away, but I don't lean into her. She looks almost happy, her eyes are wide and her lips are glossed-up red, and she seems to vibrate, bouncing on her feet. Like she's turned on instead of worried. I imagine the tampon soaking up all her blood. Her panties crusted with it.

I look at the attic—or the smoking space where the attic was—and think about the futon where we first made out. There's nothing there, just thin sticks of wood poking up like black toothpicks.

The crowd of people pushes toward the closed-off tape the cops have set up. Like they want to get singed. Like they want to see everything inside, finally. Like they've been robbed.

Even Brandy's on her tiptoes, pressing forward.

That's when I pull away from her. I haven't said a word. I'm wearing my boots, and my shit jeans, the ones I like to wear to work because I don't care if they get stained. They are soft and worn in, because I bleach them after wearing and the denim is going to fall apart soon, but I don't care. I have two pairs of these jeans and I rotate them and this is my uniform. Shit boots, worn jeans, a T-shirt I can pit out and not care about. I'm holding my keys in a wad, flipping them around my index finger.

"Will?" Brandy is saying. "Will? Are you all right?"

I nod. I tell her I'm okay.

"Just a minute," she says. She moves to talk to another woman. Mrs. Vance, maybe? I step back. Again. Again. The smoke rises up farther into the sky, where the sun is so bright it seems like it'll burn it all off.

I'm standing around the mob of people looking.

"Faulty wiring," some guy says.

"Space heaters, maybe," someone else says.

"In June?" someone answers. "Surely not."

Everyone murmurs. All these people who never talked to us, or talked to my dad and got the rough side of his tongue. They don't wait long to dish up on the failure.

I step back again, budge into a woman who's holding a baby. I apologize. The woman barely notices me, she's staring so hard at the smoky sky.

"Will?"

Brandy, pointing at me. The woman next to her, staring over at me.

"They're saying nobody was in the house, Will. But do you know where your dad is?"

I don't know. I can't see my dad's truck. Or the shitty van. Or

Roy's car. He can't be in there, but part of me thinks that it might be better if he was.

"Just the dog in a painting," I say. I don't know if anyone hears me.

I step back again. People turn to stare at me.

"There was a dog?" I hear someone say.

"Will, where are you going?" Brandy, near me. Up under my chin. Her arms trying to circle around me, but I keep moving back. Back. Back. I just want to get to my car.

I walk and walk and walk until I'm through the mob of people. I get into my car and sit there, holding my keys. Looking down at them in the little cup of my palms.

A knock comes at the window. Brandy.

"Will, your dad is here," she says. "He just showed up with Roy, do you—"

"I have to be at work."

"Will," she says, and then I put the keys into the ignition and drive. Turn the radio all the way up until I can't hear anything.

All the way to work, I see the picture of the dog in the attic. Curling up in smoke. Then ashes. Then blowing away. Less than ashes. The sky is very blue but I think I can see bits of smoke and ashes. Following me all the way to work.

I punch in. Sierra says hello, introduces me to the new waitress. She's cute. Lillian. The new cook is working through breakfast rush with the other prep cook, a girl whose name is either Jenny or Jen. Or maybe Jan. I can never remember. And she's one of those people who won't shut the fuck up, who tires you out with all their information so that you don't even want to get to know her. She's a good worker, though.

I go into the walk-in, look at the list of deliveries. It's Wednesday, so we're flush. Time to unpack and chop. There's a fresh box of tomatoes and just one cambro of diced left, for omelets. I start on that, decide I'll do lettuce next, then cheese stacks.

Carl comes over, then. Asks if I'm all right. I nod at him. He just stares for a minute; he's sucking on a huge cup of Mountain Dew from a straw. Then he ducks out.

A minute later, Sierra's standing by me: "Will, are you okay?"

I look up from my chopping, sweep a bunch of tomato guts into the trash bin.

"I'm fine," I say.

"Okay. Lemme know if you want a pop or anything. Okay?"

I nod, keep chopping. Keep my eyes on the knife.

I don't know when she leaves, but I'm about to start on lettuce when Garrett's there.

"Have you talked to your dad?"

"No," I tell him.

"You need to punch out," he says. "Your girlfriend told me you just left without saying what was up. And I . . . your dad needs you."

"I was scheduled for ten."

He shakes his head. "You don't . . . it'll be fine, Will. Just go."

"I'm finishing my shift," I say.

He says more stuff, but I'm in the walk-in, getting lettuce. Coming back out. Garrett's by the prep counter. He looks exhausted. His hair grayer. Like ashes. I wonder if they're starting to drop from the sky above my dad's house.

"You don't need to be here," he says.

I want to say, *No. No, I do.* I don't say anything, though. I need to keep standing. I need to do something. Anything. I don't want to talk or look at him.

My phone is vibrating in my pocket with texts. I would turn it off but I kind of like knowing I'm ignoring everyone.

"Fair enough," he says. "Though I think you need to be with your family. But I guess . . ." He looks up at the ceiling. "Anything I can do for you?"

"Nope."

Lettuce. Cheese. Mushrooms. Stack beef patties, then chicken portions. Then taco meat.

Sierra brings me a big chocolate milk shake, without me asking.

The new cook girl brings me a bacon cheeseburger, on my break.

Carl asks me to bring him some more lettuce so I do.

I help rack coffee cups, then bus a table of twelve, including two high chairs. Sierra uses a Hoky to sweep the cracker crumbs off the floor. I take out trash. I make salads. I restock ice cream in the beverage station. I push potatoes through the slicer for hash. I do fries for the girl cook.

I wonder if he took any pictures of it, my dad. Before it burned. I should have had Brandy take pictures.

At five after six, I'm standing outside, watching the clouds cover the sun. It feels like it might rain.

It feels like I'm going away for a long time. Like I'm saying good-bye to all these things but doing it privately. Quietly. Only in my own head. Doors to bathrooms closing, sleeping dogs curling up in smoke, in flames that nobody saw or started.

When I get to Garrett and Kristin's, they're both standing there, arms linked, watching me crawl slow down the gravel drive. Kristin has her hand over her eyes, looking at the clouds.

"Come inside," Garrett says.

We go inside, the three of us. Toward the screened porch. The wind from the rain that's surely coming is whooshing through the screens. Kicking up dust and dirt and bugs from the fields. Kristin sits on the couch where I lay with Angus that one night. She puts her hands on her knees. I sit down next to her. Take off my glasses, rub my eyes. Rub the lenses on my shirt. I kind of like how everything's blurry. The green and black field meeting the gray sky.

"I can take you off tomorrow's schedule, if you like," Garrett says softly.

"No, that's okay."

"Your mom wants you to call her," Kristin adds.

"I will."

"Are you hungry?" she asks.

I shake my head.

She gets up, then, goes into another room. I can hear her talking low, like she's on the phone. I put my glasses on.

"Your dad's upset," Garrett says.

"I know."

"He had things all finished," Garrett says. "Well, nearly."

"I know," I say.

"We can have your graduation party here," he says. "Or at your mom's."

"Whatever," I say.

"Will," he says. "It's a setback, surely. But not reason enough to postpone celebrating your accomplishments."

I look at him. I want to tell him it's no accomplishment, me graduating from Franklin. I don't want to celebrate with anyone. Especially my mom. I don't want her pity so fuck her and fuck Jay. And my dad? I can't imagine seeing my dad's face. I can't think about it without wanting to break down.

I tell him I need to go to bed. I tell him, can he just take my phone. I hand it to him and it feels heavy, like it's overstuffed with texts and electricity. I tell him to tell everyone I will call them in the morning. I tell him thank you and then I go into the bedroom that's mine now. I sit on the bed and take off my boots and I think that this bed feels like the perfect balance. I can sink into it, but it holds me up too.

I sleep, but I wake up a lot. I see my dad's face at graduation. I see my mom and Jay staring at each other. Sending messages in silence.

Before dawn, I'm awake. It's sudden, like I just know that I should open my eyes.

I think about Brandy, rolling yarn on her bed, bare naked, this same time so many months back. I think about Angus, sitting up in his bed, letting me kiss him before I left that one morning.

I know where I am. The air is no longer heavy and too thick.

I go downstairs, barefoot, in my boxers.

The house is quiet. I stand on the screened porch, feeling a wave of wind burst through the porch and then the rain itself, spraying on all sides, drenching the cornfield black and green.

A house is built of many things, my dad said. That was a year ago. I feel older than a year from that time.

Built and rebuilt, he should have said. Because he will rebuild it. I know he will. And all this will go on, between him and my mom, between him and me. Between me and myself, whoever I turn out to be, years from now.

Between me and Brandy. And me and Angus. Maybe one of those conversations will stop. Sooner rather than later. I can't decide what I think of that. I stand there, watching the rain, hearing the thunder. Seeing the lightning crack and ask for my attention. Puddles in the yard, puddles in the gravel drive, long dirty streams gathering along the furrows near the field's edge.

I stretch, cracking my neck and arms. The hair on my arms and chest stands up and I'm shivering but it feels good. I'm awake, and it's nowhere near time to go to work, but I still go into the kitchen to make coffee for when Kristin and Garrett wake up.

AUTHOR'S NOTE

THIS BOOK STARTED with a question: How would it feel to fall in love with your best friend of the same gender?

Could you separate out your love for that person from the sexual aspect?

Adolescence is when young people are just starting their sexual exploration, and in writing this book, I wanted to explore how some teenagers might come to define themselves as bisexual. Do they land on "gay" or "lesbian" first? Would they assume they were bisexual to begin with? Would it be difficult to accept you were attracted to both genders, or possibly didn't even care about gender when it came to love and sex and romance? How would you explain this to others?

The word "bisexual" never once appears in the story, and readers may wonder why Will doesn't come to identify himself in this way. That Will doesn't even consider this is an example of "bisexual erasure."

Bisexual erasure is the willful disbelief that people can be attracted to both genders, as well as the tendency to emphasize sexual identities in people that fit the observer's own narrative, e.g. a man who is bisexual is really a gay man in denial; a woman who is bisexual is just doing it for male attention. Bisexual erasure can be perpetrated by gay or straight people. To paraphrase my friend Rachel, "We don't see people romantically holding hands with two other people usually, so we assume whoever they are currently with defines their sexuality."

For instance, when Will goes on dates with Brandy, observers see a straight couple. On the other hand, Will believes that if others see him and Angus as a couple, the assumption will be that they are gay.

I don't know what Will's identity is. Even if I did know, I think it's more interesting for a reader to contemplate what he is and what he might be than for me to label him with certainty.

What I do know is that we need to work for a world where it is easier for kids like him.

For more information on bisexuality and sexuality, I suggest the following resources:

Scarleteen: www.scarleteen.com

The Bisexual Index: www.bisexualindex.org.uk

Bisexual.Org: www.bisexual.org

Advocates for Youth: www.advocatesforyouth.org

ACKNOWLEDGMENTS

I'M A TERRIBLE photographer. I nearly failed Photography in high school, actually, for not understanding how to reckon with my school-issued adjustable Yashica, as well as occasionally flipping on the light in the darkroom. In order to get a basic sense of the art of photography while writing this book, I read John Berger's *Ways of Seeing* and *On Looking* and even as a person who only took one art class in undergrad, I found them quite fascinating.

I'd like to recognize the following people for their support in the making of this book:

Michael Bourret, who takes such good care of me, seeing to things that I don't want to deal with or even attempt to understand, as well as responding to highly prurient email questions in a most unflappable way.

Andrew Karre, for launching me into this world and embedding so many wise whispers into my brain.

The cabal of Gayle, Ted, Drew, and Christa: there are too

many things to thank you for, but mainly for making me laugh.

Tess Sharpe, Betty-Jeanne Klobertanz, and Bryson McCrone, for help on issues of sexual identity.

Kristin Mesrobian and Meagan Macvie, for being early readers and constant cheerleaders.

Shelley Mlsna, for help on the nature of high school photography labs in real Minneapolis Public Schools.

The team at Harper: in particular, Erin Fitzsimmons for the lovely cover; Alyssa Miele for her editorial insight and commitment to Daryl Dixon; and Claire Caterer and Jon Howard for diligence and patience in copyediting through my slop. (Did you edit this graph too, with its snarl of colons and semicolons? Good lord . . .)

And Alexandra Cooper: I've learned so much writing this book with you. Thank you for your openness to my gross/weird ideas. Thank you for buying me cookies and cheeseburgers when you visit Minneapolis and never blinking when I bring up something off-color or opinionated. Thank you for all your patience and for seeing things I don't see. Your belief in my Fake People gives me more confidence than you can know.